A LOVE SO
CAREFULLY CONCEALED

Staci Biscamp

Harvest Creek Publishing & Design

CONROE, TEXAS

STACI BISCAMP

A LOVE SO CAREFULLY CONCEALED

Discover the Thread of God's Love
Hiding in Plain Sight

To my Husband
and
To Larry and Carolyn

You are people who showed me, here on Earth, what a true marriage of love and devotion looks like.

CONTENTS

SQUARE PEGS vs. round holes. Short for tight corners in stubborn opposition to smooth surfaces. It seems odd that a couple of fragmented sentences, poking like shards from the body of a paragraph, could so easily sum up the story of my life. But what could I expect? Jagged terrain clashing against the landscape of a seamless sky was where I called home.

Generally speaking, I've found that most things rarely fit the way they were supposed to, looking from the outside in. That is, of course, until I realized that the good Lord has never been that short-sighted. While I was working with a microscope to pick apart the shattered pieces of my life, God was using a kaleidoscope to bring all of my sharp edges back together again in a way only He can.

Things that appear visually incompatible to you and me somehow always seem to align perfectly with what God is doing from the inside. It would seem that He is a lover of hard angles and violent contradictions. Otherwise, us square pegs would have never been reconciled.

And no pin clinches this sentiment more clearly than the book of Esther from the Bible. What makes it so unique and seemingly the biggest mismatch in Hebrew scripture? Surprisingly, it is the only book in the Bible that never uses God's name.

That's right! This book dares to deviate from every other account in the written Word, detailing one of the mightiest deliverances of the Lord's people, without ever giving mention to its lead character—making it appear to the average reader that God just decided to sit this one out. It's a definite oddity, coming from a collection of writings whose sole purpose was to glorify God and magnify the very name this book so conveniently forgot to include. But, if there's anything the Bible teaches us, it's that looks can be deceiving.

God's name may never be declared in the confines of its verse, but we find Him there, nonetheless, working in the background of the story. In between every line, He can be seen mending the tears in the fabric of His people, shaping His will from judgment to redemption, brokenness to wholeness, and destruction to deliverance in every word.

Esther's story of salvation is a remarkable one. But it's the underlying theme of God's truth revealed to observable reality in such a captivating way that seems to be its intrinsic message. This young girl's circumstances reveal a thread of God's love in her life that was never really concealed at all but hiding in plain sight, only waiting to be discovered—like a vein of gold embedded in rock, or seeds lying just under the surface of the soil, moments from breaking ground.

Even the name of the book of Esther reveals this very concept. In Hebrew, the book of Esther is written *Megillah Esther* or The Scroll of Esther. However, across a Semitic spectrum, it would resonate as *Uncovering What Is Hidden.* It takes no stretch of the imagination or the flexing of mental muscle to grasp this understanding.

The Hebrew word *megillah* is derived from a word meaning to *reveal* or *uncover.* And although the name *Esther* means *star,* in Hebrew, the root forming *Esther's* name means *hidden* or *concealed.*

The spelling of the name *Esther* even kindles an audible relationship with another Hebrew word—*etzer,* meaning *treasure* or *something laid up in store.* Making the underlying theme of the book, *The Uncovering of Hidden Treasure*—that being, God with us in every verse and plotline.

We find beneath Esther's tale of woe, riches of hope, and great joy, captivating the reader with the most implausible of circumstances. Elements of this young woman's life have been so intricately woven they could have only been unraveled and bound back together by the Creator of the Universe—the One who is above the stars and their journey across the night's sky.

Poetically, this too, is yet another name for the book. The word for scroll *(megillah)* has a close cognate association with the Hebrew word *magalah,* meaning *path* or *course,* bringing an acoustic link between the two. Thus, making the name of the book *The Path of the Star,* evoking with it a sense of destiny. Hence, the very nature of these two renderings of the book's title suggests that the stars don't dictate God's movements. He has always been the underlying force dictating theirs.

Why am I telling you this? Because these same observations can be said of our own stories. To God, we were all created for such a season as this under earth's star-studded canopy, to be lights in the fabric of space and time, pointing straight to Him. God has always been marking out a course to make us shine a light on the truth of His love, mercy, and salvation in the presence of a dark world—navigating every moment, even when we don't see Him or feel Him.

Just to be clear, the book you are about to read isn't a didactic novel set out to expose the physics behind the movement of stellar or planetary bodies. Nor is it a commentary on the book of Esther. It is a book of Esther, testifying to the hidden workings of an all-knowing God.

Unlike Esther, The Lord's name is mentioned countless times, revealing His majestic thread of love throughout one life—so mankind can see that God has always been in the process of modifying our shape and polishing our sharp edges to make us perfect through the infinite love of His Son.

This book glorifies God, the name of Jesus, the work He has done, and is continuing to do for the good of those who love Him. It is a confirmation that in every circumstance, God is still sovereign. He is still above the stars.

God's story, as well as ours, reveals that there is no luck or happenstance. Everything fits right where it should, according to the Lord's purposes, to uncover His thread of love—Jesus Christ—in every word of our narrative.

He is the hidden treasure found in *God with Us—Immanuel*. He is the hidden vein of love at every turn of the page in Hebrew scripture. Jesus is the light in the dark ages between the Old and the New Testament, when it appeared that God wasn't up to much. And He is the Messiah, who was ultimately revealed in the flesh throughout the New Testament.

This word was written to encourage readers to search for Jesus, letting go of their own preferences, longing instead to hold on to His. It was written to encourage those who love the Lord to walk in relationship with Him, applying His Word to their lives so others might be inspired to unearth Him for themselves.

You see, I was not a servant of God, but now I am. I had no intimacy with Him, but now I do. So that through Him, this square peg can make an impact. And through His Spirit, I can encourage the body of believers to be patient, expectant, hopeful, thankful, and rejoicing in every circumstance. Knowing in every season, every rebuke, and every rub, that God loves them. And to trust that He sees the bigger picture because He has illustrated it Himself.

I pray that through His perfect words, believers might dig deeper into the treasures of the Bible that bring wonder to uncover that light, that scarlet thread, through every turn, revealing Jesus in ways they had never considered before. Ultimately, finding with it the greatest treasure they could ever discover in this life and in the one to come—God with them in a story of their very own.

Oh, Heavenly Father, in the name of my Savior, Jesus Christ, allow this work to reveal treasures never before seen by your servants. May it strengthen the hearts of believers, turn the heads of prodigals, and bolster the faith of both. According to Your will, allow every leaf of paper bound in this book to lead straight to You. Allow it to bring sight to the blind, hearing to the deaf, and let it by Your power, strengthen the legs of the lame. Amen and Amen.

In His grip, and He in mine,
Staci Biscamp

EPIGRAPH

Here is a trustworthy saying that deserves full acceptance: Christ Jesus came into the world to save sinners—of whom I am the worst. But for that very reason I was shown mercy so that in me, the worst of sinners, Christ Jesus might display His immense patience as an example for those who would believe in Him and receive eternal life.

1 TIMOTHY 1:15-1:16

To all those who have found it hard to believe,
even the fantastical can sit squarely in the hem of reality.

FOREWORD

HEREIN, Staci Biscamp takes readers to and through a mysterious place similarly to that of the biblical Book of Esther. And while the writings in Esther are mysterious because God is never mentioned explicitly, in *A Love So Carefully Concealed,* it's the tacit inferences that catch Staci's eye and pen: how He is, in fact present and working—but behind the scenes. Individuals who lose sight of that—as they find themselves tossed around amidst the turbulence of trying times—will no doubt benefit from Staci's treatment of her circumstances and of life, in general. I am pleased to commend the book.

Dr. Jeffrey Seif
Professor of Bible and Jewish Studies

Coincidence is God's way of remaining anonymous.
ALBERT EINSTEIN

1867

THE THOUGHT of the journey thrilled him. He could almost smell the opportunity of a chance like this. And the notion for his next grand adventure? To step into a world not his own, to write about places long hidden behind walls of indifference and false impressions, on somebody else's dime, no less.

It truly was a brilliant scheme—getting paid to furrow fields, not yet turned, in places most people had never heard of. There would be no need for toil or plow; all Sam would be taking on this voyage were his wits, a pen, and a couple of scraps of paper. The very thought of it made his senses tingle—a modest endorsement, at best, but that's all it took to make the hairs in Sam's mustache tickle his nose, bringing a steadfast confirmation to every fiber of his being.

Drawing an interesting and humorous outlook of foreign places for the one stuck in the doldrums of everyday life was far from altruistic, Sam had to admit. But, he could also recognize that his worldly insights, proclaimed across every city street and back road in America, had the potential to lift the spirits of his fellow man which was no meager contribution.

Like ink leaking through the front page of a newspaper, Sam's thoughts changed the tone of everything they touched. His words could inject a smudge-stained dose of reality to the day that slapped a smile across the faces of men, making even his harshest remarks easier to swallow.

Moreover, Sam's rousing accounts were known for rubbing the sleep from people's eyes, allowing them to see things through the lens of a fresh viewpoint. He had a gift for unraveling and patching a situation back together, however imposing, that helped people relate to a stranger's way of life. Like a bucket dropped into the darkest of wells, Sam's words could draw the soul in a way as to no longer see its own vulnerability as a character flaw—but rather as a fountain of understanding, unshakably hitched to compassion, when presented with the right opportunity.

Now, all Sam had to do was sell it. Picking up his pen, he mindlessly stroked the ends of the mustache he was so fond of and began writing his proposition. It would end up as a telegraph sent clear across the country in a matter of minutes. Pure magic, by the day's standards. He would have to get every word just right because each one was costing him a small fortune. He could see it as if it were all happening in real-time.

The story in his mind playing out, that is.

He strode into the editor's office, filled to the brim with bold assurance. He was on a mission. "I've got an idea for the paper, if you're interested," Sam groused.

"What's on your mind, Sam?" The man blustered, barely able to contain himself that Sam had just waltzed into his office with an idea. You see, Sam was dusty raw talent. His words were as real and weathered as the pair of worn-out old boots he was wearing.

The guy sitting behind the desk had always appreciated the worth of a well-written word. And that's exactly what Sam came to offer. The editor had no doubt.

Slowly, Sam began to paint a picture with broad strokes of exotic locales and customs, with as many decadently colored adjectives as he could stomach. After laying the foundation of his plan on in thick coats, he eased into his need to report them back to the rest of the world.

This is where Sam's star truly shined. His tongue was every bit the pen of a skillful writer as his hands had ever been. And by the end of every hard sale Sam had ever made pitching his stories, he always left his audience smelling every word and choking back their need for one more taste. Sam's face softened into a slow smirk as he finished his speech, knowing he had just won the guy over.

"Okay, I'm sold. How much are you going to need for this little endeavor?" The editor grimaced.

"Twelve hundred dollars, give or take. I'll be leaving on a ship anchored in New York. It's been decommissioned by the military and re-appropriated as a commercial sailing vessel. I figured I'd hitch a ride with a group of people who have commandeered it, hell-bent on reaching the Holy Land."

"All right, Sam. But I expect great things from this."

"So do I, sir. I couldn't imagine a more delightful trip. In fact, it has to be the grandest scheme of my life. Designed with the utmost frugal compunction. As I won't have to depart from one dollar in my pocket." Sam beamed, as the edges of his mustache rose on both ends like hands lifted in silent praise for a job well done.

"Well, you had better deliver, is all I've got to say, or we are both in a sling."

With that, Sam turned around and strode out of the office, none the worse for wear and even more confident, if that were possible, than when he had gone in.

That should be about the way of it, Sam thought, without a shred of doubt that would be the way things would work themselves out. He would be setting sail the afternoon of June 8th if all went according to plan.

True to his thoughts and just as confident in his devices, he received the money shortly thereafter. He booked his passage with the funds the obliging newspaperman so generously wired and waited—something Sam had never quite fully mastered.

It would be days later, as he passed hundreds of like-minded enthusiasts along a bustling pier in New York, when the providence of the trip finally struck him. As soon as Sam's feet stumbled onto that tottering ship, he couldn't seem to shake feeling like an overzealous actor fumbling through lines during his first audition on the world stage.

Peering at the ticket in his hands, Sam began to chuckle, now only noticing the name of the vessel upon which he was about to embark. Things like this always tickled Sam. The name of the steamer was *The Quaker City.*

Strolling into his stateroom, now a little steadier in his step, Sam hoped this journey and his voice as its witty mouthpiece would indeed stir the waters. And he wasn't just thinking about the changes he could invoke upon the sensibilities of his readers. Sam was expecting his words to move mountains regarding his own prospects as well.

Sam had been yearning for some time to dip his toes into the rushing waters of penning a lengthier read, and this opportunity might lead to its inspiration. One-minute commentaries from the circulation of local publications were no longer enough to satisfy. Sam wanted his words to soak up more space on the page, to leave his mark two-fold. Now was the time to pull up anchor, part the water, and level some ground, so to speak.

You see, Sam had been a great many things in his life, but becoming a writer was what eventually stuck—like mud that had vacillated for far too long between solid and liquid, only to find itself, in the end, catapulted across a room and hardened against a wall. Settling into it, however, had been more like trying on a new pair of shoes—tight and uncomfortable to get over the heel. But once the cumbersome deed was done, and the shoes were trounced around a bit in the dirt, they became the right fit. Making the thought of ever trying on any other pair after that an outrageous violation to all that was holy.

Sam hated to see a blank piece of paper he hadn't scrawled something witty, insightful, or just plain back-handedly funny upon. He had come to believe there was nothing more depressing than the first, not yet pounded letter in the corner of a blank page, and he was its remedy.

To Sam, that suspended letter sat alone, waiting for something. It waited with bated breath for the perfect word, sentence, fragmented phrase, or timely quip set in perfect order. Knowing once the shining verse finally revealed itself, each line became its own proof. And just as comparable as any divine revelation in religion, science, or mathematics.

Sam was convinced polished prose was a work of elegant perfection, its own cosmic geometry. And if done to the satisfaction of its creator, a true miracle in the universe, like a comet firing across the night's sky, drawing near enough to blaze a path of new perspective and understanding without annihilating the very audience it was meant to captivate.

1981

On a green and yellow rusted-out old swing set, sitting orphaned in her backyard, the little girl began to sway. Pushing off with her legs, giving herself momentum, she baltered them about to take flight. *It was sunny today. Not a cloud in sight,* she thought.

After what seemed like an eternity, she was finally given lift. No longer bolted to the ground, she was rocketed to the heavens. Gliding as high as her little legs could carry her, the girl noticed the sky was now filled with clouds, much to her squealing delight. Imagining they had all gathered there just to catch her, she began to flirt with each one in an intimate exchange.

"It's time to come in," her mother called out from the kitchen window, breaking through the clouds in her dreams, bringing the little girl's boundless journey to an abrupt end.

Eyes now closed, her legs slowed in their ascent, as she came to rest them back on the heavily trodden dirt under the thin vinyl seat she was sitting on. As she opened her eyes, they lingered on the dirt beneath her feet. The combination of dried mud and grass had been beaten into two small tracks from the countless times she spent creating friction in forward motion to bring her tiny swing soaring into the air. As her gaze lifted, she noticed a man staring from the picnic table on the concrete square resting behind her house.

The man didn't move. He just sat there, staring at her. The little girl knew she wasn't scared of the man. There was something comforting in the way he looked at her. He wasn't her father. Yet, he seemed to offer the same gentle gaze of a proud parent, counting the minutes on a park bench for the conclusion of playtime and the joy of their long walk home together.

The girl got up. She wasn't apprehensive, but still, best not to tell mom about this. Mom wouldn't take it too kindly if she knew there was a stranger in the backyard. The girl walked to the door, the man's eyes tracking her every step. The door opened as the little girl started to traipse through. As she turned her head to get one last glimpse of the man who had appeared out of nowhere, he was gone.

CHAPTER ONE

COMING IN

——◆——

October 9, 2019

WALKING DOWN the sidewalk, I began calculating every step. Balanced. Deliberate. Precise. Watching where my feet were going without tripping or getting run over had become an exercise in futility; I still found myself stumbling and squeezed in by an anxious mob of daily commuters. Trying with little success not to become too bothered by it, I hurried to the crosswalk, fighting back the urge to turn around. *Run.*

It didn't take long for the light to change, signaling it was time to cross over. While waiting for the crowd to thin out, I adjusted my blouse and coat before traversing the heavily trafficked street. Thinking for the hundredth time that I had lost my mind, I stared up at the well-polished tower of steel, chrome, and glass standing before me.

Sitting in one of the dirtiest urban centers in the world, I couldn't help but think it fit right in with the steady groan of congestion. The theme of sweat, toil, and grit this city seemed to crave as part of its landscape was perfectly etched into every shadow of the building's design.

Feeling more than out of place, I just shook my head. I hadn't stepped across the street yet. *Run.* I could turn around right now and forget my plan to visit the top two floors of this behemoth, home to the publishing house my feet were all too determined to reach. I could ignore everything I had been told. Nobody was going to believe me, anyway. The message I had been sent to give was going to cause a shaking in the world, like an unsteady pulse of the earth, under the thundering approach of an invading army. This information wasn't going to go over.

I was a firm believer that most people were comfortable with the lies they told themselves, trusting it was better not to know the truth. But, more than that, they liked being deceived by doubt. Because if doubt existed, if it had flesh and drew breath, things could be both true and false in men's eyes, enabling them to keep their feet firmly planted in two camps.

People were like contranyms. Two words, mirror images of themselves, looking and sounding the same but meaning the polar opposite. Like the word *dust*—meaning *to be both swept away* or *piled on*, all at the same time. It wasn't lost on me, having been apparently created from dust, that mankind was destined to be both piled up while simultaneously swept away with the dawning of each new day.

Ambiguity seemed to be part of our genetic makeup from the start. It's what made the world turn. It made it easier to move and breathe. To be swayed by the tides of a culture corrupted, desensitized by it all—a perfectly sensible solution to most. No shaking. No stirring. No invasion. Just *dust,* floating whichever way the collective wind blew. That's the way people liked it. The information I was about to deliver was going to cause a shift in the air with the warm, gentle approach of a Category 5 hurricane.

As I stepped down from the curb into the middle of the street, I looked down at my feet and noticed I didn't have any shoes on. *It was happening again.* Walking on broken glass, my feet were now shrouded in blood. I snapped my eyes shut, willing the image to be scrubbed clean with the backs of my eyelids. Blinking a couple of times, I looked again.

To my surprise, my feet were once more covered in my very sensible, worn-out, cream-colored ballet flats. Hot tears began to streak a path down my face. Overcome by the heaviness of the visions I'd been having, I let them fall. *I had to do this.*

Undeterred, I finally made it across the street to the entrance of the building. It was still early enough to see the glint of the sun's buttery rays, along with a perfect reflection of myself in the building's thick glass doors. There were no smudges from anxious fingers reaching for the door handles just yet. Instead, every fallen tear, wrinkle, and wind-swept hair was on display, sitting out of order and glaring back in defiance.

Eyeing my simple beige suit under a similar-toned trench coat, I straightened and quickly tried to iron out a couple of noncompliant folds in my shirt. Then, tucking the last bit of unruly hair behind my ear and swiping the last tear from my cheek, I swung open the double doors and walked in.

My heart began to beat a little faster under my skin, somehow knowing that just crossing this threshold it needed a kick-start. Nervously, I shoved my hands into the pockets of my coat. Lined with the hundreds of notes I'd taken, my fingers fumbled lazily over the torn-out pages, silently willing the rapid fluttering of my heart to slow its assault in my chest.

After locating the building's directory, I carefully scrolled through the list of company names. Finally, finding the one I was searching for, I drug the fingers of my right hand from the pocket it occupied to push the button for the elevator.

The doors, however, opened on their own as a man I hadn't noticed went in ahead of me. He eyed me curiously, throwing out an arm to keep the doors ajar. "You going up?" Wordlessly nodding, I stepped in behind him.

Seeing the floor number and the button corresponding to it already lit up, my body relaxed slightly. My eyes shifted, only to catch those of the man standing beside me, staring blankly in my direction. He gave me a modest smile before shuffling uncomfortably to one side of the elevator. The guy must have thought I needed the space.

It was then that I noticed the man had dropped something on the ground. I went to pick it up for him because I wasn't carrying anything in my hands. All I had was a book, my notes, and two small pictures in my pockets.

Curiously, I glanced down to find a compass with markings on one side. It was worn from the effects of time and what could have only been from a constant rubbing of something along one side of its tarnished surface. It must have been a sentimental keepsake the man received on some long-forgotten holiday—a token of love from a family member, perhaps.

Handing it back to him, he said, "Thank you," in what seemed like genuine gratitude for not having to bend down to retrieve the item himself.

Finally, the elevator reached its first stop, its doors opening, allowing the gentleman to amble out. Without turning around, he offered me a warm-hearted similitude before disappearing around the corner.

The doors closed, but then the walls of the elevator quickly screeched to a halt again as the doors opened for me to step out. Directly in front of the elevator was a door that looked entirely too small for the space it occupied.

Suddenly, I felt claustrophobic in my coat. Even my shirt's once comfortable collar was now trying to cut off my air supply. Loosening one of the buttons at my throat with one hand, the other edged towards the door and pushed it open. *I can do this.*

A receptionist sat at the entrance to the office. She was put together. Her outfit and makeup perfectly paired with the lighting in the lobby. She was breathtaking, really. But of course, she had to be. She was the first face seen by those coming in and the last face remembered by those going out. She had to leave an impression.

Looking at me, she forced a smile and said, "How can I help you?"

I told her I had an appointment with Tabitha, one of the literary agents on staff. It was then that she asked for my name. Huh. I hadn't thought about whether I wanted to continue to keep my identity a secret. Was there really any safety in anonymity?

Deciding I wasn't quite ready to reveal myself, I coaxed out the same response I managed to give when making the appointment. "Oh, sorry, guess you need that. It's Jane. Jane Doe." Did that honestly come out of my mouth? I was a writer now, for heaven's sake. A lover of words. That was the best I could do? This lady probably thought I was a complete joke.

Humiliation choking me, I winced. "I have an appointment with Tabitha at 8:15."

"Are you serious?" She asked, knitting her perfectly shaped eyebrows closer together.

Clearly annoyed, knowing that couldn't be my name, she tracked a long, slender finger down the list of names in her appointment book. Frowning, as she had apparently found mine, her brows furrowed into an even tighter line as she picked up the phone. She pushed a button and spoke softly to the voice on the other end.

While waiting quietly for a response, her eyes began to catalog every detail in my appearance. A mental reflex, I'm sure, for any possible witness statements she might be making in the near future. This lady didn't like me very much. It didn't seem like she was enamored by what she heard on the other end of the line, either, as she clucked into the phone.

Huffing as she hung up, she told me to take a seat, absently motioning to a chair sitting in front of her work area.

The soft leather of the sunken lounger looked inviting. I think I was half-hoping that when I finally sat down the thing would swallow me whole, knowing once I told someone, this would be real. There would be no turning back. *Last chance. Run.* Before I could take a seat or turn around and *bolt*, the door opened.

"Miss. Doe, please follow me," the receptionist said.

I realized at that moment if irony was anything, it was anything but dead.

To *bolt*—meaning *to sit stubbornly rooted to a foundation* or make a *run* for it, all at the same time. It would seem I was just as much a walking contradiction as everyone else.

CHAPTER TWO

GOING OUT

THE NAMES we passed along the narrow hallway started to blur with each step I took until I was ushered into an even narrower, cluttered office space. Waterfalls of manuscripts littered the floor. An oversized desk sat in the middle of the room, acting as the floor's centerpiece. A calendar was hanging slanted on the wall, set to the wrong month, while a clock sitting on the desk had fallen an hour behind.

I gathered Tabitha wasn't the type of person who was bothered by the details. And probably consistently late to all her appointments. The subtleties of the room told me more about this woman than the name hanging on the door.

Lost in my own thoughts, I didn't even notice Tabitha walk into the room. Catching me off guard, standing just inside the doorway with her head cocked to one side, she seemed to be assessing the situation. She must have talked to the receptionist. *Great.* Dismissing whatever she'd been told, she bustled deeper into the tight quarters we would share and sat down behind her desk.

Tabitha was nothing like her name. Bright-eyed, beautiful, light, and quirky weren't exactly words I would put on her list of descriptive identifiers. She was slim and wrapped head-to-toe in designer labels. Black hair sat shoulder-length and stick-straight. Choppy bangs covered a tattering of deep lines across her forehead, refusing to stay concealed. She was a beautiful woman, but there was no light in her eyes. They seemed world-weary. Hidden behind a heavy canopy of thickly coated lashes, they darted around the room, finally laser-focusing on the clock resting on her desk.

Knowing eye contact would bring a hint of intimacy to the discussion we would be having, Tabitha seemed to be wrestling with the idea. With a heavy sigh of resignation, she finally looked in my direction and asked what she could do for me.

Clearing my throat, I offered, "Yes, ma'am. I have a story to tell and thought maybe you could help me. Let me start by saying that I didn't go to school to become a writer. I was a labor and delivery nurse. A midwife of sorts. Now, though, it seems I have found a new calling. *Helping to give birth to words as a means of helping to deliver the soul,* or so I've been told."

With a combination of both confusion and dread, Tabitha's eyes returned to her desk. She was probably wondering if I had stolen that little gem from Socrates all on my own.

Like some comic book superpower, I could read every thought Tabitha was silently playing out in her mind as if they were captioned in tiny word bubbles that had won their fight with gravity and were now hovering weightlessly over her head. *Was she being punked? Had she angered one of her co-workers? Was I about to pull a gun from my coat and mow her down, right here in broad daylight? Was I one color shy of a rainbow? One sandwich short of a picnic?*

Hurriedly, I removed the coat I was wearing, exposing my very unimpressive suit underneath, hoping this simple gesture might alleviate some of her concern.

A slow exhale escaped her lips at my vain attempt to ease her mind. "Can I hang that up for you? A bag or anything else?" Without waiting for an answer, she shot up and grabbed my coat, still more than a little unnerved by my previous comment.

"I don't have anything else."

She slowly hung the coat with a sigh, the look of worry coming back full force. "You don't have a bag, a portfolio, or a copy of your manuscript?"

"No, ma'am. You see, it's not about me. It's about Him." I said as I pointed an index finger into the air, aiming it at the water-stained ceiling tiles hanging directly over our heads.

Tabitha's eyes slowly followed the direction of my finger and hesitated. "It's about who?"

"Him," I said, my eyes following the same path as my finger.

Slowly, Tabitha started catching on, and with a mild snort, she blurted, "You mean God?"

"Jesus, more specifically." I clarified.

Seeming like I may have made the biggest mistake by wasting this woman's time, she bellowed, "Miss Doe, is it? I'm sorry, but I am just a literary agent. I am not a ghostwriter, a priest, or a psychiatrist, for that matter. I wouldn't know how to help you, but I can give you some names of some people that might."

Pulling a couple of business cards from one of her overcrowded desk drawers, she stood. "This first guy is a great ghostwriter, and the second is the number of a therapist I have heard nothing but really great things about. And if you need a priest, St. Joseph's is right down the street."

I think she was expecting me to follow her lead, but I remained seated, rooted to my chair, now decided more than ever to finish what I started. Feeling a sense of urgency, thinking she was about to call security, my hands grabbed both arms of the chair I was sitting in—resolved that if I was going, the chair was coming with me. Crazy? I'd call it more like steely determination.

I proceeded to tell Tabitha if she would just listen to the story I came to tell, she might change her mind. Or, at the very least, be able to put me in contact with the right person for the job. Maybe this was how she was supposed to help. I had to be there for a reason.

Mulling it over for a second, Tabitha sat back down, still a little uneasy at the prospect of giving me one more minute. Pulling her chair in, she solemnly folded her hands, placing both elbows on her desk. Looking over at the clock and brushing the curtain of bangs from her eyes, she inclined her head. "I have about an hour to kill before my next appointment. So that's all I can spare."

Positioning myself for battle, I squared my shoulders, allowing the sweat stains under my arms to make an appearance. That wasn't exactly the statement I was going for—desperation clashing with conviction. But this was going about as well as I had expected.

"Have you ever read a book and knew it was talking about you? Something written by someone you never met? Something that exposed things you have never shared with anyone? Things written that could only be known by someone who knew you intimately?"

"No, can't say that I have," Tabitha admitted, exasperated and probably rethinking her decision to give me one more minute of her time, let alone sixty.

Realizing I might have started in the middle of the story, I furiously backpedaled. "I think I'm getting ahead of myself. I should really start from the beginning, or rather, the going out."

CHAPTER THREE

COUNTING TO TEN

"I CAN'T take it anymore. This is more than I can bear. I think I might be in more pain than most women." Skittering down my spine, another side-splitting current wrapped itself into a tight embrace around my belly, conjuring another scream from somewhere deep within me.

What good was an epidural that didn't work? That anesthesiologist had a death wish. Side-eying the antique monitor, its paper continued to spit out a mixed bag of painful curses and rich blessings in my direction. The steady stream of peaks and valleys in my current travail displayed on one line, and a wavering fetal heartbeat on the other, told me this was far from over. Allowing the frustration of my present situation to finally sink its teeth in, my body collapsed back against the bed.

At least I was able to ready myself a little before each new contraction reached its summit. Why, oh why, had I decided to become a surrogate for my brother's wife? My conscience and I needed to have a serious conversation.

The only consolation in all of this was knowing with every peak, the pain would come, and with every valley in between, I would find some measure of relief. All I could do was focus on this moment. It's what I had to do to get through this. My life and the life attached to that little heartbeat inside this vise that was now my uterus weren't going to weather this storm very well if I didn't.

I was alone in this. No, not alone. My husband was here. He just kept trying to keep me comfortable, and telling me, in no uncertain terms, that I was Wonder Woman. My sister-in-law, on the other hand, was a nervous wreck. Seconds away from a full-on panic attack, she kept wringing her hands, not daring to look in my direction.

Oh no, here it comes again. Slow, squeezing pressure, a death grip clamped around my lower abdomen. It felt as if every ounce of blood flowing through my body was now sitting squarely between my legs. The pressure was unbearable. *Just breathe,* I told myself.

The nurse in the room was like a drill sergeant. Repeating over and over again in my right ear, "Take a deep breath, hold it, and bear down. One. Two. Three. Four. Five. Six. Seven. Eight. Nine. Ten. Take another breath and bear down. Two more times, just like that. I know you are hurting, but you must stay in control. Nice, slow breathing, in through your nose and out through your mouth in between contractions."

My inner beast just wanted to punch her lights out, but I kept myself in check. Feeling more pressure with each push, I knew I was getting close. This wasn't my first rodeo, having had four kids of my own. I was just older, advanced maternal age, they called it.

The nurse checked me once more and asked me to stop pushing. Calling for the doctor, she placed a gloved hand over my perineum, knowing if I so much as sneezed, this baby was coming out. Stifling a groan, I started pushing anyway.

"It isn't me. It's my body," I protested. An undercurrent of pain, exhaustion, and hunger had honed my voice into an unintentionally sharp instrument as she pleaded for me to stop. Then, out of nowhere, the doctor breezed in and gowned up like he was preparing to save us all from a worldwide biohazard spill instead of delivering a baby.

Turning to me, he finally said, "Push."

Okay, now we're talking. Digging the tips of my fingers into the underside of my bent legs, I curled around this baby my body wanted so desperately to be rid of. Taking a deep breath, I beared down. Despite the numbness in my limbs and pain in my gut, I pushed the head out and then pushed once more, and it was over. He was here.

A beautiful little boy. John Michael, 7 lbs. 4 oz., 19 inches long.

My brother and his wife were instantly smiling through tears of joy as a lifetime of prayers had finally been answered in that tiny bundle they were now holding. I, on the other hand, was exhausted, shivering, and covered in blood and mucus. Exposed to the world, nether parts, and all—I was definitely not looking my best.

At that point, I didn't even care. I had harnessed every ounce of energy I had left on one simple question. When could I finally taste food again? It's the first form of discernment we learn as infants. So, it seemed only rational that it would be one of the first thoughts I had after trying to make sense of the ordeal my body had just been put through. I had spent three nights with a hungry belly. I could almost feel my ribs poking through the green, bloodstained gown I was wearing.

Then, out of nowhere, a dull pain on my right side refocused my attention. I couldn't breathe. Something was wrong. My husband said something to the doctor, and then everything faded.

I'd heard it's been said from those who have stared death in the eye and lived to talk about it, not to flinch. Why? Because your whole life passes before you in a blink, and you'll end up missing the recap.

But I wasn't even afforded that much. In an instant, every second of every season of the life I once had changed from reds, oranges, and greens to shades of black and white.

CHAPTER FOUR

LEWIS

WHAT HAPPENED? Everything was quiet now. I was lying in my bed at home. Light streamed in through the edges of my curtains, displaying the dust still suspended in the air, floating lazily onto my bed. It must have been a dream. *I didn't feel like I just had a baby,* I thought, as I glided my fingers along the lines of my abdomen for reassurance. My stomach was still flat under my favorite faded *Stones* concert tee. No blood. No mucus. I could breathe.

Bolting upright in the bed, I noticed the walls in my room were charred. Stained patterns from the inside of a well-used furnace dusted the sheetrock—its soot, like the dregs of past sins on display. Surely, a fire had burned in here and then been haphazardly put out. All that remained was this fire-stain, instead of the semi-gloss, eggshell-colored paint I had chosen for my walls six months ago.

Suddenly, the quiet was disrupted by heavy footfalls coming down the hall. Their weighted impressions had to be leaving a mark on the scuffed-up hardwood I knew lay just beyond the four walls of this room. Not daring to open the door, I looked under its jamb instead, only to find a man advancing in an inky black, floor-length trench coat. He was coming for me.

I ran to the opposite side of the room on instinct as the door began to pulse and bow inward. Thinking any minute now, its remains would come spiraling through the air, only to stake me to the burnt remains of the wall my body was plastered up against.

But then, as if listening to my silent pleas to stop, the door abruptly rested once more against its frame while a voice boomed from inside the room, "Go. Find your Bible, and read page 228, chapter 9, verses 1-11."

I ran to my closet without considering where the voice had come from, knowing whatever lay behind the door, that voice was keeping it at bay. I searched for the hidden tome, throwing a mess of discarded clothes out of the way. Finding it, I realized the pages had never been turned. They were stuck together, refusing to budge, as if physically affronted that I had never cracked the cover. Slicing the tips of my fingers through the edges of its thin parchment, I peeled the book open to reveal the scripture I had been commanded to read. It was from Numbers:

> *The Lord spoke to Moses in the Desert of Sinai in the first month of the second year after they came out of Egypt. He said, "Have the Israelites celebrate the Passover at the appointed time. Celebrate it at the appointed time, at twilight on the fourteenth day of this month, in accordance with all its rules and regulations."*
>
> *So Moses told the Israelites to celebrate the Passover, and they did so in the Desert of Sinai at twilight on the fourteenth day of the first month. The Israelites did everything just as the Lord commanded Moses.*
>
> *But some of them could not celebrate the Passover on that day because they were ceremonially unclean on account of a dead body. So they came to Moses and Aaron that same day and said to Moses, "We have become unclean because of a dead body, but why should we be kept from presenting the Lord's offering with the other Israelites at the appointed time?"*
>
> *Moses answered them, "Wait until I find out what the Lord commands concerning you." Then the Lord said to Moses, "Tell the Israelites: 'When any of you or your descendants are unclean because of a dead body or are away on a journey, they are still to celebrate the Lord's Passover, but they are to do it on the fourteenth day of the second month at twilight. They are to eat the lamb, together with unleavened bread and bitter herbs..."*

What was that supposed to mean? I sat in my closet and listened to the quiet, foolishly thinking it might provide me with an answer. What time was it? It had to be morning, or at the very least, early afternoon. My kids had to be up. They must be outside playing because my kids were never quiet. What was going on?

I certainly wouldn't be figuring any of this out in my pajamas. Repressing a shudder, I grabbed some clothes from the floor, pulled them on, and waited. For what? I had no idea.

Finally venturing to open the door, I walked into my living room to find a man I had never met sitting in my husband's sweat-stained recliner. He simply stood and said, "Hello. My name is Lewis. I have been waiting a very long time for you to wake up."

CHAPTER FIVE

THE TWO STONES

———◆———

WITH THAT, Lewis shouldered through the back door, ushering me in his direction. The porch that lay behind the house was overrun with discarded toys and a handful of half-dead plants. At its far end rested a neglected patio set, clinging to a host of disjointed screws dangling from their metal casings.

Lewis walked over, motioning for me to come and sit down. Trailing after him, I pulled out a chair, its legs grating against the concrete, echoing my apprehension that the seat would hold.

As I sat down, I looked out across the backyard, now only noticing how foggy it was around the house. So foggy, in fact, that I couldn't make out the back fence line or any of the houses next to mine. *How odd.* Looking back at the porch, an awkward silence stretched across the table as thick as the fog encasing the house. Deciding to act at least a little concerned, I slid a sidelong glance at Lewis and probed, "Who are you again? And what are you doing here?"

"My name is Lewis. I am here to talk to you about what God has called you to do."

"And what might that be, exactly?" Nothing about this felt real. I couldn't help the leery tone in my voice.

"He wants you to take your appreciation for words and sew them into a message of reflection and hope through the bearing of two stones. Not just any two stones. These two stones are the most precious stones ever sought. Their worth invaluable. Their metal incorruptible. They are, in fact, a foreshadowing of the instrument of all creation. They are a treasure of

God, by God, and for God. Flawless, skillfully purposed, and without blemish, pointing straight to His Son and the cross."

This guy was nuts. Two stones. What two stones was he talking about, and how did he get into my house? What was I now, a treasure hunter? An archeologist? A warrior-poet? I hated the dirt. Besides, I barely passed my Intro to English course in college. Scrubbing my hands down the front of my face, I tried to erase the annoyance I felt.

"What is the last thing you remember doing," he offered, bringing me back to the conversation, "because your purpose starts there?"

"Well, I was in the hospital. I just had a baby, and I couldn't breathe. The next thing I knew, I was lying in my bed at home. So how does that fit into all of this, Lewis? With this purpose God has for me? How does any of it have to do with finding two stones and me having a baby? I thought that was a dream."

"You weren't dreaming. You really had a baby, and you are still in the hospital. You will find the two stones, and the purpose for your life starts in that delivery room. Do you have your Bible?"

I told him it was still sitting on the floor in my closet, so he told me to go get it. Walking back into my room, I noticed the book exactly where I left it, opened to chapter nine in Numbers.

As I closed it, I vaguely recalled the scripture I had been pressed upon to read about preparing to participate in the first and second Passover. There was something about being on a long journey or being in contact with a dead body.

Walking back outside, it wasn't surprising to find Lewis still sitting there. A sinking suspicion told me I was going to be spending a lot of time with this man, whoever he was.

Lewis didn't seem to be in a hurry, so I decided not to be either. I sat down slowly and pushed the Bible in his direction. A part of me was curious about this mysterious stranger and the hidden things he wanted to share with me. Intrigued enough that I hadn't even raised an eyebrow at something he just told me—I was still in the hospital.

Lewis pushed the book back to me. "Open your Bible to Exodus 1:15-19 and read."

CHAPTER SIX

THE BIRTH STOOL

—◆—

The king of Egypt said to the Hebrew midwives, whose names were Shiphrah and Puah, "When you are helping the Hebrew women during childbirth on the delivery stool, if you see that the baby is a boy, kill him; but if it is a girl, let her live." The midwives, however, feared God and did not do what the king of Egypt had told them to do; they let the boys live. Then the king of Egypt summoned the midwives and asked them, "Why have you done this? Why have you let the boys live?" The midwives answered Pharaoh, "Hebrew women are not like Egyptian women; they are vigorous and give birth before the midwives arrive."

I LIFTED my eyes out of the scripture, only to find Lewis staring back at me. "Okay. I read it. It's talking about midwives delivering babies, defying Pharaoh, and fearing God. But I don't know what that has to do with me or these two stones I am supposed to tell everyone about. Much less, how they point to Jesus. I know you are probably aware of what I do for a living. I am a labor and delivery nurse, but other than that, how does this relate to me?"

Massaging my neck with one hand, I closed the book with the other, pushing it back to him. Then I shoved my twitching fingers back into my lap and waited for him to give me an answer my mind could somehow wrap my head around.

Lewis carefully opened the Bible back to the passage in Exodus and said, "Do you know what the Hebrew word for delivery stool is?"

Shaking my head, he continued, "It is the word *ha-abenayim*, and it literally means *the two stones*.

"In ancient Egypt, Egyptian women were known to squat on two, level birth-bricks during their labor. These two bricks were named after one of their many goddesses for childbirth. Her name was *Meskhenet*. Egyptian women believed these special bricks would offer divine provision and protection during their labor and birth experience because, in ancient times, the rates of maternal and infant mortality were extremely high.

"To the Hebrews, the name for these two bricks sounded much like their word *mishkan*, meaning *tabernacle* or *dwelling place*. The name *Meskhenet*, itself, is almost identical to another Hebrew word *miskenoth*, meaning *storehouse* or *gathering place of great service, provision, value* or *benefit*.

"This makes perfect sense because, in antiquity, gathering places of worship and centers of learning doubled as a community's treasury. The thinking, being, that these assembling places not only supplied the regions surrounding them with the means to meet their physical needs but were also considered birthing places of intellectual and spiritual provision. For the Hebrews to change the word for these two bricks to the words *ha-abenayim* is very telling."

Realizing I didn't have anything to add, he said, "This word phrase is only used one other time in the Bible, in the book of Jeremiah. Let's read it together."

He came around the table and settled next to me, opening the Bible to Jeremiah chapter eighteen, verse three, and I read:

> "*So I went down to the Potter's house, and I saw Him working at the wheel.*"

"The Him in the sentence is our Lord. He is the Potter. He was working at *the two stones*."

"What was He working on?" I said, never having been one to beat around the bush. Believing early on, the quicker the understanding, the quicker I could get what I needed. Two birds. One stone. And all of that.

"Not what was He working on, but who is He working on?" Lewis replied.

"Okay, I'll bite." I said, with a sigh, "Who is He working on, Lewis?"

"He is working on you, of course. He is turning the two stones, His Divine Instrument, molding your composition into a vessel. He is shaping you into the purposed container He intended you to be so that you can hold water—so what flows out of you is Him.

"Those two stones the Hebrews delivered on, back in Egypt, were a veiled reference to the Hebrews' reliance on God to provide, deliver, and dwell with them.

"Do you think, maybe, the midwives feared God because they saw beforehand that God met His people's needs through His Son?

"Could it be that they saw *Jehovah Jireh*, one of the many names for God, meaning *God our Provider*, in action? Because even though *Jehovah Jireh* reads *God Our Provider*, the literal meaning comes from a word that means *to see*, making the more appropriate translation, *God Will See to It*.

"The strange thing is that the word for *to reverentially fear* and a derivative of the word for *to see* are spelled the same in Hebrew. It is the word *yirah*. The midwives *feared* God because they saw *God See to It* on countless occasions, just like He did on Mt. Moriah with Abraham and Isaac—through the substitutionary exchange of His Son for man's.

"Those ladies knew there was a reason the Hebrews cried out to and had faith in their God. They saw that the Hebrews didn't rely on the pagan temples, storehouses, and wisdom traditions they were surrounded by to supply what they needed.

"The Israelites were delivered with vigor and shaped in strength and wholeness because they tabernacled with and treasured the Living God. They were brought to birth, standing on His Word, nourished by His principles, and trusting in His love to provide.

"You may not know this, but the most significant difference between the God of Israel and all the gods worshiped by the pagans in the Fertile Crescent, other than Israel's belief in one God, is that the God of Israel lives with His people. He doesn't occupy niches in walls or inanimate bricks decorated with tokens of pagan goddesses in relief. The Lord isn't conjured through ridiculous incantations, but dwells intimately with His people.

"That delivery stool back in Egypt was a foreshadowing of God's people dwelling with, provided for, covered by, and standing on the ultimate delivering instrument—Jesus Christ.

"And if you can receive it, that stool was also a type of foreshadowing of the first Passover. Remember, by standing on that stool, the Hebrew baby boys lived. It foreshadowed Jesus standing between Israel and certain death on the first Passover and, ultimately, Him standing on the cross thousands of years later, in the flesh, for that very same reason.

"Interestingly, the word for son in Hebrew is *ben*, the very same word used to mean *between*. The Lord's *Son* has always been standing *between* mankind and certain death, it seems. The Israelites just haven't been able to see that the vehicle of God's provision has always been with them through His Son, Jesus Christ.

"And I can prove it. If you were to separate the words *ha-abenayim—the two stones*, the way the Hebrews were known for doing to obscure an underlying message in the Hebrew text, it would poetically sound like *The Son of God with Us—Ha* (The) *Ben* (Son) *iah* (of God) *Im* (With us).

"If that isn't enough, the word the Egyptians used for those two birth bricks, *meskhenet*, and the Hebrew word *miskenowth,* meaning *tabernacle or storehouse*, even point to Christ with Us. *Mes* (Egyptian for Son) *Khen* (Stands) *Et* (With Us, Always)—*The Son Stands with* Us, *Always!*

"Jesus has always been the vehicle of God's provision—the Son who always stands with us and on our behalf."

CHAPTER SEVEN

THE WHEELS

———◆———

Was this guy for real? In my defense, I had been raised on a more than a healthy dose of skepticism. I was never one to take anything at face value. For me, everything was suspect and up for debate. Indecision was my second skin. Uncertainty, a never-ending side hustle; I had never been one for leaving all of my eggs in the same proverbial basket.

Lewis scowled and leaned in, invading my space so much I had to lean back. "Yes, I am for real." *Wait a minute, I didn't say that out loud.*

Lewis turned away, apparently not expecting a response, and offered flatly instead, "Do you know what an object lesson is?"

"Why don't you enlighten me, Lewis?" This conversation felt like it was starting off all kinds of wrong. I didn't think I had said anything ignorant or even mildly offensive.

"It is a teaching method that comprises using a physical object or visual aid to drive a point home. What if I told you these two wheels—or two stones—have always been the material object lessons representing the foundation for all of God's most basic spiritual truths—love and compassion? Being perfectly delivering, perfectly freeing, and perfectly redemptive.

"What if I told you these two stones reflected the nature and process of God and His Son in the Old Testament? And that in the New, Jesus came down in the flesh, the human instrument of creation and deliverance, much like the pottery wheel and the delivery stool, to show God's people the nature of God Himself and how those two stones were always meant to lead to the cross. After all, He has always been the Rock of our Salvation, the firm foundation we stand on, are delivered by, and dwell with. And, if you are willing to accept it, so much more."

Perplexed, I furiously massaged my temples. This guy made my brain hurt.

Lewis sighed. "This might be better if I give you an example."

Maybe. We would have to see, but I wasn't about to hold my breath.

CHAPTER EIGHT

THE FOUNDATION OF THE TRINITY

"WHEN YOU are building any type of structure like a house, a temple, or even a grocery store, any carpenter worth their weight will tell you how important square corners are in your foundation.

"A square corner doesn't mean all the sides are of equal length, but that the outside angles of the building are ninety degrees. Without square corners, the subfloor of any foundation will be off. The walls will lean sideways. And your roof will look like it was made by a guy with a crick in his neck.

"So, how do you get your foundation right? Well, in carpentry, in more primitive times, you could use a knotted cord, twelve lengths long, to measure out a 3-4-5 right triangle to square your corners. A triangle to square your corners? That sounds odd. But don't we do that in our faith to square our spiritual corners? Through God, the Father, God, the Son, and God, the Holy Spirit, who make up the perfect *right triangle* in the foundation of our faith.

"As believers in Christ, we believe God came down in the physical realm, the agent of creation becoming man Himself, to save us from death and separation from Him. How did He do that? Through Jesus Christ, of course!

"Jesus came to dwell among us, in the natural, to show mankind what service, worship, and true love in every season of our lives looked like. And to essentially show us the nature of God Himself. He did this with the desire for us to willingly accept Him, obey Him, and receive Him in a bond of relationship, allowing Him to redeem us.

"God knew from the garden that mankind wasn't up to the task. All they did was mess things up. They took His commands and made them stumbling blocks.

"From the start, they relied on themselves and had their fingers pointing at each other rather than accepting responsibility for their own actions and mistakes. They had sacrifice without obedience. Their offerings were never without blemish, and their remorse never involved true repentance. Sure, they were occasionally motivated, but without the key ingredient—discipline—mankind's love was always conditional.

"Humanity was given all the supplies to build their spiritual house: the knotted cord, the Law, the prophets, the Lord's writings, and the merciful, unfailing love of their Father in heaven. But left into their own hands, man took that knotted cord, tied their own hands behind their backs, and made themselves slaves to sin.

"So, God, in His infinite wisdom, sent them a carpenter to get their corners square. To become their cornerstone, in the flesh, uniting them with the Trinity, in a holy marriage wrapped in the unraveling knotted cord of His love and righteousness."

Lewis put my hand in his and asked me if that made any sense. I was confused. Where were the two stones in the story? If the two stones represented Jesus in the Old Testament, where were they in the building supplies?

I said as much as Lewis smiled.

"I'm glad you were paying attention. Remember back to your Sunday school lessons. What did Moses bring down from Mt. Sinai?"

"The Ten Commandments."

"Exactly. The simplest, purest form of the Law. And what were they written on?"

"Two stone tablets." *The two stones.* Lewis saw the glimmer of recognition in my eyes and nodded.

"If you'll remember, the first set of stones, provided by God, were destroyed by Moses because of Israel's rebellion. The first two stones represent Jesus' first emergence and rejection by man. Remember, Moses had to carve out new stones, fleshed out by man, and ascend the mountain again to be written by God in order to be re-dispatched to His people. This second set of stones represents the Second Coming of Christ on the Day of Atonement.

"According to Jewish tradition, this was the actual day Moses returned with the unbroken stones. Both sets were then placed in the Ark of the Covenant, the broken and the whole. This is a perfect foreshadowing of Christ—the Ten Words, the two stones becoming flesh, to dwell among us, broken by man, while at the same time, making them whole and at one with Him.

"You may recall that Jesus talked extensively about these two stones to His people. Not because they didn't know what was written on them, but because they didn't understand the underlying theme behind them all along was love.

"There is a scene in the New Testament where Jesus uses these two stones to get this point across. In John 8:1-11, we find Jesus defending a woman caught in adultery. Scribes and teachers of the law brought her to Jesus to trap Him in His words. They asked Him if the woman shouldn't be stoned for her sin. Jesus bent down and started writing something in the dirt. What do you think He was writing?"

"I have no idea, Lewis. I don't think it ever says if I've remembered correctly."

"You're right. It never says what Jesus wrote. Scholars for generations have pondered what He scribbled in the dust that day. Could it be something as simple as this? Could He have simply been writing the Ten Commandments in the dirt? Writing something that would confer the most benefit to both the woman and the teachers of the Law? With one simple action, Jesus silently asked them if any of them were guiltless without condemning them. He was teaching them, that maybe, instead of throwing stones to break and destroy, they should have been learning from them, to be made whole instead. Jesus showed them that understanding the principles of God should always come down to His measure of love— The Word of God, and the perfect balance between discipline and mercy, guided by The Holy Spirit."

CHAPTER NINE

HEAR AND OBEY

—◆—

I NEEDED to stand up and stretch, but I couldn't move. Anxiety had begun to weave my body into tight knots. Every limb, muscle, and fiber of my being seemed to have simultaneously rebelled against my brain, causing my extremities to remain stuck to the patio furniture.

This was obviously a lot to swallow, along with the throat-clogging alarm creeping up from my gut. Slowly but surely, the unsettled feeling eased its grip, allowing me to stand and coax my limbs from their sleep.

Lewis joined me as I walked along the fence line, the deafening silence the only words between us. It seemed the fog had lifted a little around the house, only to find its way under my scalp, clinging to my brain like a wet blanket of question marks I had no hopes of getting any answers to.

"Your thoughts?" Lewis whispered, offering me an opening to give voice to the concerns that were starting to leave a wear pattern on my gray matter.

"Why me? I guess that's the first of many I have, Lewis. I haven't been obedient to God. I'm on the B-team if you know what I mean. I don't pray. And to be honest, I dread going to church. I've been saved and baptized, but I have lived the same life I have always lived. A fornicator, an adulteress, a liar, more to myself than anyone else, a thief, an idolater, a breaker of the Sabbath, disobedient to my parents. I have taken God's purposes and made them empty and meaningless in my life. I haven't been a true witness to His character. He hasn't been my God. I may not have committed all-out murder, but I have stabbed to death countless relationships. I'm a faker. I don't tabernacle with God. I don't dwell in the temple. I live in a house of hypocrites. A white-washed tomb, like the Pyramids used to look—a sparkling oasis from a distance, but up close, filled with dead bones and a three-year-old's idea of artwork on the walls."

Lewis put his arm around my shoulder. "You may not have been faithful to God, but God has always been faithful to you. Do you remember what you used to pray all the time when you were a little girl?"

I thought for a second, reaching back into that cob-webbed corner of my mind. "I used to pray that if I ever fell away from God, He would call me back, and I would return to Him before I died."

I thought about what I just said and stopped cold in my tracks, a nervous laugh bubbling up from my throat. "Lewis, am I going to die?"

"Yes, but not today," he said with a smirk, clearly amused that he hadn't really answered the question.

"Then what am I doing here?" I pleaded, cradling my stomach, feeling like I was about to puke.

"I already told you. God has a very important purpose for you. You are His chosen vessel, bringing a message important enough to tell the whole world. And it starts and ends with Jesus.

"When you look back at your life, you see all your mistakes. You chose the world instead of God, but He never stopped loving you. You broke His heart, but He remembered your prayers.

"Think about the constellations of scars that have dotted your past. Do you think any of them were a surprise to Him? Do you think it changed His desires for your life? He took every crack and dent you or someone else put in that vessel and made it work for your good and according to His purposes. It is within this seemingly wild perspective that God moves.

"God wants people to remember He has always allowed desolation to bring fruitfulness. He has always allowed desert times to produce the meadow.

"He allows something to be made empty, so He can make it full again. Isn't this what the whole history of the Jews has shown mankind?

"A simple survey of the Old Testament reveals to the world, through the Jews, how God loves. He has always been the Creator and the Re-Creator. Our Provider. And a God of Second Chances.

"God just wants His people to realize that His provision has been through His Son—Jesus Christ. He is the only way home and back to the Father. And that entails both believing in Him and receiving Him. And the believing and receiving means changing your *want-to*. The *want-to* comes from turning away from sin and turning to God.

"A true believer acknowledges their sin, knowing they are not enough and need a Redeemer. They yearn to walk with a different perspective, no longer making excuses, or flat out skirting the very principles God holds dear."

"That doesn't sound like anything new. I mean, people know that, I think. What am I supposed to bring to the conversation?"

"You will bring a message of supernatural hope with this story in the middle of a hopeless day. It will help to open people's eyes to the truth and lift their spirits, pointing them to God. It will remind them again that anything is possible with the Lord and that He has always been in control. The author and the finisher of our story.

"It will help people remember that the Lord's whole endgame for all of mankind was never desolation but the garden. Never despair, but joy. Never graves' clothes, but a wedding garment. Never Mt. Horeb, but Moriah.

"This account will help create moments when people will decide they want to accept and reflect Jesus again. These two stones we've been talking about will be the centerpiece on the table of this story."

Lewis and I started heading back to the house. *Now what?* I thought.

He answered my question in one fluid movement as he walked to the door. "That's enough for today. I will see you tomorrow." He opened the door and started walking out when I reached up and gently touched his shoulder. "Lewis, you said I was still in the hospital. Is that where my family is? Are they okay?"

"For the moment," he replied, and then he was gone.

The fog outside the house had become thick again, so I went back inside and shut the door. Racing to my bedroom, I flopped down on the bed and buried myself under my second-hand sheets, absently rubbing the center of my chest, hoping beyond hope that it would somehow be hard enough to wake the dead.

CHAPTER TEN

ONE IN THE SAME

—◆—

EARLY THE next morning, I got up and did the usual things. Making my way into the bathroom, I showered and then got dressed. I untangled my long, unruly hair, pulling it into a tight bun without even thinking. My hands even started reaching for the toothbrush, without a thought as to whether it mattered if I brushed my teeth here or not, wherever here was.

The house looked like mine but had become different in a way I couldn't quite put my finger on. Every fixture, every appliance, looked the same. Every stick of furniture was in its place. The house's layout even had the same generic floor plan I had picked out years ago, identical to every fourth house in my neighborhood.

The bare bones were there, for all intents and purposes, but the life inside seemed hollow and disconnected. I couldn't help but think this is precisely how a lame man must feel—a refugee who had fled to a foreign land but found no refuge or means of escape.

After getting dressed, I made my way into the kitchen. Was I hungry? Well, no, but maybe my regular morning cup of coffee would be nice. There was something appealing in the civility of repetition. A cup of coffee could go a long way in bringing back some semblance of normalcy to my life. A security blanket of sorts, cautiously bubble-wrapped in monotony. I was thoroughly freaking myself out enough, as it was. After all, Lewis told me—*I am a vessel. I am a vessel.*

After making the perfect cup, I cleaned the kitchen and walked through the dining room, only to find Lewis sitting quietly at a corner of my dining room table. He was dressed in blue jeans and a crisp white T-shirt, poking out from underneath a sky-blue blazer. I couldn't help but think he looked like he was waiting for his name to be called to pick up his hot, non-fat, no-foam latte before heading off to work, where every day was casual Friday.

Startled by his presence, I jumped about three feet in the air. And so did my coffee. *So much for a security blanket.* Luckily, the cup and its contents missed my clothes and fell to the floor. Piercing the silence with a giant crash, the cup cracked into about a million pieces, scattering liquid goodness across several square feet of my adobe-brown ceramic tile. I had chosen the color specifically because it was supposed to mask messes like the one I had just made. *No such luck.*

I picked up said mess, grumbling all the way back to the table, and sat with a grunt. "Next time, make some noise or something, Lewis, so I know you are here. You scared me to death." Horrible figure of speech, I know, given the circumstances. Maybe I shouldn't have used those exact words.

As I settled in, Lewis brought out a set of pictures from the breast pocket of the jacket he was wearing and laid them on the table. They were pictures of various sets of stones, ten pictures in all. As I picked up each one, Lewis began to explain what they were and how they were used.

- The first was an ancient Egyptian birth stool.
- The second was a pottery wheel from the Ancient Near East.
- The third was a picture of Charlton Heston heaving the Ten Commandments over his head. Okay, Lewis had a sense of humor. I would have to remember that.
- The fourth was an ancient hand-mill used by maidservants for grinding grain.
- The fifth was an olive press.
- The sixth was the picture of a lodestone. Apparently, it was a naturally occurring rock with magnetic properties.
- The seventh was a picture of a woman sitting in a chair with a distaff in one hand and a spindle in her other, spinning wool.
- The eighth was an anvil and hammer.
- The ninth was a furnace used in antiquity for the baking of bread.
- The final picture was of a meadow with a sheepfold and its gate.

I laid the pictures down after examining each one. Knowing that if I believed what Lewis was telling me, each one represented Jesus in some way. "What am I looking at, Lewis?"

"We have talked about the delivery stool, the pottery wheel, and the Ten Commandments tablets. These are the other stones we will be discussing. Are you ready to continue?"

"Yes, Lewis!" I said gruffly, thinking what a waste of time it was to point out the obvious.

"The thing you must understand, first and foremost, is that the truth of God's Word is like two sides of the same coin swinging from a pendulum. The Word has the power to save, while at the same time the power to slay. That's the rub. And God's process is all in that rub.

"With every forward stroke, there is an equally important backstroke against the grain, wiping away the residue, revealing the Lord's nature and, ultimately, ours. He rubs us to reveal that with suffering, healing; with crushing, wholeness; with dying, living; with poverty, riches; with boundaries, freedom; with servitude, authority; with disparity, fruitfulness; and ultimately, with judgment, redemption. This is the juxtaposition of His very being.

"You see, God has always been in the business of rubbing away our sin, not rubbing it in. These sets of stones evoke this common theme, which can be found throughout the entirety of scripture and revealed in Christ, Himself."

CHAPTER ELEVEN

THE HAND-MILL AND THE HAND MAIDEN
———◆———

NOT WAITING to let any of that sink in, Lewis held up the picture of the hand-mill. He began explaining that the hand-mill was essentially two millstones, on a much smaller scale, that maidservants used to grind grain with. I was familiar with the other, larger millstones since I felt the weight of one around my neck most of my life.

Millstones weighed tons and were made of solid rock. One circular stone was carved into a depression track the upper stone revolved around. The grain was crushed under the weight of the upper stone and gathered in the bottom one. The hand-mill was used for the same purpose, only in a more intimate way.

Lewis explained the concept of the hand-mill, then sat back in his chair, quiet, for what seemed like forever. He loved those silent, contemplative pauses that were very quickly getting under my skin. He seemed to be thinking carefully about how he was going to proceed. Like he knew the gravity of what he had to tell me and was now cautiously pressing upon my train of thought before it jumped the track and my brain shut down.

With a voice low and edged with restraint, Lewis whispered, "Jesus is the hand-mill. He's the two stones that work the grain into a fine meal so it can be used to make bread. He prepares the meal for provision. The boundaries or edges where those two stones meet and rub together are where this takes place.

"Figuratively speaking, this is where tracks of tribulation are cut. Chords of conviction are struck. Our eyes turn to the Lord. Relationship is fostered. God's process is revealed. Provision is procured. Healing begins, and The Almighty is glorified.

"As man finds himself in circumstances that are or are not a result of his own doing, triumphs, troubles, and calamities produce an effect—the forward stroke. God uses this stroke to lead to healing, growth, and relationship. Ultimately producing a testimony from relying on Him—the backward stroke. This process covers us, keeps us fed, and feeds those in need around us, enabling us to offer help and compassion to others without feeling the need to hoard and treasure it only for ourselves.

"Have you ever considered for one moment the boy in the New Testament in John 6:9-11, who was pressed upon to give up his lunch on a hillside so thousands could eat? Have you thought perhaps, just maybe, it was the witness of this boy's belief in Christ that fed the masses that day, right along with his fish and bread? Could it be that what satisfied them as much as the miracle was his testimony, in action, about the trust he put in Christ to deliver? This boy could have told Christ and the disciples to get lost, but instead, he will forever be remembered for this act of generosity and his faith in God to provide."

I had tears running down my face, but I didn't make a sound. The words Lewis spoke hung in the air, suspended over that table, suffocating me. How many times had I been asked to offer up my lunch and declined? How many times had I been pressed to feed others with the truth of God's promises and failed miserably? I had never considered it in this way before.

Finally, Lewis said, "I want to reveal something to you that you may have never heard." He got up and left the room, quickly returning with the Bible we had used the day before tucked under his right arm. He opened it again to Exodus. He flipped to the eleventh chapter and began reading at verse four:

> So Moses said, "This is what the Lord says: 'About midnight I will go throughout Egypt. Every firstborn son in Egypt will die, from the firstborn son of Pharaoh, who sits on the throne, to the firstborn son of the female slave, who is at her hand-mill, and all the firstborn of the cattle as well."

"Do you understand what I am telling you? The firstborn son of Pharaoh and the firstborn son of the maidservant (slave girl) at her hand-mill. This is one of many instances foreshadowing Christ through the embodiment of these two stones.

"Moses was prophesying about the future death of God's Son. The hand-mill (the two stones), in the hands of the maidservant—baby Jesus, God's perfect principles of love made manifest in the flesh, in the hands of Mary, the Lord's maidservant.

"The word used here in this scripture for hand-mill is the word *recheh*. A Hebrew audience with some grasp of poetic sensibilities would connect *recheh* with the word *rechem*, a close cognate equivalent, meaning *love* and *compassion*. The word looks like this word *rechem,* as it is written in this scripture, *ha-rechayim*. The Hebrews loved to take advantage of wordplay, and this example is no exception.

"This sounds just like Jesus, doesn't it? The two stones (The Ten Commandments) that were always meant to represent love and compassion revealed in the flesh through Christ, The Son of God, With Us. Through His death, by being both the sin—represented by the first fruit of Pharaoh (inferring oppression, man as provider, and self-glorification) and the sin offering—the firstborn son of the maidservant (inferring discipline, love, mercy, humility, sacrifice, God as Provider, and glorification of Him) Jesus would bring the law of love and compassion back to life and feed us all."

CHAPTER TWELVE

GETHSEMANE

MY PULSE began to quicken, my breaths deepening, trying to keep up and drink all this in. Lewis had caught my attention. He was making perfect sense. He certainly wasn't a madman; he didn't appear to be distracted or misguided. Lewis was someone I didn't think I had the luxury of humoring or ignoring anymore, even if I still wasn't convinced.

Lewis pointed to the picture of the oil-press. I didn't notice a big difference in its design from the larger millstones, but I knew there must be a reason why it was included in the pictures on the table.

"You know, sometimes they're not given, right?"

"What aren't, Lewis?"

"The reasons why."

Okay, I know I didn't say that out loud.

Without pause, Lewis continued, "God is the Director of the Universe. Sometimes, He allows us to see what He is working on, a slight glimpse in front of the tapestry. Those are the true blessings we receive. Knowing we may never get to see it, though, should encourage us to always be watching and vigilant to walk in truth and right relationship with the Lord.

"So many people say they are saved, when, in fact, they walk deceived. They aren't watching or vigilant to walk in right relationship with God. These people are sitting next to you at church.

"People today, just as much as they did in antiquity, like to come up with their own principles, definitions, and boundary markers of what faith and belief mean. This is what tickles the ear, so to speak. The story of Gethsemane is an example of what God does and doesn't expect from us."

"What does Gethsemane mean, anyway?" I asked.

Lewis lifted up the picture of the oil-press, so it was directly in my line of sight. "This. This is how oil was pressed from olives. Under immense pressure and crushing came oil the Israelites used in lamps to bring light and to anoint kings and priests with.

"In a similar fashion, this is how God uses this vehicle (as the Ten Commandments) to bring light into our own lives, enrichment to our circumstances, and something from our suffering. It makes more malleable our hearts, allowing us to see the bigger picture—that lying at the heart of those two stones lies a breeding ground for repentance and relationship, not resentment and persecution. It is no coincidence that Jesus' most anguishing struggle was at Gethsemane. If man was afflicted in this way, then so must the Messiah be. Let's look at what it says in the Bible."

Lewis opened the scripture to Matthew 26:36 and read:

> Then Jesus went with His disciples to a place called Gethsemane, and he said to them, "Sit here while I go over there and pray." He took Peter and the two sons of Zebedee along with him, and he began to be sorrowful and troubled. Then he said to them, "My soul is overwhelmed with sorrow to the point of death. Stay here and keep watch with me."
>
> Going a little farther, he fell with his face to the ground and prayed, "My Father, if it is possible, may this cup be taken from me. Yet not as I will, but as You will."
>
> Then he turned to his disciples and found them sleeping. "Couldn't you men keep watch with me for one hour?" he asked Peter. "Watch and pray so that you will not fall into temptation. The spirit is willing but the flesh is weak."
>
> He went away a second time and prayed, "My Father, if it is not possible for this cup to be taken away unless I drink it, may your will be done."
>
> When he came back, he again found them sleeping, because their eyes were heavy. So he left them and went away once more and prayed the third time, saying the same thing.

Then he returned to the disciples and said to them, "Are you still sleeping and resting? Look, the hour has come, and the Son of Man is delivered into the hands of sinners. Rise! Let us go! Here comes my betrayer!"

Lewis looked up at me with tears in his eyes. "Jesus was so troubled. He didn't want to drink the cup of affliction that was being given to Him. Knowing He would be separated from His Father, Jesus prayed three times for it to be taken from Him; yet He continued to pray that His Father's will be done and not His own. Jesus didn't even have the support of His friends."

Lewis looked down at the picture once more. "This is where He was anointed King-Priest. In the oil-press. Not because of the crushing and pressure but because of His submission to do the will of the Father, even under those conditions. Jesus perfectly stood firm on His Father's promises and principles while being crushed and pressed. If you think about it, Jesus was pressed so deeply that His skin oozed blood that day, as if that oil-press was being used on Him in that garden.

"Peter, John, and James were sleeping. God expects us to be awake and ready, willing to do His will and not our own, by being obedient to His Word. The light the Son provides helps us live like He suffered and died.

"Jesus provided the perfect example of how men should live through the crushing and most difficult times of life.

"God's Word is much like the oil-press. It helps to restrain us and gets us through difficult situations by producing a substance expressed through every turn of the page in scripture to comfort us. It provides invaluable insight and wisdom to nourish us and light our paths, keeping our consciences ever-present and awake instead of swept away and lulled to sleep."

Lewis walked to the front door. Then without another word, he was gone. I stood in the doorframe of my lonely little house, considering what he said, wondering when the fog that seemed to cling like mildew to my house would ever go away.

CHAPTER THIRTEEN

THE LODESTONE

—◆—

IT SEEMED like a very long time before Lewis came back. The house was lonely with no one in it. So, I resolved to clean up the inside of this temporary lodging place I somehow found myself stuck in. I scrubbed the floors. Changed the sheets on the beds. All the mundane things I used to do at home.

I liked the mundane, but unfortunately, it hadn't allowed my mind a reprieve. My stubborn intellect refused to be turned off. *What was I doing here? And where was I going?* Those two questions kept playing in an endless loop inside my brain. As my thoughts returned to my family, I heard a knock at the door.

Running to answer it, I opened the door and exclaimed, "Hello, Lewis!"

Offering me nothing but a comforting smile, he walked inside.

"Are you ready to talk about the lodestone today? That is next on the list, right?"

I loved how he acted like he was uncertain and was giving me some discretion about the direction the conversation would be going today. "Yes, I think so."

Heading into the living room, we sat down on my favorite couch. Sitting in the room like an old friend, it always seemed ready for the chance to pull me in for a warm hug. The piece was certainly nothing to look at, but what it lacked in style, it more than made up for in comfort.

The armrests were decorated in coffee and water stains, seasoned over time. The cushions were deformed, causing the couch to sag in the middle, the result of countless failed attempts to make it to bed before falling asleep. Wrapping a blanket around my legs in a cotton cocoon, I sat down and burrowed in.

Pulling out the picture of the lodestone, Lewis handed it over. There was only one rock in the picture. Before I could nag him about the missing stone, he exercised his right to speak.

"The lodestone is a very singular rock. In antiquity, it was discovered that this rock drew iron to its surface. For all intents and purposes, it was essentially a permanent magnet. Can you imagine what a wonder that must have been to humanity at the time? To this day, geologists have racked their brains, developing all kinds of theories to their origin.

"The lodestone had an important purpose in the Ancient Near East. Do you know what that might be?"

"Well, the only thing I can come up with, is that it might have been used as a compass, Lewis. For navigational direction. Am I right?"

"Exactly. The word *lodestone* comes from a word meaning *to lead*. It was the *lead, way,* or *journey stone*. This object guided its user in the right direction. This is exactly what a compass does.

"And the word *compass* comes from two Latin terms meaning *together* and *a step* or *pace*—walking together, essentially. Doesn't that sound like Jesus Christ? He walked with us and suffered for us. He died and took our sin upon Himself so the whole world could get its metaphorical ship back on course.

"God covered us with His blood and became our moral compass. His Spirit came into our hearts, inking Himself onto our very souls, to direct us in the ways we should go—setting our moral straits, straight again."

"But, Lewis, I don't remember there being a verse about a lodestone referring to Christ in the Bible," I questioned.

"There is one, though. It can be found in Isaiah 53. It might not be clear, but Isaiah spoke about the Second Coming of Christ in this scripture.

"Isaiah 53 describes, in detail, the suffering, death, and atonement of sin for all of mankind accomplished by Jesus Christ. It is a futuristic verse because Isaiah is speaking to his people about something they had already done (the first Coming of Christ and His Crucifixion) for which they would repent at some future date (the Second Coming of Christ and His

Judgment). The verse in question that I would like to discuss about the lodestone can be found in Isaiah 53:2:

> *He grew up before him like a tender shoot, and like a root out of dry ground. He had no beauty or majesty to attract us to him, nothing in his appearance that we should desire him.*

"Isaiah was saying that there was no pull to the Messiah, because His chosen people were trying to be drawn with the wrong pair of eyes— physical ones, instead of spiritual ones, just like they had done so many times in the past, like demanding an earthly king they could lay their eyes on, instead of rejoicing in the Heavenly King they couldn't see, who always provided for them."

Lewis pointed again at the picture of the lodestone before adding, "Lodestones are not attractive to look at, but there is an internal inducement that pulls iron to its surface. This magnetic force can't be physically observed but inherently felt.

"Isaiah knew that one day, his brothers and sisters in Israel would see Jesus for who and what He did and finally be drawn to Him. He just didn't know when."

"Lewis, where is the other stone? It must have been the one attracted to it."

Pulling another picture out of his pocket, Lewis looked at it before handing it over to me. It was the picture of a large black stone with a large cluster of nails entangled around its crown.

CHAPTER FOURTEEN

THE DISTAFF AND THE SPINDLE

———◆———

TIME SEEMS to spin out of control when you aren't the one at the wheel. At least, that's what it seemed like to me. I didn't know what day it was. Hours had become bunched together in a jumbled heap, crowded with sleep, idleness, and the occasional random visits from Lewis.

Today was no different from any other, except I felt on edge, with an inherent need to accomplish whatever I was tasked to do here. This was new for me.

I had always been the one who did half the job. Never an early riser, I was the queen of procrastination. The enforcer of instant gratification. A woman of preferences, not principles. And a job worth doing was only worth doing if it took all of five minutes. I never gave my all to anything, least of all Jesus.

Thankfully, there was a knock at the door. Going to answer it, my throat began to bob, attempting to swallow my own hypocrisy before nausea set in.

Lewis came in and I asked him if we could go upstairs. The whole second floor had been neglected since this little staycation began, and I was quickly running out of rooms he hadn't seen.

I was going stir crazy in this house and wanted to see some change. And the only change I thought I had any control over was the scenery we would be having our little discussions in. So Lewis and I went into the den and sat down.

There was no small talk. With Lewis, everything was big. He pulled out a picture of a woman holding a wooden staff with wool wrapped around it in the bend of one arm, and a spindle hanging to gravity, turning wool into thread with the other.

"This is the distaff and spindle. The distaff is used to keep the wool you see in the picture from being tangled as it is spun on the spindle to make thread. This thread is used to make coverings, clothing for bodies, tents for shelter, carpets for flooring, and mats for bedding.

"Thread or string is essentially hair being manipulated and spun to make something new. And it was a very hot commodity in ancient times, just as much as textiles in the global market are today.

"Let me ask you something. How did the ancients prepare hair for its tasks? It was cut, bound, braided, shaped, and even burned on some occasions, right?"

"Yeah, sure," I said, as if I had any clue where Lewis was going with this.

"God is like this."

"Like what, Lewis?"

"He takes string and shapes it, just like He does with clay. After we have been pressed and turned, spun on the whorl, so to speak, and untangled to see what the pressing has revealed, a mess or a masterpiece, God always thinks, *I can work with that*. He never forsakes us, even when it feels like He has."

"We are the string in this little scenario?"

"Yes."

"I'm sorry, but I'm not following, Lewis."

"This is just like the potter with the clay on the wheel. We are just using a different medium. You see, just like string, clay never loses its composition. It remains clay, but is shaped in the way designed by its creator to be expressed. This is simply another object lesson."

"I remember what an object lesson is," I countered, rolling my eyes.

Ignoring my aggravation, Lewis continued, "God is always working for our good. No matter what the enemy's design is. God's plan will not be compromised. He will be the Potter, the Weaver, the Hunter, and the Musician if He needs to be. He works in whatever medium He chooses. Let me give you some examples."

He must have sensed that I felt lost because the feeling was growing in the deer-in-the-headlights expression written all over my face.

"God is the Weaver. The Loom is His instrument, and we are the string, carefully woven over and under each other, bent and fashioned to produce in us a new covering.

"God is the Hunter. The Bow is His Instrument, and we are the string, pulled taunt, bent into the image of it with His finger. We are the string pulled back in restraint and then released. The arrow launched and guided by the Holy Spirit, our testimony and witness in action, designed to destroy the enemy in others.

"God is the Musician, His Son, His instrument. We are the string pulled and tuned perfectly, stroked with genius precision by Him to produce a note in us. A measure of music made to share with the world, igniting in them a passion to be used by Him to make music of their own."

I sat there for a second, trying desperately to understand what he was telling me, and finally just let out a groan of exasperation. "Okay, but Jesus is supposed to be reflected in two stones, the building blocks of our faith. How do the distaff and spindle represent Him, Lewis?"

"That is a good question. And I'm glad you asked me. Did you know the distaff was also called a *rock* because it sat firmly fixed? And the spindle consisted of a weighted stone that hung to gravity like a plumb line, where the string was gathered as it was spun. Here are the two stones that help mold the thread, just like the pottery wheel helps to shape the clay. You see, without Jesus, The Word, we are just a tangled mess. A lump of clay. A hair-ball with no purpose."

Okay. That made some sense, I thought. I figured that would be the end of our lesson, but Lewis didn't get up to leave.

He added, instead, "Did you know spinning has a special holiday? In the past, and even today, people celebrate Distaff Day?"

"What is Distaff Day, Lewis?"

"It is the day after the Epiphany."

"Alright, then what is the Epiphany?"

"Epiphany is a Christian feast day that celebrates the revelations of Jesus as the Son of God. It commemorates the visit of the magi to the Christ child, and the dwelling of the Holy Spirit upon Him at the Jordan River. They are both representations in His life that declared His divinity."

This man was, infuriatingly, the slowest leak of information. A faucet hanging onto that last drop of water needed to make a container full, yet waiting for some unknown reason to do so.

"Spinning was considered women's work, and Distaff Day was the day women went back to work. It was when household work began again." Rising from where he was sitting, he looked down at me and didn't say another word.

Well, that was interesting. A remarkable game show fun fact I could throw into my bag of useless information and pull out at dinner parties when there was a lull in the conversation. Standing up, I gestured for Lewis to walk downstairs. As he walked out the door, he turned and asked me to do something.

"I want you to read Proverbs 31. There won't be a test. I just want you to read it."

After I shut the door, I grabbed my Bible and sat on the couch. Proverbs 31 was about the Wife of Noble Character. As I began reading it, I instinctively knew the scripture was more than just about one person. Sure, it reflected the individual, but more corporately, a society of people. It represented a community gathered together, clinging to and thriving on a biblical worldview. It's what a society looks like that God delights in. Then I got to a specific passage and froze. It was Proverbs 31:19:

> ... *in her hands she holds the distaff and grasps the spindle with her fingers...*

This sounded a lot like another reference to a maidservant holding two stones. Like Mary holding baby Jesus—the two stones—*ha-abenayim*, "The Son of God with Us."

And corporately, a nation holding tightly onto God's Word—grasping in their fingers, His views of love, mercy, and compassion, clothing themselves in Christ, holiness, and restraint.

I think Lewis was trying to tell me, in no uncertain terms, that it was time to wake up, not only for me but for the Body of Christ to get up and get back to work.

CHAPTER FIFTEEN

THE ANVIL AND THE HAMMER

THE NEXT day Lewis showed up bright and early. Instead of leading him in the direction of the room I wanted to converse in, he walked right past me, through the kitchen, and out the door that opened into the garage. The garage was filled with all of my husband's tools—everything you needed to get a job done. The space was a simple, two-car enclosure, with a work bench spread across the length of its back wall. The garage seemed much bigger today until I realized the cars weren't there. They must still be at the hospital.

Lewis stopped in the middle of the garage. I walked around him to see what he was looking at. There, in front of him, was an anvil and a hammer. Not the picture of an anvil and hammer but an actual anvil and hammer.

"Where did this come from, Lewis? My husband isn't a blacksmith." Looking around the garage, I waved my hands toward all the other tools hanging on the wall. "I honestly don't even know if he knows what most of these tools are used for."

Lewis waited for me to stop babbling before saying, "We are in the garage today for a reason. And it has everything to do with the anvil and hammer. It should come as no surprise that they are used for forging iron into instruments that equip us to succeed in our work and purpose. They help us to be more efficient in the time appointed to us with the tasks in our daily grind if you will.

"There is something hidden here, however. Did you know your ears have an anvil and hammer? They are two of three little bones behind your eardrum: the *malleus*, the *incus*, and the *stapes*. We know them better as the *hammer*, the *anvil*, and the *stirrup*."

He then continued explaining that a sound or voice lifted and carried in the air is transferred through vibration to the malleus in waves. As the sound vibration strikes the incus, it rubs the stapes, which is in contact with the inner ear. And without these tiny little bones, we wouldn't be able to hear or stand upright.

I listened to what he said, hesitantly deducing, "So the two stones we are talking about today are more about the anvil and hammer in the ear?"

"Yes. These two stones allow us to hear clearly so every action purposed in an array of specific instructions provided in our day-to-day can be successful. It benefits us both in our calling and our relationships. But they also help us to hear God and obey Him. To guard and keep His Word, whether in church, worship, and fellowship with our brothers and sisters in Christ or our encounters with random strangers.

"God uses these tiny little bones to protect us from ourselves, as well as from others. Isn't that what His Word does? Isn't that what Jesus does? When we hear the words that come out of our mouths that are messy, emotional, and destructive, the utter sound of it can give us pause. It can help us reflect on God's Word, and hopefully enable us to exercise restraint in the future, or even navigate a different course direction altogether, if necessary."

"That's all good, Lewis, but why are we in the garage? What does that have to do with hearing?"

"Everything. First, the word *garage* comes from a word meaning *to guard and keep*. The word for *to hear* in Hebrew is *shama*. The word for to guard and keep is *shamar*. This word looks very similar to the word *shama,* which can also mean *to stay awake.*

"The Hebrews related keeping and guarding something with vigilance to keeping both one's eyes and ears open. When we have our eyes and ears open to God's Word, doesn't it help us make better decisions in all of life's triumphs and setbacks? Isn't this what the anvil and hammer do in the ear? They help us to watch our own words and guard and obey His.

"We talked about the anvil and hammer in the ear, but the *stapes* is just as vital. The word *stapes* comes from a likely word meaning stirrup, coming itself from two Latin terms, *stare* meaning *to stand* and *pes* meaning *foot*. So, in essence, the two stones striking the stapes assist us in standing on our feet.

"It might interest you to know that the ear is essential in our physical sense of equilibrium and allows us to recognize up from down. This is what hearing and obeying God's Word does. It strikes a chord in us, helping us to stand up, walk in His will, and recognize up from down.

"And at the end of the day, everything comes down to staying awake, hearing, obeying, guarding, and keeping God's Word. This is important because when you don't hear and obey God, you leave the center of His will. There is a critical scripture that speaks of this in Luke 8:18.

> *Take care then how you hear, for to the one who has, more will be given, and from the one who has not, even what he thinks that he has will be taken away.*" (ESV)

Lewis looked at me intently and added, "People have forgotten how to hear. They have dismissed from their minds how to obey. They have let slip how to stand and walk straight in the middle of an evil day. They can't tell up from down. They say that they are awake, but they are certainly not. They do what is suitable in their own eyes, hooded in lust and selfish desire.

"People have forgotten who's in charge of everything. They have disregarded the fact that God allowed man to write His biography and continue to deny Him authority over theirs."

We headed back inside, as exhaustion and fatigue had finally set in. I excused myself and went to my room to lie down. I guess Lewis must have shown himself out. I didn't remember showing him to the door.

CHAPTER SIXTEEN

THE FURNACE

SOMETHING IN the house had stirred. It was probably the foundation settling. I lived in Texas, where there were three seasons: hot, humid, and miserable. And although the air was thick with moisture, its constant mood swings caused the soil to expand and contract.

Foundations built in these conditions liked to sink and crack, shifting a house's subfloor and everything attached. Walls creaked. Doors stuck. I was used to it, but something had woken me up.

Looking out the window, I wondered what time it was. It was still dark outside. How long had I been sleeping? It was still foggy, too. Why wouldn't this fog lift?

Knowing it was pointless to try to go back to sleep, I went to my closet and pulled on some comfortable jogging pants and a matching cotton t-shirt. I didn't know what time it was, but I was hungry. So I went to the kitchen, pre-heated the oven to 350 degrees, threw some ingredients together to make a casserole, and popped it in the oven.

As I closed the oven door, the doorbell rang. It couldn't be Lewis. He had never come at night before, but I was wrong. It wouldn't have been the first time.

Welcoming him in, we walked through the living room and into the kitchen. I went to pull an extra plate out of a cabinet, thinking he might be hungry. But before I could offer him something to eat, he stopped me and said he wouldn't be staying. He just wanted to come by and see how I was doing.

He knew where I was. At the hospital, right? He better know how I was doing. I was relying on this guy to get me out of here. There had to be another reason for the question.

"Lewis, is there another explanation for the midnight house call?" Suddenly my oven alarm went off, as if it sensed my internal unrest. I grabbed two oven mitts to grab the food bubbling up inside. As I placed the dish on top of the stove, I turned around and barked, "Well?"

"Okay, I do have another reason for coming over." He pulled out a picture of an old Israeli cooking range. A large clay vessel sat in the center of the picture's frame, supported on the ground by two large stones.

"This is a furnace. In Israel, a furnace was known by many names. The words used in the Hebrew meant *hearth, cooking range, oven, or fire-pot.* The one I want to talk about today is called a *tannur.* It was used in Israel to bake bread. The dough was prepared by rolling it into small flat discs and then placed along the walls of the *tannur* until they were done."

"Lewis, this is all really interesting, but I don't see a mystery here."

"Oh, but there is one. It may be apparent that the *tannur* represents Jesus, regarding the discussions we've been having. But what isn't so obvious is the significance of the name given to the vessel in question, and why Jesus would be represented in this way in the first place.

"There was another important *tanner* in the Bible in the New Testament. And although these words sound the same, they describe two very different things. The former, spoke of a type of cooking hearth, and the latter, described a craftsman who specialized in the drying out of animal skins to make them more resilient and durable for wearing.

"Apart from being homophones, these two words share a deeper connection. Both words deal with the use of extreme measures of heat as a means of preparation—food for eating, skins for wearing.

"The *tanner* I want to talk about today can be found in the book of Acts. His story is a sidepiece of a much greater narrative found there. This *tanner* lived in Joppa, and his name was Simon.

"Before this story plays out, we find the disciple, Peter, in Lydda, in Acts 9, visiting with the saints and healing a man named Aeneas, who had been lame for eight years. Peter was then soon called to Joppa, a city on the western coast of Israel, just a stone's throw from Lydda.

"He had been summoned because a dear woman in the faith had died. Her name was Dorcas, and according to all the widows in Joppa, she dealt in fabric, providing clothing and robes for the needy. Her body was placed in an upper room awaiting burial. Peter found his way to the house where she was laid and went to her. He prayed for her, and she was resurrected from the dead there. He then went to stay with Simon, the tanner, while he remained in the city.

"Before we continue, I want to make sure that you realize that both people in this story worked in preparing coverings for people. Dorcas, clothing for the needy, and Simon, preparing skins for coats and other coverings."

I simply nodded, silently assuring Lewis that I wasn't completely lost.

Lewis then told me that while Peter was staying at Simon's house, he had a prophetic vision about a sheet being let down from heaven with all kinds of four-footed animals, birds, and reptiles on it. He then remarked about how God told Peter to kill and eat. Peter tried to rebuke God, saying he had never eaten anything unclean, and he wasn't about to start.

"What was God's response to that, Lewis?" I blurted out, more sarcastic than inquisitive.

Lewis answered, "Acts 10:15 states, *The voice spoke to him a second time, 'Do not call anything impure that God has made clean.'*"

Then he said, "That same day, while Peter was still at Simon's house, two soldiers from Caesarea Maritima came calling and asked Peter to return back with them because a Roman centurion named Cornelius needed him. They all journeyed back to Cornelius' house, the home of a Gentile, where many people had gathered to hear about Jesus. They began to be filled with the Holy Spirit as Peter spoke. Peter then realized why he had been given the vision at Simon's house. God had, metaphorically, extended His table to all nations through Christ. It was a confirmation that salvation through Messiah Jesus, was for the Gentiles, just as much as He was for the Jews."

Lewis continued, "The face value account isn't the only takeaway from the story, however. There is a hidden measure found between these lines. Remember, every detail matters. The names used, the cities where events happened, and even the time of day, add to the rich texture God wanted the writers of scripture to convey in the Old and the New Testaments to reveal His Son.

"God is always making sure that every word, every detail, every person, and object is used to its fullest capacity so that it can be peeled like an onion, revealing Jesus in every layer. So that, in whatever plotline, He is there, even when He isn't revealed at the time. Did you know that Peter fulfilled part of the Old Testament prophecy from the book of Genesis and didn't even know it?"

"How is that Lewis?"

"First, it might interest you to know that *Dorcas'* name means *gazelle* but comes from a Greek word that means *to see*. And *Simon's* name means *to hear*. Can you see the beauty of God's Word? Could it be that Peter was sent to *Joppa*, a place that means *bright* or *enlightened* to *see* and *hear* this very specific dispensation about God's desire to cover all of mankind with His love and redemption?

"The purpose for all of humanity is laid out like this if they would only *see* and *hear* with this type of mindset. God has a special purpose for each person's life. And it is as intricately laid out as this story is, and revealed in increasing intensity every time their faith is walked out.

"Think about this. What if people realized how important their call was? What if they realized how much God loves them and how intricately laid out their own storyline was? What if they recognized that every word, every triumph, every failure, every sorrow, and every pain had a purpose? What if people saw Jesus in every move, name, and circumstance?

"Could it be that if people had a meaningful relationship with the Living God, they might resemble Him in compassion, mercy, and every loving rebuke as they served each other? Knowing with every step taken in His covenant love, they would bring glory to God, and lay out His table (or His sheet, in this case) for others to see.

"I am about to tell you something that's never been revealed before. Remember back in the Garden of Eden when God killed a sacrificial animal and covered Adam and Eve with its skin? The words used were *kethoneth,* and the word *or,* meaning *tunics of skin.*

"If you haven't already realized it, along with wordplay, the Hebrews also loved exchanging letters that sounded the same in some scripture verses to allow God's plans to be hidden in plain sight. Letters like *gimmel, khaf, qof,* and *chet,* in the Hebrew alphabet all made a *ch* sound and were used interchangeably in this way. This is how the Hebrew scribes sometimes incorporated different spellings of a word to hide a deeper meaning underneath. This account is a perfect reflection of that.

"The Hebrew word used for tunics, *kethoneth,* is the Greek equivalent of the word *chiton,* which looks and sounds invariably like the Hebrew word *chathan,* the word for *bridegroom.* And the word *or,* for *skin,* resembles another Hebrew word *or,* meaning *light.* Making the deeper revelation here, that God covered Adam and Eve in the garden with the *Bridegroom's skin* or the *Bridegroom's light.*

"Now, not only did the Hebrews like to exchange and switch letters around. They also liked to use parts of one word to join another one in a verse to reveal something in the combination of the two. If you look closely at the words, *chathan or—bridegroom's skin/light—*there seems to appear different words altogether, *ha tan nur* (the *tannur*).

"It was a *tannur* and a torch, in Genesis 15, that cut a covenant with God as a substitution for Abraham, enabling him to become the father of many nations. There is no coincidence that this new command by God in Joppa would be confirmed at a *tanner's* house, since it was the *tannur* (the object reflecting Christ as the bridegroom's skin) that was substituted for Abraham, making this very specific covenant, including many nations possible.

"With this understanding, the importance of another combination of these letters becomes glaringly apparent in another famous scripture. It can be found in Daniel 3:6, in the story about three boys thrown into a fiery furnace. The words for fiery furnace written in this scripture are *attun nur.* It makes the whole detail in Daniel 3:25, about *one like the Son of God,* (Ha Benaiah Im—The Son of God with Us, *the two stones*) in that blaze with those guys make a lot more sense.

"This scripture infers that nothing comes as a surprise to God. He is always ten steps (or *words*) ahead, literally. His plan was always to cover us in His love, and redeem us from the fire with *ha tannur,* the *bridegroom's skin—*Jesus'.

"And if you look at the word that's used for that giant picnic sheet in the sky in Simon's dream, you will find that it is the word *othone,* in the Greek, taken from the Hebrew word *etun* meaning *fine linen thread*, inferring to bind or make one. This word looks very similar to that Greek and Hebrew word for tunic, doesn't it? It also looks remarkably like the English word *atone* or to be *at one* with."

This was too much. I felt like my brain was about to explode. But Lewis apparently wasn't too concerned about the spray of hand grenades he'd already tossed at my head because he continued in the next breath with a land mine.

"That's not all. There is another takeaway here. Could it be that the central fires of our faith not only save our souls but also provide wisdom and insight in our day-to-day lives? By preparing our testimony and skin, God makes us more resilient when put to the fire, supported by the Lord, and covered in His Word."

Mic. And. Drop. I couldn't do anything but sit there staring at Lewis like a voyeur with a backstage pass. I was half-expecting him to shout, "Lewis. Out," before exiting the stage to wait for the crowd to call for an encore. *Man, I'd been to too many late-night rock concerts.*

"I want to share one more thing with you that no one has ever heard. Remember when I said the Hebrews loved to put other letters that sounded the same in a word to mask an underlying message?" I just wordlessly nodded, having nothing of my own to contribute. I felt like a preschooler at a Ph.D. seminar. What did this man want from me?

"Sometimes the *qof* sound was exchanged with the *chet* and used in this very way because they sounded the same. We can find evidence of this in the word *qatan*. It means *small, least, little, unimportant, young, weak,* or *worthless*. Doesn't *qatan* look very similar to the word *chathan,* meaning *bridegroom*? It seems *The Bridegroom* has always been with the weak and worthless, longing to cover their broken bodies with His skin if only they would repent and receive Him.

"One more thing. And this is imperative for you to understand, especially in the times you are living in. Children have a special covering, and Jesus wanted mankind to know this. Consider what Jesus was saying when He offered in Matthew 19:14:

Let the little children come to me, and do not hinder them, for the kingdom of heaven belongs to such as these.

"For ages, scholars have taken this scripture to mean that Jesus wants His people to trust Him the way all little children do their parents. But could it be that Jesus was implying something else here as well? If you look at the phrase *little children* something very startling appears. If the words in Greek are exchanged for Hebrew, they become *qatan naar*. And if you look closely, you can find the *chathan or*, *the bridegroom's light/skin* and *the tannur* there.

"So, when Isaiah speaks about a *qatan naar* leading God's people in Isaiah 11:6 it makes that verse burn a little brighter in the context of his dialogue, doesn't it? Didn't Jesus come to Earth as a little child (*qatan naar*) to cover us in His skin and lead His people into the light?

"It also appears that children are covered before birth by Jesus' skin, love, and salvation, until they reach an age of accountability and can make their own choices. The life of all mankind is important to God even before he takes his first breath, it would seem, making Psalm 139:13, '*For You formed my inward parts; You covered me in my mother's womb,*' (NKJV) take on a whole new meaning.

"Could Jesus have been telling the disciples, aside from trusting like children do their fathers, that all children are precious to Him? Shouldn't mankind cherish and protect them the way God does? And long to be covered by Him, like all little children from the womb?"

Mind. Blown. Encore, Lewis. Encore!

CHAPTER SEVENTEEN

THE SHEEPFOLD AND THE GATE

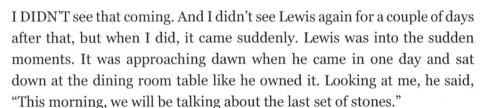

I DIDN'T see that coming. And I didn't see Lewis again for a couple of days after that, but when I did, it came suddenly. Lewis was into the sudden moments. It was approaching dawn when he came in one day and sat down at the dining room table like he owned it. Looking at me, he said, "This morning, we will be talking about the last set of stones."

He pulled the last picture out of his jacket pocket and laid it on the table. It was a picture of a sheepfold made from stone about four feet high with an opening in it, if you could call it an opening. The space was crowded by two, large, carved-out stones. There was a narrow area separating the two, providing little to no space to navigate it. Theoretically, someone could traverse it by turning to the side and wedging themselves through if they weren't concerned about taking off the top layer of skin along the way.

"Sheepfolds were used to protect sheep at night in the pasture. The gate was specifically made this way so the sheep would stay in, and the wolves would stay out."

Slowly, Lewis pulled a picture from his pants pocket and gave it to me before continuing, "There is one more picture I want to show you. This is another sheepfold gate used in Israel. Do you see anything different about it?"

"Yes, Lewis. The stone wall looks the same, but instead of a gate with two stones, there is a man lying down in between the two gateposts."

"That is the Shepherd. He stands in the threshold. He protects the sheep, just like the two stones. Protecting them from themselves and from the wolves. He keeps guard there. Doesn't Jesus do that?"

I nodded in agreement before adding, "That's it?"

"Nothing more, nothing less."

"Am I going back now, Lewis?" He knew I meant back to my body. No longer in between, but back to my life and the living.

"Yes, but we need to step outside first. There is something I want to show you before we go."

"Front or backyard, Lewis?"

"Front yard." Lewis opened the front door and walked me down the driveway and into the street. Taking my shoulders, he gently turned me to face the house. It was then that I noticed my house was the only one on the block with the front porch light on. All the other houses looked like nobody was home.

"I could have taken you anywhere in the world to share this word with you. You must know that. I could have marooned you on an exotic beach. Or perhaps, perched you upon a snow-capped mountain top. The sights would have been exquisite, breathtaking, to be sure, but this is where we had to come."

"To my house, Lewis?"

"Yes. How could we get you to give this word if your own house wasn't in order? We had to do it by building you up in the Spirit, one room at a time. God isn't distracted by the exteriors like people are. He wants to clean up the inside of the house first because when He does that, light invariably spills out onto the front porch.

"An example of what took place here can be found in Ezra-Nehemiah in the Bible if you're looking for a precedent.

"When those guys returned to Jerusalem from exile and started restoring Jerusalem to its former glory, they had the inhabitants first rebuild the walls in front of their own houses. Why do you think that is?"

"I haven't the foggiest idea, Lewis."

"Well, in the Bible, when someone faced opposite something, it was often a reflection of his own character. It gave the reader insight into what lay underneath the skin of the story's protagonist. The broken walls represented the Israelites' own brokenness and need for renewal, just like you. You had to see with this type of discernment before we could leave this place."

"So, now where to, Lewis?"

"The delivery room, of course."

Instantly, we were taken back to the delivery room where I had given birth to John. There was no one there. It was just as desolate as the street I just left. It looked like a tornado had touched down. The bed had been stripped and shoved against one wall. An oxygen mask lay abandoned on the floor. There were cords strewn all over the room. Dried blood coated the laminate hardwood floor. Opened syringes, gauze, and delivery instruments lay forgotten on a delivery table flung next to the bed.

Lewis approached a monitor that had been turned off.

A scroll was unrolled about five feet, splattered with blood, displaying a fetal heart rate and contraction pattern across its thin surface. Dangling silently from the machine, it seemed to be waiting for a nurse to come back and retrieve the recordings to explain what took place here.

Lewis looked at the paper as if he was meticulously deciphering every dip, squiggle, and line. "Do you see the valley between the two contractions? How each contraction looks like a mountain top?"

He pointed to one and remarked, "These were the times when your labor was the most painful, and those mountains seemed like they were never going to move. The end of the contraction and the valley in between were the times of rest before each new mountain ascended to its peak."

"It seems backward, Lewis, doesn't it? The mountain tops were supposed to be where you were lifted and not suffering, rejoicing in the majesty of God's glory. The valley was supposed to be the time of suffering, not the time of rest."

"And look," Lewis added, "the baby's heart rate was struggling along with each contraction, just like you were. He had to use the oxygen he had in reserve because, during those times, his provision was completely cut off too. In the valley, he also got to catch his breath."

"The contractions look like the sheepfold gate," I whispered, more to myself than to the man standing next to me. "Two large stones with a narrow valley in between."

"Yes, it does, doesn't it? Did you know the word *valley*, in Hebrew, also alluded to a trench or a trough, because to the Israelites, a valley resembled a depression track where water cut into a region's landscape?

And *trench* and *trough* are just a few synonyms for the word valley found in the Bible. Others include words like *crib* or *manger.*

"As you know, The Bread of Life (Jesus) was found in a manger, a feeding trough. In a valley, of sorts. And valleys are where rivers flow.

"In ancient times, rivers were highly regarded by the Jews because rivers brought life to arid places. They were gathering places where communities of men, beasts, and birds flocked to receive provision. It's not a far stretch to understand that the Hebrews considered valleys feeding trough for animals too.

"One of the words in the Hebrew for manger, one type of valley, is the word *urvah,* a derivative of the word *arah,* meaning to *gather* or *pluck,* because a manger is a gathering place for the plucked fodder that animals consume. And *arah* is where the Hebrews get the word *ark*—as in *The Ark of the Covenant* because all of Israel's camps gathered around it to get their spiritual nourishment (like a feeding trough).

"It makes perfect sense then that Jesus would be found in a word taken from the word for *ark* if He is The Ten Words—The Ten Commandments, made flesh, right? Or from a word that would bring flowing or living waters to mind?

"The writers of scripture wanted to communicate this. They also wanted to convey that most wisdom didn't come from mountain-top moments, but rather, after immense pressure and testing.

"They understood that discernment was found where the rub gave way to insight, and this is where Jesus is. It is the birthing place of testimony. The place where if we are listening, God persuades us to continue in our walk or hopefully results in the changing of it for our good. Both can grow us, not only in building our faith but also in giving people a witness to the covering and healing power of Jesus Christ.

"When we trust God, and hear Him, a contrite (rubbed) and convicted heart will lead to repentance in ourselves or others. This is what we leave the valley to ascend the mountain to declare to the world. And that is, in our deepest suffering—in the rub—we encounter the Living Christ. He rubs us free from sin and covers us in His love. Hearts are convicted and persuaded. Obedience is the result of that persuasion. And suffering because of something we have done or someone else has done to us, no matter how big or small always plays a crucial role.

"This is part of God's process involving us all. It was planned long before our birth. Part of this process for you has been to show people the way home and to declare who it is that transforms them and helps them keep the front porch light on.

"You have been called to show people God's ways are higher than our own. That sometimes man can't see Him, to reveal what is hidden in themselves, only to lay down a path to help bring them back into the light.

"You have been called to encourage people to be led by the Holy Spirit again, allowing the Manifest Presence of God to be revealed in mankind again. It has been a call to hope in His grace again and recognize that all people have been sought by Him, no matter how broken."

"What am I supposed to do, Lewis? I'm not important. I am no one. How can this be done?"

Lewis stared at me in quiet deliberation, as if carefully choosing each word before it was spoken. "An angel of the Lord has visited you. You are not a *no one*, but a *someone* to God. You have become pregnant with this word and you will deliver it. It will be a written testimony of God's process. A call to seek Jesus, repent and receive His salvation, freely choosing to call Him Lord. And allow Him to work through mankind, for the heavenly kingdom, by holding onto the principles God thought enough of to impart to His creation.

"A lot of people don't understand this, but Jacob's name wasn't changed to Israel because of the grudge match he had with the Angel of God. Jacob, the crooked heel-grabber, became Israel, the upright and strait-laced, because he held onto God and His Word, through every turn in the road, storm, and plot twist.

"People must take care because a shaking is coming. They must shake off selfish desire and the pride of life and cover themselves in the righteousness of Christ. The complicit state in which man has lived has almost reached its full measure. There is not much time left. A time is coming and fast approaching, as prophesied in Hosea 9:11:

Ephraim's glory will fly away like a bird—no birth, no pregnancy, no conception.

"You were chosen because a seed was planted in you long ago. A seed planted in arid, dry and withered ground, just waiting for the right conditions to bud. We have spent this time, this season, cleaning house, sweeping away the dust and preparing the soil. We have been preparing you for something new.

"You are not famous nor renowned. You are unknown to man, but you are known to God. It is now time for you to take hold of it and fulfill His purpose in you."

CHAPTER EIGHTEEN

DELIVERANCE

"LEWIS, HOW am I going to explain this to a proud and stiff-necked people? Myself included. They will want evidence about this word, about these two stones and what they mean. They aren't going to just take my word for it."

"You will tell them what the Bible tells them. Doesn't Colossians 1:16 say:

> *For in him all things were created: things in heaven and on earth, visible and invisible, whether thrones or powers or rulers or authorities; all things have been created through him and for him."*

Lewis paused and stared at me to make sure I was still following and then continued from Romans 1:19:

> *"... since what may be known about God is plain to them, because God has made it plain to them. For since the creation of the world God's invisible qualities—his eternal power and divine nature—have been clearly seen, being understood from what has been made, so that people are without excuse.*

"Look at the earth. How was it formed? By folding and separating, by shaking and falling, making old things new—by the rubbing and shifting of rather large stones. Today scientists call these stones tectonic plates, and the edges of them subduction zones.

"Buried deep in the earth's trenches where the boundaries of the earth's crusts meet, there is a rubbing. There is a descending of one surface below the other, scraping off one layer to expose another. This is where mountain building happens. It is where earthquakes tremble and volcanoes erupt, exposing themselves to the world. It's where they are reduced to ash to become something new.

"In this, there is a hidden mystery for you. It is a confirmation of His word to you. Did you know the element stibium naturally occurs as a result of volcanic activity?"

"That's nice, Lewis. Are we getting close to a point here?"

"I'm getting there," he said.

He hesitated a second and then offered, "Stibium is known by another name. Do you know what that is?"

"No, Lewis."

"It is known by the word antimony. Antimony was used in antiquity as a cosmetic. Pulverized to ash, it outlined the eyes to make them stand out, to make them more brilliant. It was considered a real eye-opener. You can find evidence of it in most Egyptian artwork. Knowing this, let's look at another scripture. Isaiah 54:11:

> *Afflicted city, lashed by storm and not comforted, I will rebuild it with stones of antimony, and lays its foundation with sapphires.* (ESV)

"The word for antimony, here in the Hebrew, is the word *puk,* which means *fair colors, paint, or dye,* or *to make something brilliant.* The word *sappir* comes from the word *saphar,* meaning to *write, proclaim, give evidence,* or *an account.*

"Could it be that through devastation and being pummeled to ash, eyes are opened, and a testimony is provided to help give an account? That this is what Jerusalem would be built on, to a discerning ear? The eye-opening experiences of life, and the testimony we glean holding onto, and covered in Jesus, God's Word, helping us through them.

"When iniquity or holiness is exposed in us, from any type of shaking or volcanic eruption in our lives, being rubbed either the right way or the wrong, a truth is revealed, giving us an opportunity to be made whole. It's much like dust that is kicked up, magma that flows after a volcanic eruption, or when the earth quakes from the rubbing together of tremendous shelves of rock deep underground. Something is always brought to the surface. The evidence from the rub breaks through, and we are given an opening for refinement and healing at its heart.

"You may not know this, but the word for the verb meaning *to heal* in Hebrew is *rapha*. It got its name because two stones were rubbed together in the mending of a garment, making the *ra-pha* sound. This is the foundation of the salvific work brought by Jesus Christ. It is in the rub where repentance starts, wholeness is sought, Jesus is found, and the Holy Spirit is heard. It leads us from a place of brokenness to insight and a turn in the right direction. Through testing, we find a testimony. True beauty from ashes.

"We could never live through the rub perfectly, so Jesus had to come and do it for us. But He still expects us to live a life of holiness. Every person in the Bible who Jesus healed was instructed to '*Go and sin no more.*' They were expected to endure the rub with what Jesus sent to help them endure it with—the Holy Spirit.

"Let me put it another way. Isn't truth what we glean from fact? And truth is reality through God's heavenly perspective. It is a contrite (rubbed) and humbled heart gleaned from missing the mark, and a holy heart gleaned from hitting it. These are how explosions, even earthquakes, can become so sweet. The shaking, the rubbing, and the turning are the real eye-openers. It is how mountains and islands are built. This is how we get beauty from ashes. It was like this from before the beginning. Even before the first two elements in the universe were struck together to produce their first spark.

"Do you remember the midwives in Exodus? Their names were *Shiphrah* and *Puah*. Doesn't that look a lot like the words *puk* and *sappir*? Two labor and delivery nurses whose own eyes were opened to the truth of *Immanuel*. Two women who trembled in fear of God and whose own eyes were opened to help deliver Israel with the delivery stool, *ha-abenayim*, the two stones—The Son of God with Us."

"Were you and your mother-in-law not labor and delivery nurses?" Lewis asked.

"How did you know that, Lewis? You knew I was, but not her."

"Are you serious?" He said with an arch in his brow.

"I thought I was being serious."

Dismissing me altogether, he said, "You will both go to Israel to accomplish something in the Spirit. Those two midwives were a foreshadowing of you and her, revealing the delivery stool, The Son of God with Us, and His process to man, in a way they can relate to."

"How is that possible, Lewis?"

"The simplest explanation I can give you is that God is not subject to time. There are those who have always considered time as linear, while others have seen it as cyclical. But it is really both at the same time—an event in the now, shining a light on one in the future. Our God is not a God of casual connections. You could say He works in designed coincidence. Every event folds back on each other, like a reflection cast upon the surface of a lake.

"In Biblical prophecy, this is called The Law of Double Reference. Examples of this can be found throughout scripture. For example, just as Pharaoh would call for the murder of the innocents of Israel in the west, Herod would later decree the murder of the innocents of Israel in the east. Just as the Red Sea parted west of Israel, the Jordan would divide east of it. And just as two midwives would fear the Lord and declare the good news that God's Son Lives in Egypt, you both will proclaim it, east of the Jordan."

"Lewis, nobody is going to believe me."

"Honestly, does this surprise you?" Lewis said, mystified by my reaction.

"Well, I guess if I am going to do this, it must help somebody, right? It must have a purpose."

"Your purpose is to do what God has called you to do and let Him worry about the rest. You are His vessel. Don't forget that. No matter how marred you've become. Remember, when God looks at you, He no longer sees you. He sees the skin of the Son you are covered in.

"One more thing. Most of the women in the Bible who brought the good news were never believed outright. People had to see for themselves. This testimony will help to rub the sleep out of their eyes so they can."

CHAPTER NINETEEN

AWAKE

I AWOKE with a startled gasp, taking massive gulps of air back into my lungs, while simultaneously pushing back death, who had resolved to stage a sit-in at my throat, protesting my right to draw breath.

My eyelids felt heavy, but I attempted to open them anyway. First one, and then the other. Everything was so bright, blinding almost. I tried laser-focusing on the shadow to my right when I heard a voice. It was familiar.

"Lewis?"

"No, honey. It's me, Jason, your husband."

Struggling to shake off the haze, I shook my head and latched onto the first thing I could—a plain, sterile wall clock hanging opposite the bed. The time read 12:00p.m. As I turned to my right, there he was, my husband, Jason. He was a complete mess. It didn't look like he had shaved in a couple of days. His hair was disheveled. His clothes, a wreck. And on my left, my parents. They didn't look much better than Jason did.

"Hello," I croaked, sounding like I had just swallowed a truckload of gravel. My head was fuzzy. Convinced my brain had been transplanted with heaps of thick cotton, I tried to focus on making one complete sentence, which was a complete disaster. But it didn't really matter. I hadn't gotten out one word before everyone started talking at once.

"Sweetie, you had an amniotic fluid embolism." My husband offered.

"You're lucky to be alive." My dad added.

"You were in a coma for almost three weeks." My mother sighed.

Three weeks? That got my vocal cords working. Questions sprang from my mouth a mile a minute. Where were my kids? Was John alright? Why did my throat hurt so much? Where was I? When can I go home? When I felt like my questions had been answered I settled back against the mattress. I was still so exhausted.

I was discharged from the hospital four days later.

I never thought being back home would feel so good. I was sleeping in my own bed. My husband was being so gentle and loving, supporting every step I made. This wasn't normal for him, not that I was complaining.

A week went by in a flash. It was now Sunday again, and my husband asked me if I wanted to go back to church. Why was he asking me that? We hadn't gone to church in years. It had become too much of a hassle when we started having kids. Life happened.

"We have a lot to be grateful for, and I think we should be running to God, instead of from Him," my husband offered, when I didn't make a move to get up.

"Okay," I said, a little hesitant to argue with the man when he was making so much sense.

It was already 9:00 a.m., so we found a church service that didn't start until 11:30. Everyone got ready, and we headed out the door. We found the church easy enough. It was right down the street from our house. We made it just in time. Eying the first empty seats in the back, we sat down before any eye contact could be made, and someone would feel it was their personal duty to come and shake our hands.

Sitting in that assembly, I listened to the preacher's wife recite Psalm 91:1. It was about dwelling in the shadow of God Almighty. I had heard that scripture more times than I would care to recount, but I had never felt such an intimate connection to it until that day.

When we got home, I went on a mission to find my Bible. Finding it layered in dust, I brushed off the cover. In faded gold lettering, my maiden name glared back at me. The Bible was one my parents had given me years ago. Tracing the letters with my hands, I let the indentation in the leather tickle the tips of my fingers. Opening the cover to reveal the first page, I began reading. No better place to start than at the beginning, right?

I read nine hundred pages in about a week. Voracious at first, but just like everything else with time, it became sluggish at best. I would read a couple of pages in scripture here and there, but never spent a lot of time in the Word or in worship, for that matter. My visits to church became more erratic, while the arguments for not going had become all too predictable.

Then, on one of the rare occasions we got out of bed and made it to church on time, after praise and worship, the offering and prayer, the pastor got up to preach. About what, I had no idea. Because right in the middle of his sermon, I heard a voice in my right ear. It was in the form of a whisper.

"Stand up." I turned around. Everyone was looking at the guy on the stage.

I turned back to the front of the church and heard it again, louder this time, "Stand up!"

I knew who it was, but I kept thinking, *I can't get up right now in the middle of the message. It is quiet. No music is playing. What if the preacher thinks I'm a lunatic? What if he asks me to go and sit back down? I would be so embarrassed.*

Once more the voice rang out, "Get up, now!"

I started to cry, and slowly stood, edging my way to the middle aisle, and up to the platform, where the preacher was giving his message. I laid down on my stomach and surrendered my life to the One who had created it. When I finished, I got up, turned around and saw my husband, Jason, crying quietly in his seat. I walked back to my chair. The preacher never missed a beat.

As I sat down, I told my husband it was time to get serious about Jesus again. I picked up my Bible and turned to the place my tattered scarlet ribbon marked the last place I'd been reading. It was Isaiah 6:

> *In the year that King Uzziah died, I saw the Lord, high and exalted, seated on a throne; and the train of his robe filled the temple. Above him were seraphim, each with six wings: With two wings they covered their faces, with two they covered their feet, and with two they were flying. And they were calling to one another:*

"Holy, holy, holy is the Lord Almighty; the whole earth is full of his glory."

At the sound of their voices the doorposts and thresholds shook, and the temple was filled with smoke.

"Woe to me!" I cried. "I am ruined! For I am a man of unclean lips, and I live among a people of unclean lips, and my eyes have seen the King, the Lord Almighty."

Then one of the seraphim flew to me with a live coal in his hand, which he had taken with tongs from the alter. With it he touched my mouth and said, "See, this has touched your lips; your guilt is taken away and your sin atoned for."

Then I heard the voice of the Lord saying, "Whom shall I send? And who will go for us?"

And I said, "Here am I. Send me!"

This was really the first day I woke up. Awakened from a coma, I had been in for far too long.

On the ride home, I kept thinking about my place in this world, and God's purpose for it. When we got home, Jason went to his office to work. The kids went off to play, and I parked myself in front of my desk, yearning to write something down. Anything, really. Before I knew it, this is what came out:

THE VESSEL

Stepping off an unsteady ship onto dry land seemed like a vast improvement to the weeks spent cast upon the mercy of a canopy of driving rain and a host of storm-swept seas. But now, standing on a piece of wood, elevated four feet off the ground, examined and prodded, in a building where butchered meat was sold; I realized it was the weather-beaten ship I preferred.

It was poetic that we, meaning me, and all the others held in captivity, were being sold in the meat market. The building we were in wasn't a building at all, but rather, a brick tent, with a furnace at one end. It was called the Kitchen. One end was used for baking and cooking, while the other was used for food preparation. The heat from the kiln blazed across the room, causing the smell of rotten flesh to roll in thick waves off its walls and bury itself under my skin.

Dressed in dirty rags and a half-beaten body, I was exposed for all to see, just like everyone else on display. Every bruise and hidden treasure had been indiscriminately uncovered. Was I worth this kind of scrutiny? Voices from the square didn't seem to think so, as they offered suggestions to my perceived value. One voice stood above the crowd, however. It was low and calm, waiting to outbid the impulsive buyer, and those who were never really interested in my purchase to fall away.

My eyes, intent on staring at my toes on that makeshift stage, lifted to meet those of the man who had just spoken. Dark pools of endless glory stared back at me. "I will pay over your asking price," he said to my captor.

"This woman is hard, not soft. Her treasures were discovered and spent years ago. She is worthless, really. You seem like a man of distinction. A man who sits in the seat of honor. The first, and not the second son. You could have sent any of your hired hands to come and pick her up to labor in your fields, for she is no good for household work. Why have you come to get her yourself? She will be a waste of your time and energy," my jailor spit out.

My eyes never wavered from my appointed patron. I waited with bated breath for the declaration that, he too, had come to the same conclusion, and now agreed with this very disagreeable old man.

"She has been tested and found wanting, but I will make her worthy. I will change her ransom into a dowry. I will marry her, and she will no longer call me master, but husband. She will remain bound to me, not against her will, but freely. No longer will she be a slave, according to the law of man. Instead, she will be enslaved to me in love, in a covenant that cannot be broken. What is the price for her life?"

The jailor hesitated, and then begrudgingly mumbled, "This one is worth what any man is willing to pay. She has so little value it would be disingenuous of me to put a fair price on her head."

My patron poured out a measure that couldn't be weighed on the jailor's scales, but overwhelmed them, turning them over altogether. The pudgy little man could not contain his delight. My Savior had just made the difference in all the credits and debts in the trader's accounts agree with the balance. Not only had the man paid for my release from captivity, but he had paid for us all.

The man approached the smallest of stages, the one my tiny feet had been perched on. Holding out a hand he said, "Let us leave this place. I will take you home now." Then, lightly taking my wrists, he turned them over to expose the palms of my hands. He took a key, loosening my bonds, before placing a kiss to both of my upturned wrists.

"What shall I call you, sir?"

"You will call me My Beloved. And I shall call you, My Darling." Looking again at my wrists, he said, "The physical chains are gone, but they have been replaced with cords of love, and a desire to please me.

"You are a prisoner, make no mistake. Not one of fear, but one of hope and expectation. You will live in that hope and trust me for all things. And in return, I will plant in your heart the things you will be consumed by and thirst for. You will find refuge there.

"You will work in my kitchen, at my hearth, stoking the flames of the central fires of the principles that I have set forth from before the beginning of time. You will bake the bread I give you for the table and pour out the foundation I have provided for everyone to drink. It will be a load to carry. A heavy load of illumination, but the gravity of it will make it light in your eyes.

"This type of life will not be what your flesh prefers. Nor will it be the preferred opinion of the rest of the world because truth cannot be captured and contained by those who still hold on so desperately to their own personal desire."

Placing my hands in His, He said, "You are in my grip, and I in yours." Then He turned and led me down the path to my new home, to my new place, to my new position.

As if waking from a mental fog, I looked down at the paper in front of me. Where had that come from?

CHAPTER TWENTY

VISIONS

AS TIME passed, I began getting more involved in the church. Our family started tithing every month, our first tenth. I had read the Bible a couple of times by then and felt good in my walk. I had gotten bolder in my witness to others, not just with unsaved family members, but with complete strangers, too. That's when the visions started.

The first one was what seemed like a daydream. I was sitting on the couch in my living room. It was a Saturday. Jason was going over some work from the office, and I was looking through unread emails on my phone. Then, suddenly, I wasn't on the couch anymore. Instead, I was in Jerusalem with my mother-in-law. We were both at the Wailing Wall, putting our own prayers in one of the cracks in the stone where the mortar had worn away and been replaced by countless other requests. I looked at the petition in my hand one last time before putting it in with the others wedged there. It simply said:

Father, tear down the abomination of desolation. Amen.

I folded the prayer and tucked it safely into one of the Wall's many crevices. Then I was right back on my couch, sitting atop the stained, square cushion I had occupied moments before my trip.

The next vision came a couple of weeks later. It was night. In this dream, I got a call from my mother-in-law, telling me to pick up a bicycle she had reserved for me. I hadn't asked for one, but she had picked it up, anyway.

I walked to her house. The garage door was wide open, so I walked in. I was about to enter through the inner door but heard my mother-in-law calling from the front of the house. I came out of the garage and peeked around the corner. Sure enough, she was standing at her front door. "You have to come in through the front door." Shrugging, I followed her instruction.

The house was an old Georgian-style, one-story with a wrap-around porch. White shudders dressed the windows. And at its entrance hung a thick, white, ranch-style door. Nestled on a quiet street, one might find in a Norman Rockwell painting, the whole scene screamed the good ole days. Times when doors were left unlocked, kids still played outside, and folks found joy in penning handwritten letters.

As you entered the house and to the left, there was a parlor. My mother-in-law only used it for formal gatherings, but for some unknown reason, she ushered me into the room. Asking her where the bicycle might be, she pointed to a square cut-out cover in the ceiling next to a built-in bookcase. It was in the attic.

Why on earth would my mother-in-law put a bicycle I was coming over to get in the attic? *The garage made a lot more sense, but okay.* Shaking my head, I simply turned to her, asking how I would retrieve it. She pointed to the built-in bookcase that went from the floor to the ceiling, directly below the opening she had pointed to earlier. Going over to it, I began to climb it like a ladder. Getting to the ceiling panel, I lifted it up and out of the way. Peaking my head inside, I saw the floor littered with thousands of clean, white porcelain dishes.

I could only turn my head a little to the right. And out of the corner of my eye, I made out the opening of another room. Dark and covered in cobwebs, a thick layer of dust covered the floor and walls. This made it almost impossible to make out the only item I could barely see in the room—half of one bicycle wheel lying against its farthest wall.

The funny thing was that the bicycle rim—the spokes and the wheel itself—looked like a shiny new dime. Not a speck of dust on it. Then I woke up. I looked at the clock. It was 3:00 in the afternoon.

I didn't go back to sleep after that.

CHAPTER TWENTY-ONE

ISRAEL

---◆---

THAT LAST dream lit a fire under me, and I started talking to my husband about going to Israel. I couldn't explain it, but I had to go. And my mother-in-law had to go with me.

We found a trip that left on the evening of September 10, 2017, and started making preparations. As the day of our trip approached, I began to feel a sense of urgency and unexplained expectation.

We touched down in Tel Aviv on September 11, 2017, and settled into our hotel room to relax. My feet were swollen from the long flight, and we had a meeting with our tour group and guide at 7:00 p.m. that night. I wanted to kick my feet up for a bit.

I had no idea what to expect. There was no agenda or grand scheme on my part. I just knew my mother-in-law and I were supposed to be there. Later that night, we met our tour guide, Eli, and were given our itinerary. We would meet in the lobby the next morning at 8:00 a.m. The meeting concluded, and we practically ran back to our respective rooms and went to bed, both ready for our journey to really begin.

Tel Aviv, Jaffa, Caesarea, Megiddo, Muhraqa, the Sea of Galilee, Cana, Nazareth, The Mount of the Beatitudes, Tabgha, Capernaum, Bet She'an, The Jordan River, Ein Karem, Bethlehem, and Jerusalem. We got to experience it all.

At Mt. Carmel, I got to sing in the church erected as a remembrance of Elijah's supernatural confrontation with the priests of Baal. I am no singer, but I raised my hand when Eli asked if anyone wanted to sing. I got up and walked right up to the altar. I turned around and started singing parts of the only song I remembered from my childhood. It was a combination of two songs about God being worthy of praise. He was more precious than silver, gold, or diamonds, and nothing I desired compared to Him. I finished the song, feeling so close to the Lord. *This was meant to be,* I thought. I was meant to come here. I was pretty sure about it, but it was confirmed at Galilee.

The day began with our tour group taking a ride on the Sea of Galilee. Eli led us onto a dock, up a gangplank, and onto a boat tethered there. We were taken out onto the lake and given a brief history of the surrounding area. Then, for some unknown reason, Eli came up to me and asked if I wanted to say something to the group. I declined. I was scared the group would get irritated. I didn't want to be "that tourist" that irritated everybody else because they talked too much. As Eli turned around, the Holy Spirit said, *"Did you just refuse to preach on the Sea of Galilee?"* Thinking better of it, I stood up and said I would love to say something.

Totally off the cuff, I spoke about what a special place this was. After all, this was where Jesus walked on water and calmed the storm. This was the place He called many of His disciples into service. And on one occasion, Jesus even went to the other side of the lake, to a town named *Kersi*. I explained that this name wouldn't be found in the Bible because, during the time of Jesus, it was known as *Gaderenes*.

I went on to tell them that Jesus came ashore there in Matthew 8:28-34 and encountered two men possessed by demons. *"What do you want with us, Son of God?" they shouted. "Have you come here to torture us before the appointed time?"* They pleaded with Jesus to throw them into a nearby herd of pigs. Jesus obliged, and the herd of pigs ran down the hill and drowned themselves right there in the lake.

Finishing the story, I turned to our tour group and said, "There is something I feel compelled to share with you. You can see from this account even demons know who God is, who His Son is. What separates you from them? There must be a difference. There can't just be an acknowledgment of who Jesus Christ is, but a true desire to give Him authority in our lives, making Him the Lord of them. This is what separates us from the world."

It got very quiet on that boat. I walked back to my seat, wondering if Eli now regretted asking me to put in my two cents.

I looked over the water, searching for Jesus along the shoreline, believing somehow, I just might find Him there. I began to cry, telling my mother-in-law that if I saw Jesus walking across the water, I would jump out of the boat and not sink like Peter did. I just wanted Jesus to come to me so I could hold him, and he could hold me. "Was that crazy?" I asked her. She looked at me and, without hesitation, said, "Of course not."

The boat started heading back to shore. Once we docked, the tour group began to unload onto the pier to make their way back to the tour bus.

I got up to follow, but Eli held me back, taking hold of my hand, and said, "Thank you," while depositing something small into my outstretched palm. I looked down, and in the middle of it was a stone—one side, smooth, and the other, ornamented with a small metal crucifix. I looked at my mother-in-law and said, "Look. Jesus did come to me."

CHAPTER TWENTY-TWO

JORDAN

OUR TRIP to Israel ended on a high note in Jerusalem. On the following day, we traveled over the Allenby Bridge into Jordan, knowing that through our descent, something special was bound to happen. I was so excited because I wanted to see where Jesus was baptized, where He was drawn from the water, completely saturated in the Holy Spirit. I wanted to see the place it rested on Him. I wanted to go up Mt. Nebo and see where Moses viewed the Promised Land. I wanted to see Petra and walk through its canyons. I wanted them to open their secrets for me, just like they had for countless others over the years.

It took us an entire day to get to Petra. The heat of the journey was almost unbearable. And even though it was dry and arid, my mother-in-law and I were so excited because it was *Rosh Hashanah*—The Jewish New Year or *Yom Teruah*—The Feast of Trumpets. *Yom Teruah* was a time-honored Jewish tradition commemorating The Jewish New Year, as it rang in new beginnings and a personal and national call for repentance.

We had brought a *shophar* (trumpet) my mother-in-law bought on her last trip to Israel with the intent of blowing it there. But somehow, we miscalculated the timing of our trip, not realizing that we would be in a Muslim country for the holiday.

Needless to say, my mother-in-law and I were bummed when we realized we were going to be in Jordan for *Yom Teruah,* but we got over it. And on the evening of September 20, 2017, we blew that *shophar* from our hotel room in Petra, because to the Hebrews, it was in the evening when the new day began, shadowed in darkness, anxiously awaiting the dawn.

The next day, we went to Petra's ruins. Walking through its narrow canyons was pure torture. And even though it was grueling, the path that seemed to bring nothing but blight sprung forth from its bud, opening to hidden treasure. A hidden treasury, to be more specific. The Treasury at Petra.

As the canyon walls began to spread like the opening of an ornate curtain across a grand stage, I caught a glimpse of a memory bubbling to the surface. I pictured two stones rubbing together to bring abundance, just like those canyon walls had done, revealing that treasury. My mother-in-law and I toured the site and deposited crosses and sinners' prayers throughout the area before we left.

That night, as I lay in bed, the sound of what seemed like a million cavalry rushed past the window outside our hotel room. I turned to my mother-in-law, and at the same time, we both said to each other, "Did you hear that?" Nodding, we stood to peer out the open frame of our hotel window, but we saw nothing. Instead, I felt an intensity that went bone deep and rocked me backwards. It felt like something had been unleashed, like an impulse skipping across the surface of time, creating a giant wave that had literally crashed right into me.

Two days later, on September 23, 2017, we ascended to Mt. Nebo. We reached the top of the mountain, our feet hovering over the plains of Jericho. I stood next to a huge metal crucifix and groaned into the distance, *"Hineni! Hineni! Hineni! Ruah HaKodesh!"* meaning, "Here I Am! Here I Am! Here I Am! Holy Spirit!" And I prayed:

> *Father, use me according to Your will and not mine. Let me be a witness like Elijah. Give me a double portion like Elisha. Let me be the apple of your eye like David. Someone after your own heart. In Jesus name, Amen.*

We drove back to Amman the next day to catch a flight back to Israel, then to Toronto, and then home. We had done it.

CHAPTER TWENTY-THREE

SOMETHING FAMILIAR

———◆———

WHEN WE got back home, I started re-reading the Bible. Beginning in Proverbs, I simply couldn't get enough. I was savoring every verse like it was my last meal. No longer were the words hard to swallow, like the countless bland-tasting aphorisms I'd read over the years from stale fortune cookies after a night of bad Chinese takeout.

This newfound consciousness reminded me of those old 3D pictures you had to stare at long and hard until you found the image hidden inside. I never could see those pictures. No matter how long I stared at them. Everyone around me could gaze at them for a second and say, "Oh, I see it," and move on, but not me. I was always missing it, the treasure that was hidden inside. Not anymore, it seemed.

Prime example: One day I was sitting on my bed, going over the first couple of chapters in Proverbs again. I had just finished reading chapter two and into chapter three, when I began reading Proverbs 3:11-15:

> *My son, do not despise the Lord's discipline, and do not resent His rebuke, because the Lord disciplines those He loves, as a father the son he delights in.*
>
> *Blessed are those who find wisdom, those who gain understanding, for she is more profitable than silver and yields better returns than gold. She is more precious than rubies; nothing you desire can compare with her.*

I felt the Holy Spirit fall on me, saying, "Doesn't that sound familiar? It should, my darling. That is what you sang to Me on Mt. Carmel.

"You see, as a child, I had you remember that song. You remembered it as any young girl would—as crowned jewels, like the kind you would use to play dress-up. My love, that song was never about jewelry worn by royalty.

"I had you remember that song because I knew thirty years later you would sing it to Me on Mt. Carmel. It would be where Elijah called fire down from heaven, and proved I was more precious than silver, more costly than gold, more beautiful than diamonds. And no earthly desire, false god, man-made king, idol, or fake wisdom tradition could compare to Me.

"You worshipped me there. You gave a witness there, just like Elijah did, proclaiming to the world, the futility of God's people having their feet planted in two camps—one standing in His Kingdom, while the other limped along in the world, worshiping everything but Him."

I began weeping big ugly tears, overwhelmed by my God, completely astonished with the planning and timing of it all. A miracle, that's what it was.

I continued reading the Proverbs and found another one that struck me. It was from Proverbs 27:5:

> *Open rebuke is better than love carefully concealed.* (Interlinear Bible)

And Proverbs 31, which speaks of The Wife of Noble Character. There was something familiar about both scriptures. My mind kept trying to take hold of it, like calloused fingers that had painstakingly searched to find purchase on a rock's edge. I prayed, glorifying God's name, the giving of His Son, Jesus Christ, my Lord, and Savior. And also, for what revelation He had given me, even though I knew I was still missing something.

CHAPTER TWENTY-FOUR

SOMETHING NEW

—◆—

I FINISHED Proverbs and then Song of Songs. After that, I decided to reread the gospels, starting with Matthew. Every word spoken by Jesus, dyed in red and dripping in His blood, was a token and reminder of what my redemption cost. It certainly wasn't cheap. The gospels were a reminder of just how important the Word is—how important words are.

I began to believe that all the world's problems could be solved with *The Word of God, a Webster's Dictionary, and a Strong's Exhaustive Concordance.* But most of all, I started to realize how important the Ten Words are—how important The Ten Commandments are.

As I began reading, I found Jesus speaking through those two stones in ways I had never put together before. Like in Matthew 4:1-4:

> *Then Jesus was led by the Spirit into the wilderness to be tempted by the devil. After fasting forty days and forty nights, he was hungry. The tempter came to Him and said, "If You are the Son of God, tell these stones to become bread."*
>
> *Jesus answered, "It is written: 'Man shall not live on bread alone, but on every word that comes from the mouth of God.'"*

I felt the Holy Spirit speak into my heart that Jesus was saying man couldn't just live on bread alone, but needed both the bread and the stones. They needed the Ten Commandments, *The Ten Words*, God's purest and simplest spiritual truth, just as much as they needed the bread.

Man could not only rely on physical provision; they had to seek spiritual satiety as well.

Then, as I continued reading, I was able to see another scripture in a similar light. Matthew 7:7-12:

Ask and it will be given to you; seek and you will find; knock and the door will be opened to you. For everyone who asks receives; the one who seeks finds; and to the one who knocks, the door will be opened. Which of you, if your son asks for bread, will give him a stone? Or if he asks for a fish, will give him a snake? If you, then, though you are evil, know how to give good gifts to your children, how much more will your Father in heaven give good gifts to those who ask Him! So in everything, do to others what you would have them do to you, for this sums up the Law and the Prophets.

The Holy Spirit once again spoke into my spirit, saying, "Good parents give their children what they ask for, but they give them what they need more. What they need may not be the things they ask for. What they need might just be the snake and the stone; just like those two objects that were given in the desert by a just God, to urge a people to repentance and wholeness. The Ten Commandments and the Brazen Serpent were both used in desert times to bring both spiritual and physical healing. And they were both foreshadowers of the Son and the Holy Spirit.

"A friend or neighbor who isn't honest and refuses to speak the truth in love is someone who flatters, even when they know what the other is doing is wrong. That is not love. Loving your neighbor as yourself and doing to others what you would have done to you doesn't mean pleasing them or tickling their ears with what they want to hear. Open rebuke is certainly better than hidden love. Mankind forgets that rebuke is a form of love."

I continued reading Matthew 7:13-14:

Enter through the narrow gate. For wide is the gate and broad is the road that leads to destruction, and many enter through it. But small is the gate and narrow the road that leads to life, and only a few find it.

Why did this resonate so much with me? I had read these scriptures countless times. So why did I see them differently now? They had become much deeper and more stripped-down. It was then that I decided maybe I should start writing a journal—a written look back to help me move forward.

CHAPTER TWENTY-FIVE

A NEW PURPOSE

———◆———

Journal Entry #1

WHEN I was a little girl, things rarely frightened me. I could sleep in my own bed at night. I didn't need the night light on. The closet door never needed to be closed before I went to sleep because the closet, for me, was like a refuge. Thin walls and heated discussions between my parents had become a perfect storm in creating the soundtrack of my childhood. That little closet was my hundred-square-foot getaway.

It was a place I could read and contemplate the scenarios of how my life would play out. My future was something that never made me worry. I had it all figured out. No hard times in any of my calculations. If I had learned anything from my parents, it's that I wouldn't settle for less.

My plan was perfect. I was going to marry Bouser from *Sha-Na-Na*. I would live in a house that stayed perfectly clean, devoid of entropy. And, I was going to have the best job in the whole wide world. I wanted to be a ferry boat driver. Okay, maybe my brother wanted to be the ferry boat driver. I just wanted to be the ferry boat. *Hey, I was five!*

As I grew up, my interests changed. At various times, I aspired to be a great many things: an actress, a singer, a paratrooper. But at the top of that list was an astronaut.

My taste in guys changed, too. The man who had now captured my heart? It would have to be, without question or doubt, the incomparable David Bowie. I can't tell you how many times I wanted to walk up to him and sing, *"Let's dance!"* And then he would twirl me around and make me the star of all his music videos.

Of course, life doesn't usually work out that way. Days ended up turning into years of unmet expectations. Realizing it was biologically impossible for me to turn into a ferry boat, that dream died. What can I say? I guess I became resolved to the fact that God knew what He was doing.

Then I realized I couldn't be an actress, either, because frankly, I couldn't act. Every emotion I had ever felt was plastered all over my face.

And you guessed it, I couldn't be a singer because I couldn't sing. My voice could crack glass, and not in a good way.

I decided against paratrooping when I found out you had to jump out of a perfectly good airplane, with the wisdom to pull your chute at the right time. I just kept thinking a wise person wouldn't have jumped in the first place.

So, astronaut it was, at least, for a while. Then one day, planning my purpose in that shoebox-of-a-closet in my room, I began thinking about the few things that *did* scare me. And one of those was outer space. This would be a big problem if I wanted to be an astronaut.

I kept imagining myself losing my grip on the shuttle during some extra-vehicular maneuver, before floating off into the void. Falling into nothingness, encapsulated in a tiny, temporary sanctuary that was my space suit, made my skin crawl.

Thoughts of waiting for my air to run out, with no one to keep me company, yell at or rely on, terrified me. A thought like that doesn't escape you. Becoming an astronaut after that didn't seem like so elegant an occupation.

Fate was finally sealed on that front, January 28, 1986.

I remember the day, specifically, because it was the day the *Challenger* space shuttle exploded on national television. I was sitting in Mrs. Holland's science class. We were all watching with unveiled awe because a teacher was going into space.

It was all so exhilarating, right up until Mrs. Holland started crying. Every other kid in the class and I was confused. We had no idea all that smoke wasn't supposed to be there. Soon after, I promptly took being an astronaut off my "to-be" list.

I grew up, got a job that kept me closer to the earth's crust, got married, and had a couple of four kids, not specifically in that order. I had a lot of conflict in my life. Ninety-nine percent of it was of my own making. And I had a near-death experience, to boot.

I had experienced a lot in my life. I had ticked off a lot of the boxes on my "to be" list. So, what was wrong with me? I knew something was missing, and I was starting to get an idea of what that might be.

Out of all the dreams and aspirations I had as a child, being devoted to Christ didn't even make the top ten. I had never imagined Jesus being the star of my story, much less the great love of my life. I never envisioned Him walking with me through the tough times, or telling me how it was, like the best friend you would love to hate, but never could. Why hadn't He captured my heart?

I did a lot of soul-searching, and finally read the Bible all the way through, instead of taking somebody else's word for it. I developed a relationship with Jesus—one that was no longer one-sided, but reciprocal. I became His dance partner, just like David—not Bowie—but the king of Israel. You know, leaping and singing and praising God for who He was and what He did for me. That is what had been missing—the need and longing to worship my Creator and Savior, and to put Him first.

Just like many Christians, I did wonder about stuff, but I never questioned God's motives or judgment of things. He was a righteous God. And besides, He knew how to multiply His investments. But like any petulant child poking their bottom lip out, I wanted to know why I had to suffer? Why did anyone have to suffer? Why did evil seem to prosper in the world? Why does God stay quiet for so long before acting sometimes or seemingly not at all? These questions weren't new. They had been around long before Job had to prove his patience.

Now, I know what you are thinking. God's ways are not our ways, and His knowledge of things is so far above our own. The Lord's understanding is unfathomable. He knows the effect before the cause has even made an appearance. And I had a healthy fear of that.

I kept thinking that the Lord was my God, but He was also my friend. I thought if I kept asking Him nicely, He might share the answer to some of these questions—according to His will, of course. Days, weeks, and years went by with no answer, but I kept praying and worshiping Him. Through the good and the bad, He became the love of my life, and I wanted everyone to feel the way I did.

CHAPTER TWENTY-SIX

THE GREATEST LOVE STORY EVER TOLD

Journal Entry #2

WHEN YOU think of love stories, most people imagine star-crossed lovers being torn from one another's arms. An unquenchable passion. Heartbreaking deceit. Or maybe even unrequited love. Names that come to mind in these unfortunate scenarios include names like Romeo and Juliet, Lancelot and Guinevere, Antony and Cleopatra, or maybe even Rhett and Scarlet.

The story always begins with a chance meeting. Fierce eye contact. Pulses racing. Palms sweating. Then a brief verbal interlude, followed by some incredibly insurmountable conflict, resulting in hasty words of a love that will never die. Finally, the story ends in complete tragedy—a predictable cliché—leaving the people being entertained by said story, feeling heartbroken, ripped off and left wanting.

My story begins with star-crossed lovers.

My God, from across the universe, saw me, planned me, drew me out of the dark, and placed me in my mother's womb—with a hope and a future united with Him, filled with devotion, praise, and an unconditional love for my Creator. Yet even knowing before my birth that I would break His heart, He made me anyway.

I grew up searching for my love, finding it in the frivolities of life, in countless doomed relationships, and in accumulated possessions that didn't last. I was left wanting. I went down a path I had planned for myself.

One of self-reliance instead of the one designed by my love and soulmate. I was separated from My Love because I was unfaithful, a sinner, and weak to the temptations of this world.

But my story's hero, the One who loved me before my first breath, became my Champion. He placed my sin on Himself and battled the enemy for my cause so I could be reconciled to My Love.

Jesus Christ died for me. He overcame death and became my justification in the heavens. Imputed by His righteousness and covered in His grace, He laid me before the Lord.

My story differs from all the rest. My story differs from all the rest because mine is true. I live in His love every day, trying to walk in obedience, an obedience that can only come from the guidance of the Holy Spirit.

I feel loved completely, in the most intimate relationship I have ever known. Every day, unable to wait for the chance to talk to Him, spend time with Him, to glorify His name, and be the instrument of light He has always called me to be.

Do you think that is the end of the story? Of course, it's not. It is just one of a multitude. And there can be a love story even more powerful than the one I have shared with you today. That love story is your own. We all have a love like this if we seek Him, trust Him, and accept Him. And the title of this epic love story, you ask—Jesus and [*Insert Your Name Here*].

Dear Lord,
I love You so much. Thank You for Your loving kindness to me and to the world. Direct me in all things, Lord. Give me discernment and answer my questions according to Your will. I ask these things in the name of Jesus, Amen and Amen.

CHAPTER TWENTY-SEVEN

A HUSBAND

—◆—

YOU KNOW what they say about prayers. *Watch what you ask for; you might just get it.*

One day at church, the pastor started talking about this astronaut he knew. Now the word *astronaut* always made me perk up and sit a little taller in my chair. I don't think I had ever stopped harboring that childhood fantasy of one day sailing amongst the stars.

My interest was piqued.

This astronaut, the one the pastor was going on about, had apparently gone to my pastor's church years ago. On one occasion, he and his wife had gone out to dinner with the astronaut and his wife. As you can imagine, questions mounted in the pastor's mind. To sit at a table with someone who had joined the ranks of a select few, venturing past the boundaries of our atmosphere, made for a far from boring dinner conversation.

"How does it feel up there?" The pastor probed. This particular astronaut had been in outer space before and was now gearing up to return as the commander of the next shuttle mission.

The pastor continued with a flurry of questions. "Isn't it scary? Coming back into the earth's atmosphere? All that heat, pressure, and friction? Getting the angle and trajectory just right, so you don't go barreling off into space? It has got to be nerve-wracking."

Sitting on pins and needles, the pastor waited for the guy's response. The astronaut turned to him, shrugged, and simply said, "It's the only way home."

The astronaut in the pastor's story was Rick Husband. He was the commander of the *Colombia STS-107* mission. Unfortunately, upon re-entry into earth's atmosphere on February 1, 2003, the shuttle's protective covering failed, breaking up over parts of the Texas sky. Sadly, the crew was lost.

My pastor presided over the astronaut's funeral. The pastor went on to say, that after the service he was invited back to the family's home, where a few friends and family had gathered. It was there that the astronaut's wife pulled him aside.

She explained that astronauts had to fill out a sort of "last wishes" form before every shuttle launch, in case of any catastrophic event. She led the pastor into her husband's office, and there, neatly laying in the center of his desk, was a single sheet of paper. The astronaut's wife called the pastor to come closer and pointed to the last line on the page. It was a message to the pastor from her husband that said, "Please tell them about Jesus, Steve. He means so much to me."

Sitting motionless in my chair in that church, I felt the breath of God. "Here is the answer to your questions. Just like two stones being rubbed together to produce heat and fire, through friction and immense pressure, this is how you are refined. The friction between these barriers strips you bare, exposing something lying underneath. This draws you closer to me and helps to reshape our relationship. This is what helps bring holiness. This is what produces testimony.

"It's a truth spoken amid heartache and evidence for the hope you have and live by. It is in the valley and not the mountain top where you grow. It has always been in the trenches, the narrowing places, within the boundaries I have laid down before the beginning of time. Or within the confines of being hemmed in on all sides by the enemy. This is where your heart becomes contrite, and you find rest. This is where you see yourself and turn to Me, realizing you could never battle sin on your own. This is where you find that I have always been right there in the trench with you, offering to take up your cause, giving you the gift of atonement if you would only repent and receive it.

"My Son, Jesus, your Husband, came to earth so that all men could see this. His outer covering was stripped bare to cover you with. Accepting

Him as your Savior to cover you and lead you through this life is your choice, but it's the only way home. And it doesn't come without suffering and brokenness, in whatever form that takes, because you have to first recognize that you are not enough before you can ever turn to me to be made whole. It is only through this understanding that real discovery is made, and true intimacy and healing is fostered."

When I got home from church, I immediately called my best friend, Sheila Joy, to tell her about the revelation God had just given me, and how He had done it.

After I finished the story, she added, "You remember the day the *Colombia* went down, don't you? It was when we were roommates before you got married. We were both working as labor and delivery nurses. I remember the day so well because my mom, Sheila Elizabeth, was visiting from out of town. I was upset because I had to work the night before, but you said you would keep her entertained.

"When I got home, you and Mom were sitting on the back porch having a cup of coffee. It was about 8:30 in the morning. You guys were talking about how foggy it was around the house. I told you I had heard on the radio the *Columbia* had broken up over parts of our area, and that the already poor air quality would be worse that day. It was one of the reasons why there was so much fog around the house."

Why did all of this sound so familiar, like footsteps in a dream I had already taken?

CHAPTER TWENTY-EIGHT

FOOTSTEPS

Journal Entry #3

WHEN I was a child, my parents had a picture on the wall in our living room of an endless beachside landscape. The ocean was as far as the eye could see, with waves gently lapping white clouds of foam upon the soft sand. A single set of footprints lay peacefully and deliberately upon that sand in a path that seemed to extend the entire length of the beach.

And although this wasn't a living picture, I could hear the stillness on that beach. I could smell the salty air and feel it brush its hand against my face. Everything was in gentle order. Every pebble of sand was knocked purposefully in the furrow of each footprint molded in its path. Every wave crashed exactly on time against the break, and every ray of sunlight captured this heavenly dance that brought forth the dawn.

As a child, I knew there was always writing on this picture, but I couldn't read at the time so I asked my mom what the words meant. She told me they were a poem about Jesus. Satisfied with that response, I didn't ask her about it again.

As time went on, I grew up. I passed that picture every day as I left the comfort of my parents' house, venturing out into the world, only to come home, either full of joy, or crushed by the circumstances of the day.

I can't tell you when I read the words of the poem on that picture, but I eventually did. It was a poem about the trials of life and having the misperception that Jesus was never there for the person who made the tracks in the sand when they were hurting or sad. And Jesus lovingly tells the author, the one set of footprints were His, in every trial. And that He had been carrying her through every difficult experience. She had never walked alone.

I didn't quite understand that because I hadn't been out on my own yet. I had no self-driven experiences. I had nothing to regret or feel ashamed about. No roads had been traveled. My respective stone hadn't started rolling yet. I went to school, church, fought with my siblings, and hung out with my friends. Life ebbed on.

That picture continued to hang on the wall in the living room of my parent's home, but now that I didn't live there anymore, I wasn't reminded every day that my God was with me. He was for me, not against me. My self-reliance became bold, and I started making some really big mistakes in my life. Some were not so tragic, and some changed my life forever.

I remember one night when I was consoling myself over my last bitter disappointment. My mind wandered to that confounded picture. I became angry and was resolute that those feet in the sand weren't Jesus'. They were mine. Where had He been all those times when I needed Him? I decided right then, maybe not consciously, but determined, all the same, to put God on the back burner.

Over the years, that picture began to fade and was now more dusty than clean when I went to Mom and Dad's house. You could still make out the words with some effort, but I never did.

But then something happened.

In the valley of the mistakes I had made, hurt and damaged by circumstances I couldn't change, I found the Lord again. Slowly, I started to talk to Him again. The room that I had closed myself up in all those years ago, with no doors or windows, had now become a room with no walls. God heard everything I said.

Now when I went to the house where I grew up and passed that worn-out old picture, I finally understood what the words meant, and that realization brought me a lot of joy. I began to grow in my walk with the Lord. I started spending time in the Word every day, worshipping Him, talking to Him through prayer, and sharing the love I had for Him in my actions to the people around me.

Then, one day, while I was visiting with my parents at their home, my eyes fluttered over to that picture, still hanging in the same place it had for forty years, and something tickled me about it. I saw that picture through a new set of eyes.

The one set of footprints was indeed Jesus' in the sand, but it wasn't just because He was carrying me this time. It was because I was behind Him, clumsily, balancing from one foot to the other, trying to mirror every step in the sand with His. Seeking after my God, knowing He had established my path, and desiring ever so desperately to always walk in His will.

CHAPTER TWENTY-NINE

THE BOOK OF LIFE

$\blacklozenge$

MY JOURNAL entries became more and more about Jesus. I knew I was heading in the right direction. And I wanted to continue down that path, even with baby steps, if it meant I was moving forward. I wanted everyone to feel this way—chasing a high that wasn't destructive but renewing.

I started believing the Bible was written just for me. And I think that's what it is supposed to do. Written with such precision and divine care, the Bible was penned with each person's name purposefully expressed in its pages. It's a "right now" word for every person and every circumstance. It is a living, breathing thing. A book of life—a tree of life. Its branches, the pages, the leaves, its words, flittering off the parchment and into our hearts in every season, refining them to accomplish God's holy plans.

Every time I read scripture, I realized I was given exactly what I needed to hear, exactly when I needed to hear it. A word was rarely revealed suddenly in its entirety, but over time through prayer and fellowship with those I was yoked with.

I continued to read the Bible, feeling like I was running toward something just beyond the line of the horizon. Something I couldn't see but could certainly feel. A breakthrough was coming, like the first shard of light piercing the sky at dawn. I just didn't know when or where it might come.

CHAPTER THIRTY

REVELATION

———◆———

PRAYER IS a powerful thing. It is a direct line to the Almighty. A vocal love letter between you and your Husband. A worship service for one or more, destined from before time and directly inserted into it. Its very design brings people closer to their God. For their voices to ascend into the heavens, seeking Him in every decision of their lives, searching and wanting to give Him the desires of His heart through theirs.

Prayer isn't the recounting of a laundry list of things we yearn for. It isn't the rubbing of a proverbial bottle, expecting God to just snap His fingers and make it so. Prayer involves thankfulness, gratitude, worship, self-abasement, and then supplication.

Prayer is an outward expression of our inner belief that we know God is higher than all our circumstances. He has all authority in our lives, and He sees what we need an infinite number of steps before we do. Prayer involves confession and frees us from the burdens our flesh likes to keep in its clutches—making our hands free to walk together with Him.

So many of us like the talk. We like the sound of our voices and want to pat ourselves on the back. More often than not, we don't walk out the faith we profess in our prayer and daily life.

Taking parts of the Bible as gospel, while considering the rest mere suggestions to be weighed and measured by our own hearts, as opposed to His, have become commonplace. Prayer has become telling God what the truth is, instead of Him telling us. We are seeing, but blind. Hearing, but genuinely deaf. Having the legs to walk, but completely weak in the knees.

Talking isn't enough to guard against fire hazards. I was one of the people who once believed it was. Just like some of the Jews, after Lazarus died, in John 11:38, said, *"Could not he who opened the eyes of the blind man have kept this man from dying?"* Just like them, I didn't realize that it is not just about seeing, but that there must be a dying too; a dying to yourself, and living for God, and in His love.

I thought I was saved as a young adult, and that I could act any way I wanted to without a relationship with Christ because He had already paid for my sins. After all, I was saved by grace, not works. I had cheapened that word. Grace. It was far from cheap. It came at the ultimate price, the death of Jesus Christ, but I had made it a byword because there was no change in my *want to*. There was no repentance, no change in my perspective.

If I had knocked on God's door at the time, he would have told me, "I never knew you," and turned me out into the dark so I could gnash my teeth. It terrified me to think other people could be living under that same assumption—believing they were saved, when, in fact, they had been wholly deceived.

Jesus, our Lord and Savior, who lived a perfect life, because we couldn't, took our sin on Himself. He was nailed to two beams of wood. He took our curse, was crucified, died, and came back to life. He had to die, and so do we. We have to die to ourselves, submitting our will to His, our desires to His. Giving Him the authority. This is salvation.

Jesus didn't just save us on that tree. He was the example of how to live our lives there. The cross wasn't only a symbol of salvation and redemption, but an ox-goad, to pierce our own hearts and keep us on the right path. That upon seeing it, the cross would represent the price that was paid there.

I wanted everyone to know that. It was a matter of life and death. Salvation wasn't just about seeing and hearing, but about repenting and obeying. Bending the knee didn't just mean kneeling upon it in worship, but about lifting it to take a step in the Lord's direction. Should I write something about this? I needed to talk to the Father. So, I did the only thing I could. I prayed.

The Lord's answer came at Christmas time. We were at a Christmas service when the pastor decided to change things up a bit. The sermon was titled *"A Mary Christmas."* And he was talking about what happened before the rest of the story. He asked us to turn in our Bibles to Luke 1:26-38:

> *In the sixth month of Elizabeth's pregnancy, God sent the angel Gabriel to Nazareth, a town in Galilee, to a virgin pledged to be married to a man named Joseph, a descendant of David. The virgin's name was Mary. The angel went to her and said, "Greetings, you who are highly favored! The Lord is with you."*
>
> *Mary was greatly troubled at his words and wondered what kind of greeting this might be. But the angel said to her, "Do not be afraid, Mary; you have found favor with God. You will conceive and give birth to a son, and you are to call him Jesus. He will be great and will be called the Son of the Most High. The Lord God will give him the throne of his father David, and he will reign over Jacob's descendants forever; his kingdom will never end."*
>
> *"How will this be," Mary asked the angel, "since I am a virgin?" The angel answered, "The Holy Spirit will come on you, and the power of the Most High will overshadow you. So the holy one to be born will be called the Son of God. Even Elizabeth your relative is going to have a child in her old age, and she who was said to be unable to conceive is in her sixth month. For no word from God will ever fail."*
>
> *"I am the Lord's servant," Mary answered. "May your word to me be fulfilled." Then the angel left her.*

The pastor wanted to convey the message of being a willing servant to God without whining, grumbling, or backtalk. How many of us submit our will to God's, as Mary did?

Then something strange happened. I started remembering a scene as if I were viewing it from afar. A picture of two large stones. And then, slowly, every scene in my life started playing out in reverse, one right after the other. I saw God's love so carefully concealed under the surface of my life, waiting patiently to be revealed under the right circumstances. It was as if every scar, memory, and broken dream had become infused with gold, and I had just struck it rich. I remembered Lewis, the time we spent at my house, the fog, the pictures, and the message I had been given to share with the world.

It's not a coincidence that it would be revealed when our world had fallen so far from a biblical worldview. It would be during the time of a worldwide spiritual pandemic. It would be during a time when the will of God was worthless. A baby's life was deemed unimportant. The marriage covenant between a man and a woman was without value.

When the selfish desires of men reigned so supreme in the world that even personal pronouns had become something to be hijacked and placed under his control, while every one of God's most basic spiritual truths was under attack. It would come when a pestilence had descended, and everything was upside down. It would be in a time like this a word would have to be brought.

God had just shown me a glimpse of the front of His tapestry, so I could see a clear picture of His nature, His process, and His love. I saw how perfect His timing was. Nothing was quite what it seemed. I could see that His way was better, even if I didn't understand it.

I realized God's presence had always been in my life, never seen in my time, but His. And that returning to Him and the Word through Jesus Christ brought relationship and uncovered His presence, process, and better judgment. God's way strengthened me. It brought me to conviction. God showed me that self-examination in that relationship with Him fostered a submission to honoring Him. And it revealed His purposes for my life, instead of me submitting to the things that only satisfied my flesh.

CHAPTER THIRTY-ONE

RECEPTION

—◆—

THE TRUTH of God's work brought me back to Tabitha's office. Enraptured by the story I had been telling her, Tabitha blurted out, "Is that it?" I knew she was expecting something more.

Didn't she have somewhere to be? She had an appointment she was going to miss. "I thought you had a meeting. We have gone a little over the hour you gave me to tell my story," I said, pointing to the clock on her desk.

"That's okay," she clambered, "Is there more? There has to be more, right?"

"There is."

"Well?"

"Are you sure you have the time?"

Looking back at the clock and turning beet red, she realized it was behind. Now she knew I was already aware of it, but asked anyway. "Did you know the clock was wrong?"

"Yes," I replied, "but I thought it would be rude to point it out since we had only just met. But since you realized it now, I might as well tell you your calendar on the wall is wrong, too."

Looking over my shoulder, she saw the calendar and sighed. "You are very observant."

"Not in my own right, I assure you."

"Well, it appears that I am going to be late anyway, so you might as well humor me and finish the story."

CHAPTER THIRTY-TWO

THE SABBATH

WHEN I got home from church, Jason told me someone was on the phone waiting to speak to me. That was funny because the phone hadn't made a sound. Taking it from him and placing it up to my ear, the only thing I was greeted with was a dial tone.

Asking Jason if he was playing with me, he responded with a profuse shaking of his head. "Honey, someone did call. He must have hung up; he'll call back if it's important."

The day slowly lulled into Sunday evening. We all snuck off to our designated little nooks, where we could kick our shoes off. My corner was the bedroom. I loved Sunday evening; it being the last respite before the next dreaded work week.

After my "big sleep," I returned to work. "Big sleep" refers to my near-death experience in labor and delivery. But I couldn't go back to being a labor and delivery nurse. It was just too weird working down the hall from where I almost died.

So, I had gone back to school and got my Master of Science in Nursing, specializing in family medicine. Taking care of people from cradle to grave, on a regular nine-to-five schedule, seemed like an upgrade from the endless nights that bled from one to the other doing shift work. It was more laid back, not so much drama.

And my body was getting older. I couldn't be jumping on gurneys, jetting down the hall for emergency surgery anymore. The office work wasn't bad. It was mentally trying, but mostly provided me with something to occupy my time.

Settling into bed, I heard the phone ring. Getting up and trudging back into the living room, I expected Jason to hand me the phone. But to my surprise, he was still sitting on the couch in the same position I left him in.

"Did you hear that?"

"Did I hear what?"

"The phone rang again."

"I didn't hear anything, babe."

Going back to the bedroom, I relented that I must have been hearing things. As I picked up my feet to shove them back under the covers, the phone rang again. Whirling out of bed, my body moved faster than my feet could carry it, and I stumbled back into the living room while simultaneously blurting out, "There it is again! Did you hear it?" My husband just stared at me. He had never seen me move so fast.

"No," was all he could get out before the phone rang again. Picking up the receiver before the ring tone could get off another blast, I shouted, "Hello?"

"I've been waiting for you," was all he said.

There was no mistaking that voice. "Lewis?"

"Yes, it's me. I need to talk to you."

"Right now?"

"Yes."

"And you're calling me on the phone?"

"Yes. How would you like me to contact you? The last time you were in a coma. Would you rather us meet under those conditions? It can be arranged if you like."

I couldn't tell if he was kidding or not, but I wasn't taking any chances. "No way!"

"Good, because we haven't the time. I called to tell you, now that you have accepted what I've told you, you must receive it."

"That sounds awfully mysterious, Lewis. I thought we didn't have the time."

"We don't. Do you remember the two stones we talked about?"

"Yes. Do you want me to give you a recap, Lewis?" I quietly asked.

"If you don't mind."

"Those stones are the foreshadowing of Jesus, right? And Jesus lies in the narrow hollow of every rub, every trial, every triumph, every circumstance in our lives. He's there to cover us, to suffer with us, to grow us, and to make us whole again. He is there to cover every sin exposed in every tribulation. And through His saving grace, Jesus gives us another chance to make a first impression. Those two stones, those Ten Words, in the flesh as Christ, have always been there to rub away our sins and rub off on us.

"The rub is both literal and metaphorical. In trying times, those two stones expose what needs correction, bring us to conviction, and help us take that first step on the beaten path toward holiness. The rub fashions us into who He intended us to be. A one-of-a-kind creation, and vessel with a unique purpose for the time He has allotted us. He rubs our broken vessel, making it whole again in His love. Have I missed anything, Lewis?"

"That sounds pretty good, but do you remember what I said about one of the purposes of this message? The rub is supposed to get people to read and obey the Word, not to just read it and act like they never did. And that can only happen by being sensitive to the Holy Spirit.

"When someone is saved they receive the Holy Spirit in their vessel, sometimes baptized immediately with it. However, sometimes the Holy Spirit is unheard, neglected, or even rejected altogether because there is no relationship with God.

"It's like having Jesus as a neighbor you don't have a relationship with. You wave at Him when you drive by His house as He's cutting the grass. You say 'Hi' casually when you walk the dog around the neighborhood. You accept that Jesus exists and lives down the street from you, but you have never invited Him in for dinner. It's an acquaintance, not a relationship.

"Making Jesus an acquaintance isn't enough for salvation. Opening your hand to His is the acceptance, but enclosing your hand in His is its intimate consummation. Think about that for a minute. Envision your hand extended out to Him and firmly in His grip, but yours never enfolded in it? It screams a lack of intimacy, doesn't it?

"This message isn't just about accepting God's role and process in your life, but about the receiving of it that matters as well. It is the receiving of it that takes the inner reflection of our hearts and causes a change in our outward behavior. Taking God's Word, which we hide so carefully in our hearts and give infinite value to, becomes the catalyst in our physical display to the world, bringing it full circle.

"The word given to you should encourage others to examine their own spiritual journey with God and yearn to walk with Him hand-in-hand. It should help to show them that their own story has always led to His. And that through the Holy Spirit, God brings inward reflection, not the condemnation and judgment of others."

"Okay," I said. That seemed logical.

"You have accepted who Jesus is. You have been baptized in the Holy Spirit, and now you will walk boldly in it. These past few years have been a slow working through of a process. The journey you have taken together has been like the mining, cutting, and polishing of a rare jewel—that over time, has produced a testimony so captivating it shines a light in areas of a room, long since covered in darkness. It has worked out this way so you could understand God's pace, His purpose, and then proclaim it to the world."

"I said, okay, Lewis? What else do you want me to say? I'm in!"

"Yes, you are."

"So, let me guess. Are we going to be talking about two stones again? One of the things I do remember in my brief brush with death is that God doesn't change. He is the same yesterday, today and tomorrow."

"That is true. We will be talking about the two stones, among other things," he offered with a smirk.

"Well, what are we waiting for, Lewis?"

CHAPTER THIRTY-THREE

THE CAPSTONE AND THE CORNERSTONE

In 1969, an archeology student named James Fleming made a serendipitous discovery. As he was taking pictures of the Golden Gate on the eastern side of the temple complex, he fell through some softened ground and limestone about eight feet into a Muslim mass grave, because it had heavily rained the night before.

The area in front of the Golden Gate had been marked and fashioned as a Muslim cemetery. By making the area a cemetery, the Muslim community could assign the area with sacred status, so that it couldn't be dug up.

It seemed that God had other ideas. When James fell through the tomb, he had his camera with him. As he was looking for a way out through the bones of the dead he noticed several stones in a buried wall that looked a lot like an arch. He snapped a shot of it, climbed out of the tomb, and went to find his professor.

He told his professor everything he had seen, and they both hurried back to the site the next day, but the hole had already been filled in with cement. Someone hadn't wanted them digging around underneath the Eastern gate.

Now this was unfortunate because they were unable to get a better look at what James had found. What had been so special about this find was that the arch was directly under the present Golden Gate. It proved that there had been a gate there in the past. So, was it evidence that the stones found were the gate Jesus *entered under during His triumphal entrance into Jerusalem the week before the crucifixion? It obviously couldn't be confirmed or denied.*

I READ the article repeatedly from *Biblical Archaeology Review 9:1, January/February* 1983, having received it in the mail a couple of days ago. The article was by James Fleming and titled "The Undiscovered Gate Beneath Jerusalem's Golden Gate." The review came in an unmarked envelope, but there was no question about who it was from. Lewis hadn't made contact since that first call. It got me wondering when I might hear from him again.

The work week flew by, and on Saturday, while taking a stroll around the man-made lake in my subdivision with my dog, I saw Lewis standing where the water's edge met the lake's grassy embankment. My dog started going crazy at the sight of him and rushed forward, pulling me along for the ride.

"Hello, Lewis. I thought you had forgotten about me."

"How could I forget you? Did you get the article I sent?" *Boy, he wasn't wasting any time.*

"You know I did. I read it, of course, but what's got me puzzled is how this relates to this narrative God wants me to share."

"Thought you might be, so I brought a picture of James' discovery. Look at it and tell me what you see."

I took the picture from his hand with one of my own, trying desperately to hold on to my dog with the other, who was going nuts, trying to attack a family of ducks who had made the little lake their home.

The picture was of three stones in an arch covered by another heap of stones. Wait. They weren't stones. What I was looking at were heaps of skeletons piled on top of each other. The arch itself was only slightly visible above the jumbled mound of remains.

"Do you see the stone to the far right?" Lewis said.

"Yes. I see it. What about it, Lewis?" Why was it every time I was around this man I felt three steps behind?

"It is called the capstone, and it is the last stone always placed in a gate's arch. It connects the two sides of an arch together. It might appear that the capstone is the one taking the brunt of the load, but its load is the lightest."

"How could that be, Lewis?"

"Simply by thrusting the weight equally down the sides of the stones below it. The stone navigates the weight down the supports of the wall to the cornerstone."

I saw where he was going with this. "Jesus is the cornerstone, right?"

"He is both. We find in 1 Peter 2:7 a verse which says:

The stone the builders have rejected has become the cornerstone.

"The word used for *cornerstone* in Greek here is *akrogoniaios*, which means both *capstone* and *cornerstone*. Jesus is both the capstone and the cornerstone, the head and the foundation of our lives.

"Many people accept Him as the cornerstone, but not the capstone. And the capstone is where the Holy Spirit speaks. The capstone is also called the *copestone* or the *keystone*. The word *copestone* comes from a word meaning to *come to blows with* or *to meet in battle*. It can also mean *covering stone*.

"When the disciples met in the upper room after the crucifixion and received the Holy Spirit, there was a sound of a violently blowing wind, the appearance of tongues of fire above them, and they were given the ability to speak in different languages. They spoke differently, with power, boldness, and authority. They were given the ability to deal more effectively with difficult situations. They had become tested, brought to maturity, and more capable of dealing successfully with every trial.

"Upon salvation, every believer is indwelled with the Holy Spirit, but may not be baptized in Him. He could be lying unheeded. Not to say some don't receive the baptism in the Holy Spirit right away. Some people become very sensitive to the Holy Spirit early, and some later. We are all different and have different purposes in God's grand design. And, at the end of the day, that benefits us all. You have to have ones who hear early to encourage those and support the ones who hear later, right? These late bloomers are ones who accept the foundational framework of the gospel, but who still don't allow God to be their head and shield, the One who meets the enemy in every battle."

"Lewis, it's a little irritating that some hear immediately and others don't. But I guess that's what Jesus meant in John 21:22 when Peter was grumbling about his path with Jesus and John's path with Him. Jesus pretty much said, *'Don't worry about John's walk. Worry about your own and follow me,'"* I mumbled.

"His ways are not our ways. God's ways of increase are not the same as ours because we see the world with physical eyes instead of spiritual ones. The Lord's loving kindness, grace, mercy, and compassion are nothing like ours. We cannot comprehend every step and its purpose in our path, but God does. He sees the bigger picture and what confers the greatest benefit. This is why having faith and listening to His Spirit is so important."

I figured out just what that meant the following week at work. Monday morning had been uneventful. Treating sore throats, refilling prescriptions, and cutting off unsightly warts had been the extent of excitement for the day.

It was now after 1:00 p.m. when I saw my first afternoon patient. Walking into the room, I noticed a small woman with a set of the most expressive eyes I had ever seen. She was one of my regulars. She was from Ireland, and I inadvertently tried to immolate her accent every time she came in.

The woman was nice enough, but I didn't know her very well. Honestly, how could you truly know anyone in a fifteen-minute appointment slot? She never made small talk in all the times I had seen her. I really knew nothing personal about her.

Today, she seemed a little lost, hopeless, really. We went over her last set of lab work. I refilled her medications and gave her a new lab requisition form to follow up on some previous lab results I was concerned about.

After we concluded the reason for her appointment, I felt led by the Holy Spirit to ask her if she would like me to pray with her. I knew something hadn't been resolved during our visit. I told her that prayer comforted me when I was having a hard time dealing with the circumstances in my life that were just too hard to handle.

She turned to me and said, "If I wanted religious consolation, I would go to church and not to the doctor." She was angry. Swallowing my irritation, I apologized, explaining that I hadn't meant to offend her. I gave her the lab slip, and she left.

Feeling dejected, I started talking to God. *Had I heard wrong? What was that all about? I hadn't deserved that.* I got no response. I finished the day in a slump, wondering if there was any way I could have salvaged that situation. Had I reflected God during the appointment? I spent the whole night second-guessing myself.

The next day I was running late for work. It wasn't because I was running late. Circumstances were beyond my control—code for—I was on drop-off duty for school with my kids, and at the last minute, one of them complained of a stomachache and barricaded himself in the bathroom.

Needless to say, I arrived at work twenty minutes later than I usually did. Now, you must walk past the lab to get to my office. As I headed down the hallway, I noticed someone. My little fighting Irish woman was waiting there to get her labs drawn.

She looked at me, saw that I was limping on my right leg, and said, "What happened to you?"

"Oh, it's nothing. I can never remember who I tell, but I have multiple sclerosis. Some days are worse than others. I can mask the limp well, but I am having a bad day today. It's all good, though. God is in control."

The woman's face immediately changed. I could see a wave of regret cover her face the instant she remembered how she treated me the day before. In that moment, she probably realized I wasn't just some random person offering trivial platitudes. I hadn't been disingenuous in my willingness to comfort her, or somehow emotionally detached to the effects of pain and suffering. I had MS—Multiple Scars. And that day she could see them.

"I hope you start feeling better," came tumbling out of her mouth.

"I will. Thank you," I replied.

I walked past her with that limp, knowing sometimes God allows the limp to help people truly walk straight. As I turned the corner in the hallway, I burst into tears, praising the Lord for His perfect timing and will. I was late that day on purpose—His.

I decided to tell Lewis all about it the next time I saw him. "Lewis, I saw that appointment differently after that little encounter in the hallway. The exam room had become a testing ground for both of us. God wanted to know how she would respond to Him through me and how I would respond to offense through her. He wanted to see if I would reflect the light of His Son or the darkness of the world around us. God could only use that appointment if I stood on His foundation and followed the urging of the Holy Spirit to reflect His Son.

"God's way couldn't have been planned by me. It could have only been carried out walking in His will, led by His Spirit, so God could be glorified in that hallway the next day, leaving His mark on both of us.

"Now, all I can say is, on the day of the appointment, I was sensitive to the Holy Spirit, and the woman hadn't been. I don't know whether she was saved or not. I don't know her heart, but I also know there was no coincidence I saw her in the hall the next day. I believe it was so we could both hear from the Lord. And the Holy Spirit is how we hear God. Am I on the right track, Lewis?"

"Yes. The Holy Spirit is how we have relationship with God and walk out our lives in His will. If we can't hear Him, how can there be relationship? If there is no relationship, one should wonder, why not? One should ask themselves, *Have I completely and continually rejected and resisted the Holy Spirit, the person in the Godhead Jesus died to send me?* Which is a rejection of Jesus, Himself. If the answer is yes, a sincere self-examination should be done before God about their relationship.

"Make no mistake, Jesus spoke about this. When one isn't hearing, has never heard or obeyed the urging of the Holy Spirit through a rejection of Him, salvation cannot be claimed because there is a willful opposition to repentance. This is the blasphemy of the Holy Spirit Jesus spoke about in the Word. It is a total rejection of Jesus' message, of His urging and a continual, willful walk with the enemy, putting God, forever, on the opposite side of the battlefield.

"If that is the case, salvation through Jesus Christ may have never been obtained in the first place. That is something no one can answer for another. Mankind can't see into the hearts of men; only God can.

"And I'm not saying Christ-followers never sin. All of mankind sins, even the elect. But the 'want-to' is changed. And who brings the change in the *want-to*? It is the Holy Spirit. With His urging, you don't want to simply talk the talk; you want to walk the walk, no matter the limp, because you have Jesus to hold on to."

CHAPTER THIRTY-FOUR

THE ROMAN MILE

CAN I just say how much I hate to exercise? Unfortunately, it became clear that my leg and right arm muscles would get weaker faster by using them less. The thing about multiple sclerosis and nerve damage is that it causes muscle atrophy in an already weakened extremity, compounding an already progressive process.

I already couldn't run anymore because an electric current flowing through an invisible magnetic chain had been securely tethered to the end of my right leg, making it impossible to keep my stride without falling. Every time the useless limb was lifted, it seemed to be fighting the forces of gravity. So I became relegated to shuffling and limping along. And that was okay for a while.

But not anymore. I needed to get back out there. So, walking around the lake in my neighborhood became part of my daily routine.

As I was making my second loop around the lake one day, I saw the back of a very familiar head. Lewis was walking ahead of me. He slowed his pace so I could catch up, and finally, when my step was in line with his, he offered a "hello."

"Hello, Lewis. Have you come to be my personal trainer today?"

"Haven't I already been doing that?" He smiled.

"I guess you're right," I added, smiling more to myself than to him. "So, if you're not here to clock my time or critique my form, it must be because you want to talk about those two stones again?"

A simple nod was all I got.

Eyeing a bench ahead of us, I asked if we might sit down. I was exhausted.

"Of course, but I am here to talk about both the timing of your steps and the weighing of them."

"Lewis, you know it drives me crazy when you just don't tell me what's going on."

"Yes, but there is a reason for it, as you well know."

My mind went back to my conversation with the Fighting Irish. "Duly noted."

"Did you know Jesus had many parables about the two stones?"

"No, not really," I responded.

"Why wouldn't you? If the two stones are representative of Him, why wouldn't He speak about them to His people? The reason why those stones haven't been seen in this way is because they have been hidden until now. This is part of your message."

"Then I guess we better get started," giving him the go-ahead to get the revealing underway. We were burning daylight.

"Do you remember the comment Jesus makes in Matthew 5:41?"

If anyone forces you to go one mile, go with them two miles.

"This one comment speaks to those two stones. It may not appear so clear, but what Jesus was referring to alluded to the Roman mile. In Jesus' day, Roman soldiers could have any non-citizen of Rome carry their pack for one Roman mile with no payment or permission. These Roman miles were marked along the roads by small pillars along the wayside. Essentially, the first stone marked the first mile, and the subsequent stone marked the second.

"Jesus was saying, among other things, that not only were we responsible for bearing each other's burdens but to do it with joy, walking in His way and according to His Words—Ten, to be exact. This is how we love God and our fellow man. That is when we glorify Him. This is where the currency of our relationship with Him is spent and revealed in the transaction. Bringing an even greater abundance. Do you understand what I mean?" he asked.

"I think so. At work, I pass the lab every day while walking to my office. When I walk by anyone sitting in the chairs outside the lab, I've made a habit of telling them, 'Jesus loves you,' as they wait for their turn with the needle. I always try to make eye contact, so they know those three words were spoken in sincerity.

"One day, I was running late. Again. There seems to be a pattern here, Lewis! Anyway, as I reached the door to the office building, I noticed every chair was filled. There must have been twenty people waiting to get their blood drawn. What was so special about that day? I had no idea. There had never been that many people in the hallway before.

"Smiling a little to myself, I knew God was about to do a mighty work. And He was allowing me to play a small part in it. So I quickly walked past those in the hall and told them how much Jesus loved them. I must have repeated it ten times when I saw a gentleman stand up out of the corner of my eye.

"Turning to face the man, I noticed he was around fifty years old. It was also glaringly apparent that he suffered from a significant mental and physical disability, probably due to a birth accident. The man's hands were drawn in, and he had difficulty making eye contact. He turned to me and yelled at the top of his lungs, 'Jesus loves you, too.' Clapping to himself, the man sat back down. I smiled and said, 'Thank you so much for reminding me.'

"Tears began to fall as I continued down the hall to my office. Not because of anything I had done. I thought I was going to be doing this great work with the help of the Holy Spirit for Jesus that morning, but He had other intentions. That day, those people showed up at that appointed time. Not because of me, but because of God's perfectly balanced turning of events. He wanted me to see that He uses every one of us to fulfill His divine purposes. And that His way of glorification always brings a double portion.

"The way I intended for God to be glorified in the hallway was good, but His execution of it was exquisite. God's grace was magnified tenfold when that gentleman stood up and gave everything he had—a pure and innocent love for our Savior, Jesus Christ. We had both gone the distance, and walked in God's will that morning, rubbing each other with His love so that it could be expressed to everyone in that hallway."

Lewis sat quietly and listened to every word before replying, "You both carried the message the first mile. But it was God all along, driving it home."

CHAPTER THIRTY-FIVE

JACOB'S WELL

AS WE continued sitting on the bench, now surrounded in silence, I began to wonder what time it was. How long had we been out here? As if knowing where my train had gotten off the track, Lewis offered, "Before you go, I need to talk to you about one more thing."

Looking at my watch, I replied, "I would love to, Lewis, but my husband is going to be wondering where I've been. I wouldn't be surprised at this point if he hasn't called a search party."

"What husband are you referring to? You've had many." Looking back at Lewis, I was a little startled by his comment, wondering if I had it in me to let the insult go unanswered. He had never used his words to rub me so harshly before.

"Was I being rough or just truthful? That wasn't spoken to condemn you, but to show you something. It was only spoken for your good." Not caring, even a little bit, I stood with a world-sized chip on my shoulder, ready to walk away when he added, "Do you remember the account in John 4:4-42, about the Samaritan woman at the well in the New Testament?"

"Yes, but what does that have to do with me?"

"Everything."

Sitting back down, still annoyed by his comment, I encouraged myself not to take offense. *Okay*, I thought. *I am not going to let what he said ruin the rest of my day.* Turning to him, I muttered, "Well?"

"Remember when Jesus was resting by the well in Samaria while His disciples went out to go grab lunch? Seeing a Samaritan woman coming to draw some water from the well, He asked her to give Him a drink. But she didn't know what He would draw water with. The woman knew Jews wouldn't touch anything she offered, because to them, Samaritans were filthy. And they were considered pagans as far as the Hebrews were concerned, just like those found in Egypt, Assyria, and Babylon. So how was He going to get a drink from her?

"He showed her. And instead of giving Jesus something to drink, He satisfied *her* thirst and fed her with His words. They shared a metaphorical meal together and created a covenant while His boys were off procuring dinner.

"Remember, they went to buy food and when they returned, Jesus wasn't hungry anymore. Why is that, do you think? Could it be because Jesus had already broken bread with the woman? They had feasted and drank on the testimony of His love for her, and the insight His Word poured into her heart.

"Through Him, she was able to see the foundational love brought by an all-knowing God and got to drink straight from the well—The Word of God, in the Flesh. She tasted, touched, smelled, and was made to see with full understanding her sin in every point of her life so that she could be moved by it. She could see herself and her iniquity reflected in those waters for what they were and ran to tell others how Jesus had revealed it to her—through the gentle, but firm, rub of The Word.

"Remember, every word in the Bible is important. Jesus does and says everything for a reason. So, there must have been a reason Jesus sat down at that well to meet with that woman. And remember, anytime someone sat next to something or opposite something in the Bible, it was most likely a reflection of that person's moral character or purpose. In this case, Jesus' reflection was that well.

"In the Hebrew, the word meaning well is the word *beer, bet-aleph-resh*. But there is another word with two meanings that is spelled the same as this one that really opens up this scripture. The first is the word *baar,* meaning *to make distinct, plainly seen,* or *to declare.* And the second is a word that means *written words on tablets of stone.*

"Also remember, Jesus spoke Aramaic. And even though Hebrew and Aramaic are closely linked, some of their words are spelled differently. One of those words is the word for son. In Hebrew, the word is *ben,* but in

Aramaic, it's the word *bar, bet-resh*. And this word is closely linked to the word the Hebrews used for the word meaning well.

"This word *bar* has many derivatives. They include words that mean *son, to purify* or *select, grain* or *corn, to test metal, to feed* and a word for *covenant*. So, Jesus was the two stones inscribed on tablets, revealed in the flesh as Christ, to make plain and distinct this woman's life story and her sin—to purify her, feed her and to covenant with her. And if you are willing to accept it, you are the Samaritan women spoken of in scripture."

"What?" I said incredulously. "Are you telling me a book written over two thousand years ago was specifically written with me in mind?"

"Why is that so hard to believe? It was written specifically in mind for every person who has, and who will ever live. Their specific purpose in God's will is written there, too, if they would only seek it out. God's time isn't like ours. There have been many women at the well. And more corporately, other nations, besides ours, who have taken other husbands, denying the one true God, and have instead embraced idolatry and their own fleshly desire. For this point in time, the Samaritan woman Jesus has spoken to is you. This is the Turner's work."

"Turner's work? What on earth are you talking about, Lewis?"

"Turner's work is a term used in the Old Testament by Isaiah. It was what Hebrews called a well-set hairdo, tightly bound into perfection. It was also considered a hammered work, or rounded work beaten from one piece of metal to stand or cover the furnished pieces of the tabernacle. We are all the Turner's work."

"Lewis, are you trying to tell me God is a hairstylist or a blacksmith?"

"Neither. What I am trying to tell you is God is the Beautifier and the Master of any medium. Try to imagine every hair on your head as a mark of every point in time in your life, whether considered good or bad. From the deepest darkness to the brightest light. It is a mark of every trial, every tribulation, every devastation, cause for joy, or corner in the wall where those two elements intersected. God takes those hairs, lifts them up, and redeems them into a beautifully manicured work, with the sole intent of readying you for your wedding. This is His process. He beautifies you and covers you.

"God wants you to see that in every turn, He is stretching you to your fullest capacity, so you can see Jesus there suffering with you, fully understand His grace, and be moved by it. It is this grace, this joy, this light you take from the rub and share with others."

"That is all well and good, no pun intended. Okay, maybe a little intended, Lewis. So, Jesus represents the two stones as the well in this account?"

"Yes, the physical two stones in this story are the well itself. Spiritually, and more importantly, Jesus represents the well, and the woman reflects Him in her walk. Do you see a pattern emerging here? No longer is Jesus, Himself, the two stones, walking alone, but you are with Him, as a perfect reflection of that well, both of you working in collaboration with each other as one. You have hidden His Word in your heart, and His manifestations of love for you there, to walk out this life as a reflection of Him. This is what keeps you at the center of His will. Isn't that the takeaway from Psalm 119.11?

I have hidden your word in my heart that I might not sin against you.

"You have been given a connection that no one else has put together. Now you are running to the village to tell the people about a man who told you everything you've ever done. You have kept an intimate connection with the Holy Spirit, so you could point out to others where they can find Jacob's well—in Jesus."

CHAPTER THIRTY-SIX

THE TWO MITES

WOW. This was all becoming too much. The weight of these words. Standing abruptly, I barked, "I have to go home, Lewis."

"That's what I have been waiting to hear." He said, sighing. "Let me walk with you."

"I don't think you understand, Lewis. I can't handle this. It feels too overwhelming. I am shaking on the inside, with the magnitude resting on my shoulders. I feel as if it is about to crush me."

"You are supposed to feel this way. It is called a mantle for that very reason. It is supposed to be too heavy for you to carry by yourself. It is meant to be carried together with the Lord and with others.

"The weight of this word is one of the reasons God has drawn it out of you so slowly. It would be too much to hear at one time. It had to be extended out, completing your preparation in faith to meet the demands and expectations of your Father. He has done this with every believer who receives Him. You have to receive Him fully to see Him, to talk to Him, to know Him. This is what salvation is. It's not just a couple of words, surreptitiously spoken as a get-out-of-Hell-free card and quickly tossed to the side. That isn't knowing Him. But you know Him. This brings us to our next two stones."

We had been walking for a while, and I could now see my house from where we were. This early morning walk had been more than I expected or bargained for. "Lay it on me, Lewis."

"Don't worry, I will. Do you remember the story of the woman with the two mites?"

"Of course I do, Lewis. She was the woman the Lord saw toss two coins into the offering at the Temple. He told the disciples the rich gave from their wealth, but the woman gave out of her poverty. And she had given more than they had, even if they had technically given more money than her."

"Exactly. But this story is more powerful than that. In Mark 12:41-44, it says Jesus sat opposite the treasury. Remember, every word and every detail in the Bible matters, just like every word and detail in our own lives do. When Jesus sat opposite anything, it was a reflection of Jesus' identity. The treasury was a significant revelation of who Jesus is. He is the offering, the true treasure, and what provides provision to the Temple.

"If you recall, Jesus was watching how people were giving their tribute, out of pure humility or pride and self-righteousness—all of themselves or just in part. This woman gave her all. She completely submitted to God, knowing that she was lacking something only He could provide. She gave all she had to live on. Those two stones. They were tokens of her remembrance of what God had done in her life. She valued His provision above all things. She was grateful for His wisdom, His way, for every turn, every rub and every pressing moment revealing Him and His Word to her. She may have been lacking according to the eyes of men, but her spiritual storehouse was overflowing.

"The word used here in scripture, for the coins she tossed into the offering, is the word *leptos,* meaning *small* or *something peeled* or *refined*. Could it be this woman gave all she had because she trusted in God to provide, that it was His Word that delivered her, and made her heart contrite and refined? Could it be that she knew where the Lord's provision came from and where He dwelled? Could it be that His Word meant everything to her? It was true treasure to her, compelling her to give Him her own two cents—her testimony about His love for her and mankind. Isn't that what you are doing, writing about this?"

"You are saying I am the woman with the two mites now? Lewis, come on!"

"What? Do you still not believe? Will you not trust that God knows the end from the beginning?"

"How can I believe this, Lewis? How can God use somebody like me?"

"You sound just like Gideon. Do you need more confirmation that this is all the truth, just like he did?"

"Yes, Lewis!"

"As I've told you, every word in scripture matters. Every word and action Jesus said and did was for a reason. There is a word in Hebrew that means *poor* or *in lack*. It is the word *misken*. It is spelled almost exactly like the word *miskenoth*, meaning storehouse or treasury. And *miskenoth* is the word I shared with you so long ago about those two birth bricks back in Egypt that were used as a delivery stool. Could it be the poor widow knew it was the Son of God, Jesus Christ, who delivered and provided, and that's why she cast the two stones (*ha-abenayim*, the Son of God with Us) into the pot? Could it be that you are the woman revealing the *miskenoth*, casting those two stones at Jesus' feet because you know that He has always been God's delivering instrument, His source of provision for mankind, and the true tabernacle of love for which the prophets spoke? You are poor and have played the fool so many times, ignoring where your help comes from. But now you know it is Jesus (the *miskenoth*—the Son who Stands with Us, the *ha-abenayim*—the Son of God with Us) who has always provided, standing on our behalf. And you are casting those two stones out so that the whole world can see they were always reflective of Jesus and His role in our salvation."

"What do you want me to do with this? Do you expect me to write about it?"

"Exactly!"

"I am no writer, Lewis. I am writing some, mostly just journal entries. I don't know if they are going to amount to anything."

"I am saying for this appointed time in existence you are the woman with the two mites. Don't worry about what your writing amounts to. Continue to write what His Spirit tells you to, remembering that God has fashioned every weight in the bag."

CHAPTER THIRTY-SEVEN

KNOWING THE PRICE OF EVERYTHING AND THE VALUE OF NOTHING

———◆———

GETTING HOME after our little jaunt around the lake, I thought it might be a good time to do some of that writing Lewis said I was destined to do. It had been a couple of weeks since my last journal entry. Thinking about Lewis' last remarks, I looked up the phrase he had spoken about on our way home. It was from Proverbs 16:11:

> *Honest scales and balances belong to the Lord; all the weights in the bag are of His making.*

I had to write this down.

Journal Entry #161

Shuffling from one exhibit to the next in an art museum, people usually stand and walk past others in-frame, picnicking, perched on polo ponies, perfectly poised and posed, portraits frozen in time. People consider and contemplate the thoughts of the artist, never caring to speak to the person right beside them. They are constantly thinking to themselves, *"How can I relate to this picture? What does it say about me? Am I reflected in its canvas? I wonder how much this painting is worth. What's its price? What's its true value?"*

Trying to relate to inanimate objects—a canvas, a landscape, a portrait or piece of contemporary art, people usually expose the most defiling things about themselves. A revelation of wasted time in self-indulgence that can never be held or recaptured.

With an inflated view of the world and themselves, most people have forgotten where the gallery has always been, the world around them. Listening, talking, hearing, relating, and engaging in fellowship with the people in their circle and those circling around it. Pressing each other into a true work of art, squeezing out iniquity, in love, replacing it with fine oil, insight, or a stiffened spine, all in the hopes of standing straight and walking tall—taking on the shape of a true masterpiece.

Isn't that what Christ does for us? He expects more than a hasty shuffling from room to room in this assembled collection called life. He expects conviction, self-abasement, humility, and mourning so He can make us stand and shine. He wants us to know that we are all a part of the instillation and are expected to bend our will to stand in His.

Standing near someone, declining a shoulder to bear their burdens with them, speaking in truth with love and an authentic compassion that can't be faked or marketed, but plainly seen is what makes us captivating to God. This is what true love to God is. This is what has true value and reflects His character. God has always been the Artist; the world, His gallery. What kind of art do you want to be? He gives you the choice. One of high price or high value.

Christ lived in human form, to be the example of the service and love He commands to see in us. He was stretched out and laid bare for those who would be willing to see. A price paid, our salvation bought, so God could be intimately reconnected to us again and weave His thread of hope and love into our very souls. He wants to make us rich in His love.

God always knew what our value was to Him. Worth the burden of our sin placed on His shoulders. A yoke He didn't deserve to carry, the separation from complete unity with the Father, all done for our old canvas to have a new covering. He has always wanted to be reunited with us in a holy kiss, replacing the one Judas gave Him in the garden with one of true value. A love that can't be measured with thirty pieces of silver.

Looking at the last line of the verse, a feeling of such sorrow filled me. I had been Judas for such a long time. Had others felt this way? Just as the thought crossed my mind, the phone rang. It could only be one person. Lewis. My husband brought me the phone and said, "It's Lewis, again. Should I be worried? Has someone else captured your heart?"

"Only Jesus, honey," I said. Before I could speak into the receiver, Lewis bellowed, "That was well done. The journal entry, I mean. You are really paying attention. Are you ready for the next two stones?"

CHAPTER THIRTY-EIGHT

THE ALABASTER JAR

"I GUESS so, Lewis."

"Well then, tell me a story."

"What?"

"Tell me a story."

"About what? I thought you were the one telling stories so I could understand my place here, Lewis. Anyway, isn't this what I've been doing? Telling His story through mine?"

"Yes. This is just another example of that. I want you to tell me something remarkable that has happened at work. Something that can't be explained in the natural, but only supernaturally."

"Haven't I been doing that with the testimony I gave you about the Irish woman and the man in the hall? This seems so redundant."

"It might seem that way, but every measure taken, every insight revealed is drawing you toward your destiny. It is drawing you nearer to Him. Every discovery brings a deeper vein of intimacy, does it not? What better way to reveal these wonderful turns in your life than when He has showed His love for you and others? Now, I want you to tell me a story about something that involved something you wrote."

"How do you know about that?"

"Is that a serious question?" Lewis said with one brow raised in consternation.

Guess not, I thought.

"Good," he said. "Now tell me the story."

So, I began. "Guess I can describe what I wrote as divinely inspired, only to be divinely revealed why the next day, as I realized there had been a purpose for its message the whole time. Long before the thought had ever crossed my mind. But you already knew that didn't you, Lewis?"

"Yep." Seriously! That's all I got.

Rolling my eyes, I continued, "Having finished writing my journal entry on *The Greatest Love Story Ever Told* the day before, I shared it with my receptionist, Ella, who checked in all my patients at the front desk. After I finished the story, we started talking about what inspired me to write it. Before I knew it, 8:00a.m. had rolled around; it was time for my first patient to arrive.

"Getting to my desk, I looked over the variety of ailments I would be treating for the day. No one was coming in having chest pain, abdominal cramping or the dreaded headache that always made a diagnosis a little more daunting. It was going to be a good day.

"My first couple of patients were nothing but snotty noses and sore throats. All typical for the season we were in. The day was shaping up to be as boring as countless others, short of an act of God.

"At 9:11a.m., the medical assistant brought back a familiar patient I had known for a while. She was pleasant, in her mid-fifties, looking younger than the age reflected on her demographic sheet. She had obviously taken care of herself.

"She came to the office because she had developed a full-body rash. She had something called erythema multiforme. A big name for a rather self-limiting process. It was characterized by red circular patches covering her upper and lower extremities. It was an easy diagnosis to make. One I didn't have to take too much time to come up with.

"The rash was usually caused by a reaction to a medication. I just needed her to stop whatever it was she was taking and put her on some steroids. It would clear up eventually.

"Walking out of the room to get my prescription pad, I noticed a shiny gold speck hanging from her shirt. It caught my eye because at the end of it, hanging loosely in the folds of her blouse, was a cross.

"Not knowing why except to say that led by the Holy Spirit, I asked her if I could read the journal entry to her I had written the day before. Humoring me, she obliged.

"Reading it to her, I quickly realized she was crying. Hesitating and apologizing profusely, I offered to stop. She begged me to continue, adding, 'When you get done, there is something you need to know.'

"Agreeing, I finished the story and looked up to notice that she still had silent tears streaming down her face. Only now, they were falling into her smile. She wiped them away and cleared her throat to speak.

"She said, 'About a year ago, you saw me and did a well-woman exam. My pap smear results came back a few days later, revealing I had human papillomavirus, a sexually transmitted disease. You explained that I would have to be followed up by a gynecologist for further treatment. You gave me a business card of someone you recommended and sent me on my way.

"'It took me about a month to make the appointment because I was embarrassed by the predicament I found myself in. The day I went to see the doctor, as I was signing in, a wave of shame fell over me. It was so great it almost knocked me off my feet. My mind had become so overwhelmed by every wrong decision that led me to that exact moment. Then, as I went to sit down, I received a text message from my best friend.

"'Now, the funny thing is not that she texted me. We texted each other all the time. But that day I hadn't told anyone where I was going, what I was thinking, or what I was doing because of the shame I was drowning myself in. Her text message to me was this:

You are altogether beautiful, my darling, there is no blemish in you. Song of Songs 4:7.

"'My best friend didn't know where I was going. She had no idea what I was feeling, but God did. When you started reading the story, it reminded me of the text message I got that day.

"'I felt like God wanted me to tell you since you were the one who sent me to that appointment in the first place. Now here I am, covered in blemishes again, needing your help. It just seemed like more than a coincidence.'"

I continued, "Lewis, a true miracle was playing out in my exam room. We seemed to both let the glory of God's wonder fill the empty space between us. When I finally spoke up, I let her in on what God had already shown me.

'Are you ready for God to blow your mind right now?' I asked her. And wide-eyed, she exclaimed, 'Of course!'

"Lewis, I led her to the reception desk and called Ella over to where we were both standing. When she came around the corner, I asked her to share what we had talked about that morning with the woman standing next to me.

"Ella confirmed that I read the story I wrote the day before to her. Then I asked her what inspired me to write it. She turned to the woman and said, '*Song of Songs*.'

"The woman looked at me and started crying even harder than she had in the exam room. We hugged and clung to each other in that moment, so grateful for what God had done."

The story was over, but I wanted Lewis to know what I had taken from it. He needed to know that appointment had been divinely planned and executed with such pinpoint precision to reveal God in every aspect of it. A plan that could only have reached its full potential, through the woman and me, as we both walked in the center of God's will, guided by His Spirit. Me telling my story to her, and her telling hers to me, revealing God's love so carefully hidden there.

There was nothing on the other end of the phone. Had I been cut off and talking to dead air this whole time? Well, if that was the case, I wasn't going to repeat myself. Lewis could just forget it. As my hand reached to hang up the receiver, Lewis piped into it, "That was powerful, wasn't it?"

"Yes, it was, Lewis."

"Now I can tell you about the alabaster jar."

"The alabaster jar?"

"The one the woman opened and anointed Jesus' head with at Simon the Leper's house in Matthew 26:6-13. Remember, she poured out an expensive perfume over His head to prepare Him for burial.

"The disciples got upset because they couldn't understand the true nature of the act, but Jesus did. You see, the woman knew she had the

Lord to thank for the grace His deliverance brought her. It was worth everything to her. She knew that Jesus was who took her from a state of deficiency to a true state of wholeness and abundance just like the widow with the two mites.

"The perfume was the aroma of her testimony, praise, love and worship that consummated her relationship with her Savior. She laid her praise upon Jesus' head, giving Him all the glory for it.

"She did this beforehand, Jesus said, making Him ready for His burial, because the ointment poured over Him was myrrh. Myrrh was known in antiquity for being used to embalm the dead.

"You have done this beforehand, making ready for His return and the marriage supper of the Lamb, because myrrh was also used in the 'oil of joy.' Myrrh proclaimed to others, through the senses, the consummation of a marriage.

"Myrrh was also used to mark the tabernacle; the place of the Lord's provision; the place where true treasure was found—the *miskenoth*.

"You are the one who has proclaimed that Jesus is the *miskenoth*, the treasure house, the tabernacle, the *ha-abenayim*, (the Son of God, delivering, dwelling, and becoming 'at one' with us)."

"Are you saying that now I am the woman with the alabaster jar?" I asked.

"Yes. For this appointed season, you are. She did all she could and so will you."

"This is outrageous. Just too much! And the two stones?"

"In the account in the Bible, the hollowed-out jar was one stone and the lid that covered it was the other. The word for alabaster in Hebrew is *shayish*, an alliteration for *meshi*, meaning *costly garment*—derived from *mashah*—meaning *son* (in Egyptian), and *to draw out* of the water, inferring purification and deliverance (in Hebrew).

"And the word for *perfume, spice, embalm* or *to ripen* in Hebrew is the word *chanat*. If you put these words together, you are presented with *meshi chanat*—a Son's costly garment that delivers, purifies, preserves, and brings to a state of maturity and fruitfulness. Sounds an awful lot like Jesus, doesn't it? And the word *miskenoth*!

"On another note, it also shouldn't be lost on you that both you and your patient were being ministered to in that exam room. The Father was speaking directly to you through that woman, just as much as He was speaking to her, through you.

"It shouldn't escape you that the woman came in covered in blemishes and you treated her again. He wanted you to know that you are worthy to carry this message to the world. Because of His Son, you are altogether beautiful. There is no blemish in you, either. *The Son, who purifies and delivers, has prepared, preserved, and ripened you for this very moment.* Through His Spirit, you will inject a dose of some much-needed steroids back into the Body of God's people to help hasten His return."

Lewis had to be wrong. He must have banged his head. It couldn't be me. I was no one.

"Why not you? When you laid down at that church, with your face to the floor, surrendering to your Father, He heard you.

"When you read your Bible verse that day, what scripture did you read? It was from Isaiah, right? Isaiah, feeling unworthy, said very much the same thing, didn't he? But God placed a hot stone in his mouth and made him ready. Has not God placed these same stones, His Holy Spirit-filled words in your mouth? And when you were standing on Mt. Nebo, what did you shout, standing above the plains of Jericho?"

With a whisper shout, I said, "Hineni, Lord."

"So, who will go for Him?" Lewis said.

Replying from a memory I had almost forgotten. "Here I am. Send me."

"Yes, here you are."

"But Lewis, you have made it abundantly clear God doesn't change. God's habits, His process, His character have never changed. If that's so, every person God has ever used in a big way, He has called by name. Twice! *Abraham, Abraham. Samuel, Samuel. Moses, Moses. Jacob, Jacob.* You see where I'm going with this? He's never called me by name, Lewis."

"Where is your trust? Of course, He called you by name."

"When, because I don't remember that?"

"When you were at the church, minding your own business in that chair you loved to plant yourself in. Didn't you hear a voice telling you to stand up twice and then one final blast to get up? God told you to stand up. Twice! Now, can you tell me the name you were given at birth?"

"You know what my name is, Lewis."

"Just humor me."

"Staci." I blurted out.

"That's right. And the name, *Staci,* is a short form of the word *anastasis,* from the Greek. And it means *to stand up!* He did call you by name. Twice!"

Well, what could I say to that?

CHAPTER THIRTY-NINE

A DAY AT THE PHARMACY

THE WORD *scar* comes from a Greek word that means *to burn*. Whoever said that trials by fire were refining should be shot. Fires might be refining, but that word seemed like a gross underestimation of the process. Multiple sclerosis means *many scars* which meant I had a whole lot of burning go on.

And I was an expert on the matter, if the MRIs of my brain and spinal cord could be admitted as proof. Corroborating evidence cut across my white matter and shredded myelin sheath with the precision of an executioner's blade. The result, an out-of-control wildfire trailing up and down every nerve in my body, without a control line or airtanker in sight.

The kicker was it was all my own doing. The medical community considered multiple sclerosis an autoimmune disorder. In short, my body's own defense system was working with a less than average intelligence—it was unable to distinguish my nervous system from the common cold. *Go figure.*

The MS I'd been battling for the last several years was wreaking havoc on my body, and always seemed to get worse during the summer. Heat was my kryptonite. Who knew nerve impulses liked a nice cool environment in which to travel?

During the summer months, weighing out how I spent my energy took its toll. *Sing in church or blow dry my hair? Have lunch with my kids or take a shower?* These were the types of questions floating through my mind on the daily.

It's also why I found myself schlepping it to the pharmacy more often during the hottest days of the summer more than in any other season of the year. Unfortunate fact—today was one of those days.

Pulling into the pharmacy and seeing the drive-thru line wrapped around the building, I pulled my car into the nearest parking space and walked in. The automated doors opened, blowing a cool gust of air in my direction. *Man, that felt good.*

Strolling to the back of the store, I eyed an aisle of impulse buys, before noticing the line inside was just as long as the one for the drive-thru. Taking a number from the pharmacy desk, I went back to the section of the store I was safe in. The greeting and birthday card section. Why? Because there wasn't any chance I would splurge on something I didn't need, like a singing toothbrush or an over-priced ear-cleaner. *Let's just say, Lesson. Learned.*

In all honesty, by reading those cards, I could pretend I was someone else. Just here to grab a card on the way to the office for a co-worker. Or dropping in for a last minute buy for a birthday party, instead of picking up medication to numb my brain to the endless burning and lightning bolts taking up residence in my spinal cord and extremities. Besides, I was a sucker for bumper-sticker insight. You could always find some of the wisest words condensed into a couple of lines on them. Postcards to nowhere but the soul, I called them.

Browsing the endless rows, my fingers skimmed the tops of every category, before seeing one that caught my eye. It was under the header, *Just for You.* Picking up the card under it, a shiver skittered up my arm and down the rest of my body. Could the feeling have been from my wonky nerves? Sure. But I was starting to be one of those people who saw signs in everything. *Thanks, Lewis.*

There was nothing on the outside of the card. It was plain. And to be honest, I don't even know why I picked it up. The cover had nothing to draw me. No color, just stark white. Opening it revealed a poem in some of the most unimpressive script I had ever seen. I read the title a couple of times before reading the poem in its entirety.

Poetry Unseen

Words, skillfully weaved,
Vacillating vows of love or of curse.
Falling, to yield light,
In space, in time, in verse.

Called to be light,
Arcs, bent in the night, remotely gleam,
Suspended on strings of time and gravity.

Darkness' true form finally seen,
The reality of God,
Suspended in disbelief.

Instruments of sin and piety span,
The stones' revelation,
The true nature of man.

To defy, to deceive, oh dastardly dance,
What once was hidden,
Now, its expanse.

Words maliciously, inadvertently spoken,
Breaking to pieces, the already broken.

Tumbling, terrifically they tread,
Descending into depths,
They bleed, they've bled.

Broken paths, repeatedly beaten, a violent offense,
Thine street, oh dreaded street,
Of inconsequence.

Closing the card, the intercom drilled out the number in my hot little hand over the loudspeaker. Turning around to make my way to the register, I bumped into Lewis. When was he going to stop doing that? "Lewis! You scared me. Again."

"That wasn't my intention." Glancing at what was in my hand, he asked, "Did you like the card?"

"Just a wild guess, but did you happen to write it?"

"Yes." He offered, towering over me.

"I kind of figured, but how did you know I wouldn't have decided to go down the *As Seen on TV* aisle instead? I liked that row, too." I was just kidding, of course, but it was fun to see the look on his face.

"How do you know there isn't something *Just for You* in that aisle, as well? Your Father knows you." No way, I thought. Was there really? I wanted to go look but wouldn't dare.

Lewis and I walked up to the pharmacy counter and paid for my prescriptions. On the way out the door Lewis asked me if I wouldn't mind sitting down for a minute in the pharmacy's in-store clinic. He pointed out a chair, so I sat. Glancing over at my prescription bag, he pointed to the picture on the front. It was a symbol for medicinal preparation—the mortar and pestle.

"Let me guess, Lewis. Am I the mortar and pestle now?"

"Of course not. That belongs to God alone. He is the only judge and healer of the heart. Do you want to know who you are?"

"I have a sinking suspicion you are about to tell me whether I want to know or not."

"Yes, I am. There is a reference in the Bible about the mortar and pestle that does speak of your purpose, though not in so many words. In Matthew 13:33 it says:

> *He told them still another parable: 'The kingdom of heaven is like yeast that a woman took and mixed into about sixty pounds of flour until it worked all through the dough."*

Lewis waited and then said, "You are the woman working the dough. The kneading trough, or mortar—one stone, and your right hand in His power—the pestle, spreading His Word throughout the world with your testimony. Yet there is still a mystery you don't see."

Looking down at the card, he said, "I am glad you liked the poem because it is a part of this mystery, too. You see, in the Old Testament, a poem set to musical notes was called a *zamar,* one of many that the Hebrews used for the word *gazelle.* The thinking, being that they both dealt with gentle rubbing—gently strumming chords, the former, and the light touching of a gazelle's feet upon the grass as they glide across a meadow, the latter.

"This may seem new to you, but you have read these poems hundreds of times. You just knew them by a different name. In the Greek, they are known as the Psalms, from the word *psao* meaning *to rub.*

"Some voices are meant to be God's *psalms*, rubbing mankind with a prophetic word. They are voices meant to work in concert, within the Body of Christ, all with a distinct value, purpose, and worth to the whole. Many people don't understand this, but the Psalms aren't just a book of poetry set to music. It's a book of prophecy, just as powerful as Daniel, Isaiah, or Ezekiel. Your voice was always meant to prophesy, revealing Christ Jesus in this way.

"God doesn't want you to beat the mortar. He wants you to knead the dough. Help it rise. He wants you to lift your voice in praise to your Savior with your words, plead with mankind to repent, and to declare something to them that is short in coming.

"The poem you just read is an example of a specific type of poem, maybe not in structure, but in content. It is called a *ghazal*, an Arabic word comparative to the word *zamar* and *gazelle. Ghazals* are words woven together as a display of unrequited love, vocally expressed from the view of God to His creation, usually through pain and loss.

"The poem you read today is a poetic display of the lamentation of the loss and separation of God from His creation. It reveals His unrequited selfless love for us through the redemptive blood of His Son. And God's ultimate *ghazal* or *psalm*, was made flesh in Jesus Christ.

"Did you know Song of Songs is itself a type of psalm—*zamar* or *ghazal*? The greatest one ever written, in fact. And did you know this song is recited during the time of Passover?

"The Hebrews consider Passover a time of redemptive love between God and His people. Could it be, without even knowing it, the Hebrews sang and prophesied about Christ and His display of unrequited, redemptive love for mankind in reciting the Song of Songs during Passover?

"I know this is a lot to wrap your head around. You must have questions."

"No, not right now," I said.

"I'm surprised. Not one question?"

"Well, the card I read right before the one you wrote said, '*Never miss an opportunity to be quiet.*' I think that was just for me, too."

CHAPTER FORTY

THE B-TEAM

—◆—

FEELING THE urge to write, I quickly drove home and parked myself in front of my desk, pen and paper in hand. It didn't take long for my pen to massage the pages in my journal, the storehouse of my thoughts. Thoughts about life, liberty, and the pursuit of happiness flew onto empty lines. Not happiness, in and of itself, but a pursuit of it through Christ. I jotted everything down. Discovering my place in this world. What brought me hope. What brought me joy. What made me happy. And what was it that brought me joy? And true happiness? Finally realizing that God never expected perfection, only my desire and willingness to be perfected by Him.

Journal Entry #216

I'm on the B-Team. Always have been. The "B" doesn't stand for beautiful, breathtaking or brilliant. It isn't the beginning of some new, hip, cool mnemonic. It's simply the letter after the "A" in the alphabet. Not first, but second. Not honors, but passing. Not the all-star, but the relief. The one who gets called into the game to waste thirty seconds on the clock so the all-star can catch their breath and jump right back into it. While I, on the other hand, return to the end of the bench, counting the seconds to the end. Graduated forty-sixth in my class, missing the top ten percent by three people. Took the long track, not the fast track in college, and managed to get my bachelor's degree in fourteen years.

I saw myself in the books I read. Not as the heroine, but the sidekick, or some random ancillary character or object that gets time in the plot line to stretch out the story. You know, the one that drives the reader to ecstatic anticipation. A small satisfaction, in an altogether conspicuous conclusion—that was me. Never the main character in the book, but always its object lesson.

Remember *The Story of the Three Bears?* I was the porridge that was too hot or too cold. The chair that was too big or too small. The bed that was too hard or too soft. I was never just right.

Then one day, I picked up a book that changed my life. Wandering around my house, trying not to get entrenched in yet another Netflix marathon available to me, I glanced over at my Bible and decided it was time to read it. Having had the thing for over thirty years, I was never gripped by it. I figured it was time.

Spending more time in the Word, I started drawing closer to God, finding out what relationship with Him truly meant. You know the feeling you get when you fall in love for the first time, and you can't think about anything but him? You can't wait to get home, to only to sit by the phone, and wait for his call? That's how I started feeling about Jesus. Anytime I wanted to talk to Him, all I had to do was sing a worship song, lift my arms in praise, or read the Bible. Jesus overwhelmed my thoughts so much that I began to drown myself in His love.

I was seeing myself in so many people in the Bible. I was the woman at the well, the tax-collector, the leper, the lame and the blind man, but I was also Peter, Paul, Moses, David and countless others. They reminded me they were on the B-team, too—broken.

God loves the B-team so much Jesus came to earth and became the B-team for me: beaten, battered, bruised, and brought to death. He took my place so I could take my rightful place at the table He prepared for me. And you know what? My seat is reserved in a chair that's not too big or too small or breaks into a million pieces when I sit in it but is fashioned just for me—one that's just right. How do I know? Let's just say that I know the carpenter.

Now I call that kneading the dough.

CHAPTER FORTY-ONE

THE GIRL IN THE COURTYARD, THE GIRL AT THE GATE

———◆———

AN ENTIRE week went by until I saw Lewis again. He showed up while I was sitting in my car, waiting patiently for the gate to my subdivision to open. My week had been filled with doctor's appointments, trips to pick up my kids, treks to the corner-store, the gas station.

On this occasion, perishable items were melting in the trunk of my car from the short jaunt to the grocery store and back. They were in desperate need of finding their way into my refrigerator. If only this ridiculous gate would open!

Punching the code into the gate's access panel, I kept getting denied. I would just have to wait until someone else came by and opened the gate for me so my car could pull in behind them.

Glancing in my rearview, expecting the said car to arrive any minute, Lewis' big head occupied the space in the mirror from the back seat. Jumping nearly out of my skin and blurting out at the same time, I yelled, "Lewis, that's it! You have to give me a head's up when you are going to make yourself known."

"That's not how this works, and you know it. I apparently can't get that across to you."

"What are you doing in my car? Did you come to help me carry in my groceries?"

"No, I just saw another opportunity to talk to you about your purpose," he supplied.

"At the gate to my subdivision?"

"Yes."

"My ice cream is melting. So, let's hear it, Lewis."

"Do you remember Peter in the courtyard of the High Priest?"

"Yes, Lewis. It's where Peter was tested. It's where he denied knowing Jesus."

"That's right. Do you remember who questioned him about his faith?"

"I thought it was a couple of people."

"That's true. Many people, still to this day, have been purposed in this role. Not in a role of judgment, but of encouraging self-reflection and examination. They are called life guardsmen, gate keepers.

"If you remember, in the gospel of Mark, a servant girl asked Peter if it was Jesus he followed. It was a simple question, yet Peter denied Him. Then as Peter attempted to pass through the gate, that servant girl asked him the same question again."

Lewis looked pointedly at me. "You are the girl in the courtyard, and at the gate, asking those who believe they are saved to reflect and examine themselves in the same light. You are testing their metal. You are asking them to examine their own relationship and faith in Jesus Christ, the same way Peter did thousands of years before. You are here to ask them if they identify with Christ. Do they find their identity in Him?"

"How does this have anything to do with the two stones?"

"You will see. In Ecclesiastes 3:5, we find that there is:

... a time to scatter stones and a time to gather them.

"From a Hebrew perspective, scattering stones meant more than tossing them around. It was considered a means of separating and dividing one substance from another—to make what was mixed in more visible. In the story, this servant girl was dividing the situation, opening it up for Peter by confronting him with what he didn't want to see.

"The servant girl rubbed Peter to produce an effect in him. The girl was one stone and Peter the other. Poetic, since *Peter's* very name means stone. He was rubbed in the courtyard and by the gate so he could gather what was drawn out of his and the girl's discourse, learn from it, and then be moved into action.

"The girl was standing at the dividing line—the metaphorical threshold, acting as a sieve, of sorts, that separated those living inside the sheepfold from those who slept out in the dark. She was pointing out the place that separated those who truly identified with Christ and belonged to Him. The girl was like a beacon of light at the threshold, showing Peter where the distinction lay.

"Do you remember when I had you stand outside and face your house? This is who God has called you to be. You are the porch light, just like this girl was.

"Peter got to see quite clearly what side of the dividing line he was on. The rub exposed his denial, his pride, his guilt, his shame, his remorse, and his grief, all of which revealed that he hadn't submitted himself completely to his Savior or found his identity in the Lord."

Taking this all in, I asked, "So, what makes Peter any different from Judas, Lewis?"

"The difference is Judas was never saved. He felt bad, sure, but he didn't persevere in the faith and grow. He had no change in his *want-to*. He had no renewing of his mind, no change of heart. He just gave in and gave up. Judas' eyes were always fixed on himself rather than on God. He was always coveting, immersed in his own devices, plans, and desires, and how he might confer the greatest personal benefit from Jesus' life. He had no regard for the will of God. Judas was motivated by self-interests rather than true worship.

"Peter, on the other hand, was brokenhearted. He left that place of denial weeping, but he returned to his brothers in Jerusalem. He persevered and saw the risen Christ. God knew his heart. God just wanted Peter to examine and know his own rather than shy away from what he saw. He wanted Peter to change and grow from the insight procured in that courtyard and walk in a right relationship with his Redeemer. This is what God, working through you, wants everyone to see—the rubbing isn't punishment. It brings revelation. And only through division (breaking down a situation to see to the heart of it) can multiplication be obtained."

"Lewis, I have been working on a poem of my own since our last encounter. Let's just say you inspired me to write it. I think it speaks to what we're talking about. You want to hear it?" Without hesitation, he said, "Of course I want to hear it."

"It's called:

The Velvet Touch

The comfort of conformity,
Sometimes then, and even now,
The perversity of love,
Never constancy,
Always willing to bow.
Molded in velvet majesty,
Scraping softly,
Not to offend.
But are we not called,
To fiercely fight,
To defend,
To rub boldly,
To scrub soundly,
The metal of men?"

CHAPTER FORTY-TWO

HIDDEN TREASURE

IT WAS the end of the summer when I saw Lewis again. I had lost my job at the clinic and was now spending a lot more time at home. It didn't seem right that I wasn't working anymore, but my spirit had prayed for God to open doors that needed to be opened and close those that needed to be closed. Then, out of nowhere, I got one slammed right in my face.

Exactly a month before I lost my job, I had a dream that worried me. In the dream, I was sitting in my office looking out the window when a flock of ravens came swarming around the building. Getting down on my knees, I sought forgiveness from God. Upon waking, I had an uncanny feeling I was about to enter a new season of my life.

A month to the day of the dream, I was abruptly called into my boss's office and let go. Production deficit, he called it, meaning in the nicest way possible, that I wasn't bringing in as much revenue as he had hoped. I didn't blame him. My boss was a God-fearing man. Confident in his faith. But, like everyone else, he had bills to pay and mouths to feed. I certainly understood that. Besides, I had asked God to shut a door if it needed to be closed. He answered my prayer, just not in the way I expected. Not working anymore left me with quite a bit of time to read and do some more writing, so that's what I did.

On the last day of summer break, deciding to take the kids somewhere, I piled them into the car and headed to an indoor rock-climbing park to expend some of their pent-up energy. While they were occupied forty feet off the ground, I thought it would be a good time to read.

I walked to the seating area, found a table and chair closest to the window, and parked myself in a very uncomfortable chair. Looking up to see my kids still ascending the wall, I smiled, thinking this was the perfect time to get lost in something else. Leaning over to dig into the bag next to me, I realized my bag wasn't there. Glancing down at the floor, half-expecting it to have fallen, my pulse quickened. Maybe I left it in the car, but that couldn't be because I distinctly remembered bringing it in. Standing up to try and locate it, Lewis came around the corner carrying my bag in his outstretched arm.

"That bag doesn't become you, Lewis."

"That's because it belongs to you, my dear."

Wanting to fill him in on what had been going on in my life, I said, "I guess you know I lost my job."

"Yes, I know, but it was time."

"Time for what, Lewis?"

"Time for something new." It was then he asked for my phone. Giving it to him, he immediately tapped the camera icon and started thumbing through pictures I had stored from my trip to Israel. It seemed he was looking for something in particular.

"Lewis, can I help you find something?"

Shaking his head, he voiced, "Do you remember when you went to Jordan?"

Of course, I did. "Yes."

He showed me a picture of myself with my arms in the air on the top of Mt. Nebo, looking over the valley and into Jericho. "I know you stood on that mountain and shouted, 'Here I am, Here I am, Here I am Holy Spirit.' But what I want to know is if you remember what you were thinking at that exact moment?"

Thinking about it for a second, I replied, "Sure. I remembered praying that I wanted God to use me in a mighty way. I not only wanted to see the Promised Land, but to cross over into it. I wanted to be used like Elijah, have a double portion like Elisha, have God's glory be revealed to me like Moses. Be the apple of God's eye, like David. But mostly, I wanted to be smack dab in the center of God's will for my life."

"Well, God heard your prayer. This season is about fully realizing it. When Moses asked God to show him His glory, what did God have Moses do?"

"Honestly, I don't remember," realizing it had been a while since I had read that passage.

I grabbed my Bible from my bag and flipped it to Exodus until I found the answer staring back at me. Right there in Exodus 33:19-23, Lewis began reading:

And the Lord said, "I will cause all my goodness to pass in front of you, and I will proclaim my name, the Lord, in your presence. I will have mercy on whom I will have mercy, and I will have compassion on whom I will have compassion. But," he said, "you cannot see my face, for no one may see my face and live."

Then the Lord said, "There is a place near me where you may stand on a rock. When my glory passes by, I will put you in a cleft in the rock and cover you with my hand until I have passed by. Then I will remove my hand and you will see my back; but my face must not be seen."

Lewis abruptly stopped his narration and looked up at my kids climbing the plastic rock face and smiled. "God has revealed His glory to you just like He did for Moses, and it is written in the Bible in the New Testament."

"Where might that be, Lewis? I must have missed it."

"Don't worry because I am about to show you. When Moses went up Mt. Sinai, God showed Moses what He is showing you, and that is His process. God made Moses stand on that rock and placed him in between the cleft's edges to point out Moses' iniquity, God's omniscience, omnipresence, and His omnipotence.

"God pressed Moses in that fissure to literally press His mantle onto him, facilitating in Moses, a state of humility, repentance, wonder and the power of God's grace.

As God passed over him, Moses could see the edges of God's tender mercies in every aspect of his past. He saw how God loved him, but also how He rebuked, chastened, and disciplined him. He saw every

198 · STACI BISCAMP

circumstance from being watched by Miriam, to being found by Pharoah's daughter, to finding a way to be nursed by his own mother, to the very name he was given, as providence.

"He even saw the trouble he found himself in, and his great escape to Midian under a power much greater than his own. He saw God in every detail. This is why Moses' face shone so brightly. The turning in those two edges of that fissure caused a spark. Moses could see with clarity his inner nature, and how God expressed it out so change could occur, no longer leaving him being pressed by them, but enlightened instead.

"Did you know the word *face*, in the Hebrew, comes from a word that means *to turn*. Being pressed and rubbed brings light and change. Just like the ending of each new day, as the sun rubs against the edges of a seemingly endless horizon, only to re-emerge back above it at dawn.

"When Moses came down the mountain, he had to cover his face with a veil because God's people didn't want a light to shine on their own iniquity and be changed by it. They had their eyes firmly fixed on the tangible. They wanted to obey the rituals God prescribed in the flesh, but they couldn't be bothered at the time by any intrinsic change. This sadly reflected their inability to hold on to those things that were intangible. They liked keeping God at arm's length, with no real desire to hold on to Him in a personal way. They were still hiding and holding out there in the wilderness. The same can be said for many of us. And a veil still covers those eyes today."

"Lewis, so where in the New Testament does this point to me?"

"Do you remember in the Bible when Mary became a witness to Jesus' resurrection? She saw the angel and the grave clothes separated from the *soudarion* (the sweat-cloth used to cover Jesus' face and eyes), knowing exactly what they meant.

"Mary wept because a veil was lifted from her own face and eyes so she could see that Jesus had taken away her sin for good and even left her a change of clothes. Those graves' clothes had now become a wedding garment that Jesus had just paid the ultimate price for so that Mary would never have to wipe the sweat from her own brow again. The work was done.

"And those graves' clothes that I spoke of? The ones that were separated from the head-cloth? It was called an *othone* meaning *fine linen garment*. Like one that a *bridegroom* or *chathan* would wear. Jesus left His covering there.

"What did Jesus tell Mary to do instead of holding onto the fact that He was the Son of God-*HaBenaiah* and the sacrificial covering for His people? He told her to go and report everything back to the disciples, *'I am ascending to my Father and your Father, to my God and your God.'* He wanted her to report to the disciples they were redeemed into sonship by His death and resurrection. That they were sons and daughters of God too because of His covering.

"Do you know you were allowed to see the two edges of the stone tomb and its seal, rolling away from each other, and the purpose for it? That right at their center, is where healing begins. Those two stones became flesh, in Jesus Christ, reflecting Him at the very heart of them—two stones that became flesh to satisfy the Law, but also to be a true and faithful example of it for us. Showing us both justification and sanctification working together in constant concert with each other. There cannot be one without the other.

"Even the thief on the cross showed evidence of sanctification when he expressed his belief in who Christ was and rebuked the other thief for mocking Jesus. The repentant thief had a definite change of heart.

"In this appointed season, the Body of Christ has been sleeping and ineffective. They have been a dead body. Their eyes have been closed. It's time to wake them up, before time runs out.

"You were born for such a time as this. To declare what was proclaimed over you from the Torah on the day of your birth."

"What are you talking about, Lewis?"

"You were born May 30, 1975, were you not, at 2:17 in the afternoon? That day fell on a Friday. But in Israel, which is eight hours ahead, it was already the Sabbath.

"And on the Sabbath day, a scheduled set of readings from the Torah are proclaimed from synagogues all over the world. Do you want to know what scripture was declared on that Sabbath day in Jerusalem?"

"I'm a little hesitant to ask. You have a tone in your voice shooting shivers down into my toes. Don't get me wrong, I want to know. I have to hear it, but I'm having that overwhelmed feeling again."

"It was from Numbers, chapter 9, verses 1-11."

Feeling both clammy and hot, all at the same time, I stood utterly astonished.

"I can tell by the look in your eyes you understand. It was from the scripture God woke you up with all those years ago, long before you had an intimate relationship with Him. It was about people preparing for the Passover, the First and a Second; the one that was for those who missed the first because they had been on a long journey or on account of being in contact with a dead body.

"Mt. Nebo, where you made your request to God to be a mighty witness to His Word, was also known as *Pisgah*. It comes from the word *pasag,* which means to *pass between*. It requires no great verbal leap to see that the word *pasag* would look and sound to the Hebrews like the word *pesach*—the word for *Passover*.

"The First Passover took place in Egypt, west of Israel, and the Second took place up on Mt. Nebo, east of Israel—right where you cried out to God and received this word. The First Passover represented Jesus' first visit, and the Second Passover represents His return—a first occurrence, representing a later event. You were chosen long ago to help prepare the world for God's return.

"If you need evidence, the book of Revelations is full of prophecy, reminiscent of the ten plagues afflicting Egypt before the first Passover. Diseases, drought, earthquakes, scorching fire from the sun, darkness, sores, impure spirits looking like frogs, and a sea turned to blood, all seem to precede the wedding supper of the Lamb, and the Second Passover— the glorious return of our Lord, as it reveals in Revelation 19:11-13.

I saw heaven standing open and there before me was a white horse, whose rider is called Faithful and True. With justice he judges and wages war. His eyes are like blazing fire, and on his head are many crowns. He has a name written on him that no one knows but he himself. He is dressed in a robe dipped in blood, and his name is the Word of God.

"Do you understand?" Lewis asked.

I looked up at my kids. *So how long did we have until this glorious event? I had things to do.*

The kids had all reached the top of the rock and were now repelling down. Lewis peered up at them, before saying, "You have been given this word, and now it's time to come back down the mountain, just like Moses did, and tell God's people about His Instrument. God has put into your possession those two stones to help bring the dead body of God's people to life again before Christ's return."

CHAPTER FORTY-THREE

A TREASURE FOUND IN HEARTACHE

———◆———

Journal Entry #311

HOW MANY times have we wondered why? What was God thinking? These are questions we want the answers to in some of the most challenging times of our lives. Whether it be the death of a loved one, a broken marriage, an unrequited love, or a deflated dream.

During those times, we want our ways to be God's ways. Fortunately for us, it's not how God does things. Remember, He wants a relationship with us. He wants us to seek Him, to be invested, and to desire to be close to Him.

If we only give a superficial glance at the chapters of the Bible, we can't find what's buried beneath and draw nearer to Him. It is only when we dig deeper that we find true revelation and insight into the ways of our Father in heaven. The search is what leads to the knowledge of God's very essence, stoking the fires of intimacy, and resulting in a complete submission of our will to His.

Judah, the person, not the place, and the circumstances of his birth are the perfect examples of how God uses His Word to grow us to maturity in relationship with Him. Let me tell you a story from Genesis 29:16-30:21.

Once upon a time, there was this guy. Let's call him Jacob. Now Jacob was not the nicest kid on the playground. And where we meet Jacob in his story, he has just stolen his brother's birthright and his blessing. He's fled his hometown, knowing if his brother catches up to him, it will precipitate a very hairy situation, which is all very à propos, since Jacob's brother's name is *Esau*, which, in Hebrew, either means *to make* or something *rough* and *hairy*.

Jacob flees to the town his mother tells him to seek refuge in. He finds it in the house of his uncle, Laban. While there, Jacob falls madly in love with Laban's daughter, Rachel, and hastily goes about finding a way to procure her hand in marriage.

Now, Uncle Laban is a shrewd guy and makes a deal with Jacob saying, "Hey, Jacob, let's make a deal. Why don't you work with me for seven years and at the end of it you can marry my daughter?" Jacob seems okay with this little setup and works really hard.

With the time of his indentured service coming to an end, Jacob goes to Laban, wanting Rachel's hand. However, Laban doesn't want to get rid of his cheap labor, so he tells Jacob, "Sure, no problem."

But then, veiled and under a cover of darkness, Laban brings his first daughter to Jacob to wed. He makes love to her, but at dawn, Jacob realizes he has married the wrong girl and confronts Laban about it.

Then Laban says, "Hey, Jacob. Listen, it is a custom here to wed the older daughter before the younger. It's only right for you to take my oldest daughter, Leah, first. Keep her, and after the bridal week is over, you can have Rachel too, for another seven years of service." Frustrated, to say the least, Jacob agrees, now having two wives while being put under Laban's arm for another seven years. What could the guy do but continue working hard and begin raising a family? So, that's what he did.

Everything seemed to be all right with the world. Well, that depends on who's perspective you are viewing it from. It seems Rachel is happy. She has the heart of the man she loves. Laban seems happy. He has successfully manipulated Jacob for another seven years of service, and now has two daughters off his hands.

It does appear that Jacob is suffering, but more from circumstances he brought upon himself. He is the one who isn't satisfied with one wife and stuck around for another.

Remember, he's also the one who stole his brother's birthright and blessing. Jacob didn't seem to have a problem fleeing the whirlwind his actions created in Canaan. It seems, however, the whirlwind followed him all the way to his uncle's house.

The one person who never gets the limelight is Leah. I always felt so bad for her because, from the story, it at least appeared like she really loved Jacob and didn't do anything to deserve his apathy.

Leah spent her entire life yearning for a love Jacob had already given to someone else. Leah spent every day watching Rachel get the intimate love she longed for. Leah had to sit at the family dinner table every night and watch that love grow.

Life went on, and Leah started having children with Jacob. When she had her first son, she named him Reuben. Names mean something in the Bible and often reflect the nature of a person or a set of circumstances. *Reuben* means, *Behold, a son.* By branding him, Reuben, Leah was saying God saw her heartbreak and gave her a son hoping that Jacob would love her, or so the Bible says.

As time went on, Leah could *see* that having Reuben didn't change a thing. Leah became pregnant again and had another son. She named him *Simeon* because God had heard her pain about feeling unloved and named him, *hears.* She *heard,* too, but having a sense of hearing didn't change a thing either. Poor Leah. She had yet another son and named him *Levi,* meaning, *joined,* believing God would surely strengthen the bond she had with Jacob because she was bound to him now with a cord of three strings, so to speak. Unfortunately for Leah, she would be disappointed again.

During all the years Leah kept having babies, Rachel was barren. Leah had given Jacob three sons, and he still loved a woman who couldn't give him children more. The heartbreak Leah felt must have been punctuated by that fact.

She must have realized at some point, it didn't matter how many children she had with Jacob, he would never feel more for her. Time went by, and Leah became pregnant again. She had another son, but this time, instead of becoming engulfed by the things she couldn't have, or change, she *praised* God for what He had given her. Leah could *see her Father, hear her Father,* and *was joined with Him* through every circumstance. This time she named her son *Judah,* meaning to *cast up praise* because that's what she did.

After reading this story for the first time, I was pretty upset. I wrestled with God about it. How could God let this gal suffer so much? We already know she wasn't a beauty. By her very description in the Bible, Leah had no physical attributes that appealed to Jacob. She had "weak eyes" according to scripture. What this meant exactly is anyone's guess. Maybe she wasn't pretty, or literally, couldn't stay awake. Maybe, spiritually, she was way too weak and tempted by her own selfish desire. Leah's name actually means *weary* in Hebrew. The girl was apparently tired, suffered much, and had an unrequited love for a man she had to watch give his love to another woman, in her own house, no less!

It was remarkable to me that she worked her body to the bone, ended up having a total of seven children, and remained loyal, not only to Jacob, but his entire family.

I just couldn't understand God at all. At that point, I was glad my ways weren't God's ways. Confused and angry, I read the story again a few months later, finally realizing the reason for my irritation. I knew exactly how Leah felt because this same thing had happened to me. Knowing no matter what Leah did, she was never going to be good enough, but it didn't stop her from hoping for something better.

Once Leah realized her hope was misplaced in Jacob, and should have always been placed in the Lord, she began to praise Him, ergo the name Judah, given to her fourth son. She had apparently come full circle, her weary eyes, made bright again.

I began to understand God wants all of us to hope in Him, even when we feel weary, because that's when His light shines the brightest. He wants us all to see Him, to hear Him, to obey Him, and be joined with Him, so our praise of Him means something.

God had an unrequited love for me, even when I had misplaced my hope, trust and love in the world, and in men, for such a long time. Boy was that a punch to the gut. I immediately felt ashamed the moment I felt it, but then the Holy Spirit came and whispered something in my ear.

"You only see the back side of my tapestry. There is just so much more you can't see, hear, or will ever be able to put together. You can't see my face, but I can show you the boundaries of my love.

"I want you to know, even though Leah suffered in this life, she ultimately trusted in Me. You see, my darling, suffering was always meant to help solidify faith in Me, not destroy it. It was always meant to make the weak and weary strong again; that through that very weakness, I am their strength.

"I want you to know when Leah got to the gates of heaven, I had her turn around, and I showed her the future. She saw a man hanging from a cross, suffering in silence, for the sin of the world—not His sin, but the world's. Leah looked at Me and asked who the man was. I told her, '*For those whose eyes are weary, Behold, a Son, Who Heard and Obeyed, and Joined All of mankind to Me in the covenant of His blood. Give Him Praise, for He is the Messiah*. He is the Savior, Jesus Christ, who was born into the world to save mankind and bring him back into right relationship with God.' I told Leah that He was from the tribe of Judah.

"Leah looked at Me with tears in her eyes, and an unmistakable glint of recognition in them. 'That's right, Leah. The Savior of the world came from your son, from your line, not from Rachel's. My love, you were never the hated wife. Always remember I know the end from the beginning, and My plans for increase are perfect, far above, and just more than."

I felt a sudden sense of peace, like I had peaked into the window of God's own heart. He had placed me in the crevice of the Rock to make my own weary eyes bright again.

Lewis was right. That's when I truly started believing in the inconceivable in my own life.

CHAPTER FORTY-FOUR

JOSEPH TO JOSHUA

THAT NIGHT I had a dream.

I was walking on a beach with God's hand in mine. We were walking side by side, but I couldn't see His face. I found myself trembling and staring blankly at our path together. Each depression in the sand, shaking me, silently screaming at me to pay attention. Then I woke up.

Clearly disappointed, I knew I would have to ask Lewis about it. Tumbling out of bed, peering at my toes, I half-hoped I would find the remnants of that sandy exchange still clinging to the bottoms of my feet.

After getting dressed, I ambled into the kitchen. The coffee pot was there, just waiting to be put to good use. My husband was in the shower. My kids were still asleep. I would not be waking them up. This was my quiet time.

I toiled away at the pot, waited for the coffee to brew, poured myself a cup, and then walked outside. Finding my favorite spot on the porch, I settled in. Deep in thought, the sun began to open its eyes over the horizon and glisten across the dew in the grass. Hearing a slight crunching of earth beneath hastily approaching feet, I turned to find Lewis striding towards me. Dragging a chair close to mine, he sat down.

"Hello."

"Hello, Lewis. It's kind of early this morning, isn't it?"

"No, I am right on time," he responded, offering me a small smile.

"So, what brought you here today?"

"I came to talk to you about Joseph and Joshua."

"What?"

"The two people from the Old Testament that are at the center of the dream you had last night."

"The one where I was walking with God but couldn't see His face?"

"There is a reason for it. God was telling you, it doesn't matter what He looked like, but how He acted, how He walked. He wants you to know it doesn't matter what's above His shoulders, because between them is where His dominion rests, where His mantle sits, and where this word you've been given resides."

In this world, I learned really quick that if you didn't have anything to add to a conversation, then it was probably best for all involved to remain quiet. So, I let the silence spill into the area between us, waiting for Lewis to continue. He didn't disappoint.

"What rests between two shoulder blades? The neck, right? It is where two companions are yoked together. The neck is what lifts and bends the head. It represents where the true strength of the body lies. This is where we find Jesus. Remember, He sits in the 'in-between.' There is confirmation of this at the end of the book of Joshua, if you can receive it?"

"Why in Joshua, Lewis?"

"You have to remember Joshua is a kind of foreshadowing from the Old Testament of Jesus in the New. The names Joshua and Jesus both mean *The Lord is Salvation.* In Joshua 24:30, Joshua renews God's covenant with the people, and then he dies. Joshua was buried in the border (the dividing line) of his inheritance at *Timnath Serah* (the Territory of the Sun, or Remnant) in the hill country of *Ephraim* (Double Fruit) North *Tsaphon* (Hidden Treasure because it is spelled the same, in Hebrew, as the word for north) in Mt *Gaash* (Shaking).

"Names in the Word joined together in scripture can sometimes offer hidden meaning as a subtext to the story. Here we find Joshua (Jesus) in the border (in-between), the territory of the Sun, a double fruit, a hidden treasure in the shaking, just like when two massive plates of the earth's crust rub together to produce mountain ranges seen thousands of years later.

"The verses go on to tell us that Joseph's bones were buried at *Shekem*, on the *neck*, between the shoulders, because that's what *Shekem* means.

"Now, we know the Hebrews loved wordplay just as much as the next guy, only they seemed to do it better than most. As we have already discussed, words are often rearranged, or a letter is changed altogether for effect. Much to the chagrin of those who love to try and refute the Word, there are no scribal errors in the Bible—everything is precisely where it is meant to be.

"One of the words the Hebrews liked to use in this regard was the word *shakam*, with an equivalent cognate word *shakan* (only the last letter is different). *Shakan* means storehouse, to dwell or tabernacle with, and is the same word the Hebrews give for the word *neighbor*. This word is where we get the word *shekinah—the dwelling divine presence of the Lord*.

"It makes perfect sense, doesn't it? If God's presence rests upon our necks, it should make it much easier to lift our heads to Him in praise and decline them in submission to His will. The neck is where burdens are carried. It separates our head from the rest of our bodies and directs which way our heads turn. To the Hebrews, allowing the Lord to rest where our burdens are carried took the weight off their shoulders, and placed them squarely on His."

I was so lost. Were we ever going to get to the point?

"The correlation between Joseph and Joshua may not be evident until I share more information about Joseph's name. *Joseph,* in Hebrew, means *He increases* and is closely related to the word *asoph,* meaning *storehouse of provision*, because that is where the increase is gathered. Another word closely linked to both words is the word *suph,* meaning *come to an end, perish, storm wind* or *hurricane*—a shaking all its own.

"The Egyptians must have realized what Joseph brought to their community because they changed his name to *Zaphenath-Paneah—The Hidden Treasure Revealed in the Turn* or *The Hidden Brought to Light*. Remember, to the Egyptians, Joseph was a Revealer of what was Hidden, A Revealer of Secrets (like interpreting those dreams confined and floating around in their pretty little heads).

"Joseph and Joshua were both buried in places and associated with names correlating to abundance and healing found in places of turning— whether from the earth turning over in an earthquake, the violent turning of winds during a hurricane, the turning from one day to the next, or simply the turning of one's head away from sin (because, metaphorically, that's what the neck helps the head do).

"This is no coincidence, because Joseph and Joshua are both precursors of the physical manifestation of God in the flesh. They foreshadow the coming of Christ—the One who calmed the storm. And once and for all, took our burdens and covered our stiff necks in His glory and perfection, turning them in the right direction.

"Joseph and Joshua brought a double portion, interceded for their people, and extended their tents. Jesus did the same. He interceded for His people, took our burdens, and brought a double portion. And this happened during a quake, no less—remember, there was an earthquake that made the ground tremble when Christ was crucified. And Jesus extended His tent—bringing increase and healing to the whole world. These men were a reflection of Christ. From the first deliverer of Israel in *Genesis* to the last deliverer of Israel mentioned in *Deuteronomy*—the first and last books of the Torah.

"Joseph and Joshua represented Jesus as a man, but they were also images of Him as a dividing line. Two, to be exact that can be found between two altars and the temple. The *deleth* or door—between the altar and the Holy Place, and the *paroketh,* or veil—between the altar of incense and the Holy of Holies.

"You had that dream because the walk from the altar to the temple is the path that people have forgotten. There is a call to remembrance in it. From the altar to the temple, from the heart to the head, from death to life, from the cradle to the grave. Wasn't this the theme of Christ's ministry?"

"Yes, Lewis."

"To dig a little deeper, let's look at the words for these two dividing lines. First, the word *deleth* comes from the word *dalah,* meaning *to let down, be made low, to put in motion,* or *to be pressed or drawn out of the water.* It was used figuratively as a word meaning *to deliver.* This makes sense because during a woman's parturition she is brought low, rocking back and forth, toiling, as the baby is drawn out of the amniotic fluid. The door represents Jesus. The Agent of Deliverance.

"The word *paroketh,* on the other hand, comes from the word *perek,* meaning *harshness, severity,* or *cruelty.* When Jesus was crucified, that veil was torn. No longer was there a curtain of cruelty hanging there. Jesus died so we could pass through and dwell with God covered in His curtain of love and compassion instead. What covers our worthless necks and ushers us into the Lord's throne room is the cover of the Son of God's love and the true reflection of what the Word was intended to do—turn our stubborn heads and hearts to Him.

"Isn't that what man is called to do? To mourn their sin and be brought low enough to a state of humility and repentance, so they can move forward with their eyes wide open, and their hearts focused on better things—like the Law of love and compassion, instead of a curtain of cruelty? This is what strengthens man's shoulders. This is what brings wholeness and abundance. Isn't this what Jesus accomplished to perfection on the cross?

"Man's cruel interpretation of The Law itself was crucified there, so the true Spirit of the Law—love—could be resurrected to new life and dwell in us. Somehow, we have forgotten that in the rub, in the quaking, in the storm, we are called to resemble and testify to what Jesus has done for mankind. No one sees His glory anymore. The walk from the altar to the Temple is so short, but it's necessary.

"It's not just about accepting that what was done on the altar really happened, but about repenting of our sin, and receiving Jesus' sacrifice wholly and walking into God's presence with His Son's mantle on. It's about covering our necks with Jesus' robe because that's what brings abundance (Joseph) and deliverance (Joshua)."

CHAPTER FORTY-FIVE

THORNS AND THISTLES

A COUPLE of days later, I was out working in the yard because frankly it started looking like a jungle. The last heatwave of the summer had finally diminished into the cooler breezes of the fall. The summer was the season I didn't get much done. Most of my time was spent indoors, holding up the couch. Fall was always the time when I could stand back up again and get back to work. And it was time. The yard certainly wasn't going to manicure itself.

I had been out there for about two hours, plowing through the weeds, when I got an unexpected surprise. Cutting back a hedge of knock-out roses, Lewis came out of the garage with a trash can. Looking up, my hand hastily grabbed the edge of one of the bushes. The wrong thing to do. Knock-out roses are beautiful. They can endure the harshest of conditions but are covered in thorns. Lewis walked over and took the thornbush from my hand and put it in the garbage can he was holding.

"Thank you, Lewis. What brought you to the house today?" I said, as my fingers stroked the thorns piercing my skin.

"I came to talk about those thorns in your hands."

"Why? Are you planning on helping me get them out?"

"Technically, yes, but not in the way you are thinking. Remember when we talked about the sheep gate and that Jesus was the gate?"

I simply nodded, waiting for him to continue.

"Historically, thorns have been used synonymously with iniquity, sin and pain. Remember, the earliest written words were not words at all, but pictures. The earliest alphabets used a thorn or hook to represent one of its letters. The letter in Hebrew was the letter *vav*.

"Throughout the Bible, thorns pointed to detestable things, iniquity, darkness, and a place where seeds refuse to grow. Thorns were used as metaphors for kindling in consuming fires because that was apparently all they were suitable for. Ultimately, they were a token of God's curse and judgment. Thorns cling; they hurt. They can't be shaken off. They re-inflict the same pain in the same spot repeatedly. That sounds like the epitome of a curse, doesn't it?"

Lewis took my hands in his and turned them over to expose the two little thorns digging into the palm of my hand. "God takes the things representing pain, sin, evil and confusion—those thorns in peoples' lives, and what the enemy meant for harm—and turns them into seeds.

"We can find evidence of this in the New Testament in the crown Jesus wore at Calvary. God took a token of sin and re-appropriated it to represent the truest, most beautiful, unconditional shield of love ever known to man.

"Did you know in the Ancient Near East, shepherds would hedge the top of their folds with thorns? It was the hedge of thorns that helped to keep the robbers and wolves at bay. It was the very first prototype for barbed wire, if you can imagine that, and it was just as much a hedge of protection.

"Isn't it interesting that something as small and as arbitrary as a thorn could stand for such complete evil, while at the same time representing something that shielded and protected? Our Good Shepherd, Jesus Christ, is our hedge of protection. He had a crown of thorns placed on His head as a token of our sin. It dug into His scalp and couldn't be shaken loose.

"The crown He took carried the weight of the world's sins—taking them forever off our heads and laying them squarely on His. He took His crown of righteousness, abundance, and grace and placed it on our heads, exchanging it for our crown of division, cruelty, and destruction. The sin became a sin offering. The thorns became, in that very moment, a symbol of pure love, taking our death and exchanging it for His life. Instead of the thorn and the briar, He made the cypress and the myrtle grow. From the point of desolation came life. Jesus became the thorn and lined our broken-down sheepfolds to protect us from the true enemy, ourselves.

"The reason I am telling you all this lies in the New Testament when Jesus asks the disciples if they could gather grapes from thorn bushes or figs from thistles. The obvious answer is, of course, not.

"But if you can receive it, Jesus was also implying that yes, if transformed by His blood and His love, they can forever be changed into fruit of the vine and the fig tree. Thorns and thistles do represent sin, but they can also be seen as goads and tokens to bring transformation, with God's guidance and grace. This is how thorns shield. That is how they protect. That is how they help to bring about something new."

"That is very interesting, Lewis, but what does that have to do with me?"

"Did you know the name Mary has roots in several words. Her name can be derived from an Egyptian word *mri*, meaning to love; the Hebrew word *mara*, meaning *rebellion*; the word *marach,* meaning to rub; or the word *mor*, the Hebrew word for *myrrh*. The latter, being a derivative of the word *marar,* meaning to be *bitter* or *strong*. It also has implications in another word, *mur,* meaning *to exchange*. The thought being that mankind is called to exchange bitterness for love and strength."

"Myrrh was produced from a bitter herb used in the holy incense burned in the Temple in Jerusalem. It was also one of the gifts the magi brought from the East to celebrate the birth of Christ. The mystery I am here to share with you doesn't lie in this special resin but in the plant that it came from. The myrrh bush had to be cut to let its resin ooze out. The only problem? Take a look at what the myrrh bush looks like."

He pointed to my hands. "This. It is covered in long, piercing thorns. Thorns that can easily cut and injure the hands reaching out for them. Mary, the mother of Christ, whose name implies rebellion, bitterness, a harsh aftertaste, strength, love, to rub or to change, held Jesus in her womb. One might even say from conception, Jesus was surrounded by a matrix of thorns. He was delivered through them, overcame them on the cross, and now sits at the right hand of the Father."

"Yes, Lewis, but what does this have to do with me?" I said, frustrated, for the umpteenth time.

"Everything. The word you are to take to the world will seem like a thorn in the side. It will not be palatable to many. It will leave a harsh aftertaste, but it is necessary to open some eyes, and help to change the hearts of many more so they can see the transformative love of God's grace.

"When Jesus spoke about thorns and thistles, He said people would be known by their fruit. Could it be through living in His Word and in His love, He can exchange thorns and bring grapes from them? He can take thistles and bring figs from them? Your word will help people see that the change in our moral character, evolving into the nature of our Savior's can come from some of the most piercing times in our lives. I would say that constitutes as fruit only the Holy Spirit can bring, don't you?"

I didn't answer. I just looked at those two little thorns in my hands and wondered.

CHAPTER FORTY-SIX

THE BINDRESS OF THE GAZELLES

The two most important days in your life are the day you are born and the day you find out why.

—MARK TWAIN

THOSE WORDS hung in the air for a second before they came crashing into me like a head-on collision. My husband, busy stoking the grill, opened the back door. "Lunch is ready."

Turning to Lewis, I asked, "Are you staying for lunch?"

"Sure," Lewis replied. We set the table, called the kids in to eat, and then sat around the table waiting to fill our plates.

Lunch took about fifteen minutes to eat. We were starving. The kids asked to be excused, and once they received their leave, they bolted from the table.

"Not so fast." I blurted out. "We need to clean the table off." Returning slowly to the table, as if their shoes were stuck in cement, pouting with every step, they picked up their plates and placed them in the sink. Lewis even picked up his plate and brought it to me. "Lewis, you don't have to do that. You are our guest."

"Yes, I do. The plates aren't going to walk themselves into the kitchen for cleaning." I must have gotten those dishes at a yard sale. Some of them were even chipped, but Lewis was treating each one like fine china.

"Are you ready?"

"Ready for what, Lewis? We aren't done for the day? I just don't think I can handle anymore."

"No. We are not done. We still have to talk about your name."

"Don't you mean my purpose?"

Lewis looked at me intently, his voice wrapped in careful hesitation. "I mean both."

"Haven't we been doing this the whole time? How much longer is it going to take?"

"As long as it does. The Lord reveals things in His time, never in ours. Besides, you need confirmation, don't you? Confirmation for you must come slowly, through many circumstances and people, to reflect the process in which God works. It must be this way so you will know it is God, and only He could make the puzzle pieces fit so perfectly. This is how others will know these are far from vain imaginings, and that He has chosen you for this particular word in time."

"I get it, Lewis. Let's just go upstairs and talk." We made it to the second floor landing and found a place in the den. "This place looks familiar." Lewis pointed out.

"That's right. We were here while I was sleeping." I said with a wink.

"It's good we should be here now. Do you remember the dream you had about the bike your mother-in-law gave you? You were surprised when she called, but you still went to go pick it up. She made you come through the front door and then made you climb up to the attic because that's where she put it. You climbed the ladder, removed one of the ceiling tiles, and poked your head through. Do you remember what you saw?"

"Yes, Lewis. Spanning from my left to directly in front of me, there was a floor full of shining, priceless dishes. They looked like ones you might find in a wedding registry. From the number of place settings, they must have cost a fortune."

"They did. And what did you see to the right?"

"There was another room off to the right. In it was the bicycle. But I could only make out a part of one wheel, not the whole bike. The wheel was sparkling and clean, just like the dishes. The room the bike occupied, however, was covered in dust and cobwebs."

Lewis sat listening closely to every word. I assume it was to make sure no detail had been left out. Then, with caution, he replied, "Now is the time for the full revelation of that dream. Those dishes represent all believers washed in the blood of Christ and waiting in the upper room; all having received God's perfect gift of salvation through Jesus Christ, counting down to the wedding reception. They are waiting expectantly for God's instruction and their seating arrangement."

"It is important that you understand the vessels were clean and shining, not only because they were purified, but because they hadn't been sitting around collecting dust. They had allowed God to fill their vessels with His glory. They weren't just sitting idle in the attic, unused and ineffective.

"Remember, the inside of the vessel is where the Holy Spirit lives, and it is the outside that reflects His cohabitation. The vessel is poured out so it can be refilled over and over again, giving a whole new meaning to the term, *dinner service*. Do you understand me so far?"

"I think so, Lewis."

"Good." He said, not even catching his breath as he continued. "The wheel represents God, the Son, the agent of salvation, Jesus Christ, through all revolution of space and time. And the room the wheel is in represents the Jewish nation. It was covered in dust and cobwebs because they have not accepted nor received Christ as the vehicle to their salvation. But they will at the appointed time. Do you understand?"

"Yes, Lewis."

"This word you bring will help gather followers back to their Savior. You are just one of many who have been called to prepare the vessels for Christ's return. You see, His First Passover was the rehearsal dinner, and the Second is the wedding reception.

"I am about to tell you something that's going to be hard to take, but it is imperative that you do, so please listen.

"There are enough people out in the world today who don't believe the Bible speaks about the histories of individual people. They have become desensitized, thinking every account only speaks about a group.

"You must understand at the heart of every collective, there is the individual. Like atoms that make up molecules, that make up elements, that make up substances, that make up the universe we see all around us. Everything starts on a subatomic scale of sorts.

"Every individual was a real person with real experiences. Some of them so fantastical it's easier to believe their story only spoke of a group or was allegorical in nature. But everything that has happened to you, and has yet to be revealed, will glaringly declare to others that even the seemingly fantastical can sit squarely in the hem of reality."

"You know I need confirmation, right, Lewis?"

CHAPTER FORTY-SEVEN

TABITHA

———◆———

"Do you remember Tabitha? From the New Testament?"

"Yes. She was the first resurrection of the dead documented after the ascension of Christ in the book of Acts by Peter."

"That is right. And do you know what Tabitha means?"

"The name *Tabitha* comes from the Aramaic word *tabya* and corresponds, Hebraically, to the word *tsbiy*, meaning *gazelle* or *beautiful and honored.*"

Lewis proceeded to tell me all about gazelles, including their defining characteristics, their collective herd behaviors, and how they were symbolically related to righteousness from a Jewish perspective.

He told me gazelles were considered beautiful on account of their long, sleek, lean frames, special markings, and expressive eyes. To the Jews, a gazelle's eyes were their most highly regarded feature. Described as large and bright, their almond shaped orbs communicated a sense of knowing, of carefully examining and clearly seeing what laid all around them. Moreover, they were considered a wise species. Compared to other beasts, gazelles seemed to have the ability to reason and understand the world around them in ways others couldn't.

Lewis continued telling me gazelles were highly alert and constantly on the lookout for predators. They had incredible 'hind' sight, a necessity for eluding their enemies. Gazelles were revered for their swiftness, leaping capabilities and their ability to overcome any test in agility or endurance. As a herd, they moved across the earth like a flowing river cutting across a landscape. And flowing rivers shine. This is why they became a symbol of enlightenment. And why the nation of Israel was known worldwide as *The Land of the Gazelle.*

Lewis then explained that some of the same words meaning *gazelle* in the Hebrew were also used in the Bible to mean *roebuck, doe, deer, hind* and *mountain goat.*

After the nature lesson, he showed me a picture of a gazelle. They were beautiful. Lewis waited for me to examine the picture thoroughly before he continued, saying, "Look at the picture of the gazelle once more and pay close attention to their eyes."

Taking the picture, my own eyes focused on those of the gazelle's. "They are big and beautiful, Lewis. They have long eyelashes. They are brown and almond shaped. What do you want me to say?"

"Doesn't it look like their eyes are painted with stibium? You know, the cosmetic used to brighten and open up the eyes used back in Egypt."

"I suppose so. But what does that have to do with me?"

"I'm getting there, Staci."

CHAPTER FORTY-EIGHT

THE WOMEN AT THE WHEEL

"WHAT WAS Tabitha known for in Bible scripture?"

"Well, in Acts 9, it talks about her making robes and other clothing for believers, especially widows, Lewis."

"She was a weaver, a spinner, or an embroiderer of cloth, perhaps? We know she worked in textiles. She brought together cloth to cover the people with, especially those whose husbands were dead—those who were lacking or lived in deficiency with no means of support. She helped carry burdens. She offered alms of mercy and compassion. And when she passed away, she was washed and placed in an upper room and was resurrected there. Let's take a closer look at the details of her story.

"Tabitha was buried in *Joppa*, a town that gets its name from the Hebrew word *yaphah*, meaning *bright, fair*, and *beautiful*. She was a gazelle living in the light, bringing that light to others. This is what you are.

"Long ago, you were given the revelation of the two stones representing Jesus throughout the Word. Do you remember what they were?"

"Yes, Lewis. It was the word for pottery wheel and birth stool. It was used by the midwives in Egypt to help the Israelite women labor on. It helped deliver them."

"Do you remember what you did for fourteen years before you became a nurse practitioner?"

"Of course, Lewis. I haven't completely lost my memory. Honestly, it hasn't been that long ago. You are making me feel like an old lady. I was a labor and delivery nurse."

"So, you prepared women for delivery. You monitored their progress, eased their pain, got them to breathe right, pushed with them and then cared for them afterwards. You gave them instruction and encouragement during the delivery process and then in the postpartum period. Some had husbands and some didn't."

"Yes. That is all true."

"You have been a life guardsman. Let me ask you a question. What were the names of the two midwives who helped deliver the generation of Jews all those years ago in Egypt?"

"Shiphrah and Puah."

"Do you remember what their names mean?"

"No, honestly, not without having to look it up," I had to admit.

"*Shiphrah* comes from a word that means *to be clear, glistening, fair*, or *beautiful*, like the clearness of dawn on a cloudless day. This word shares the same origin as another word. The word *shophar*. It means *ram's horn*. Could the similarity between these two words be that *shophars* were known for their clarity of sound and ability to cut with precision through the air as instruments of proclamation?

"And *Puah* comes from the word *yaphah* meaning *fair, bright, shining and beautiful*. Does this sound familiar? This name clearly resembles several words in Hebrew.

"The first is the word *puach,* meaning *to breathe* or *to blow*. The second is the word *paah,* meaning *to cleave to pieces*. The third is the word *piach,* meaning *soot* or *ashes from a furnace*. Another is the word *poh,* meaning *here*. And last is the word *puk,* meaning *paint,* or *fair colors*, as in a crushed powder used to decorate the eyes. It was considered a real eye-opener. In Hebrew thought, it resembled the darkness that marked a gazelle's eyes and opened them up.

"The similarities in this word group have a common theme of blowing or possibly spreading a word via the mouth about beauty from ashes that helps to open people's eyes. All of which makes sense because the word for mouth is the word *peh,* another word that fits perfectly in this word grouping. Apparently, these two women, Shiphrah and Puah, were real eye-openers themselves. They were witnesses to the Living Word of God— The first to see God's Son providing for His people.

"Remember when I told you that Shiphrah and Puah were a foreshadowing of you and your mother-in-law? And that God works in the Law of Double Reference? Remember when I told you that if two midwives would be a part of a major deliverance west of Israel, there would have to be two midwives east of Israel as well?"

My stomach started churning, my body on full tilt. Skin pebbling. Hair standing on end. The whole nine. *Or ten, depending on how you looked at it.* I knew Lewis was about to tell me something that was about to change the course of my life.

"Puah and Shiphrah's names can also be translated, by a discerning ear, to *Blow the Shophar*. When you and your mother-in-law went to Jordan, you were both so disappointed that you didn't get to blow that shophar in Jerusalem on *Yom Teruah*. But God knew what He was doing. You blew the shophar east of the Jordan, in Petra, and left crosses and sinner's prayers there instead. You presented a testimony and fulfilled God's plan without even knowing it."

What was he talking about? I must have missed something. Before I could even ask, he cut me off.

"And now God has given you this testimony, and these insights, to encircle the eyes of the gazelles to open them up. Puah and Shiphrah worked the wheel back in Egypt. Tabitha worked it in Israel. Now you will work it to help bring insight and revival.

"Many women in the Bible worked the wheel. Tabitha, the Wife of noble character mentioned in Proverbs 31, and Lydia from Thyatira, just to name a few. Women played a pretty important role in the Word."

Lewis had given me a lot to think about. Pondering what he just told me for a minute, I followed him down the stairs. Lewis let himself out. I made sure my kids and my husband were still occupied and then went to my room to pray. As I read through the Word, I realized Lewis was right. Women had a pretty important role in the Bible.

CHAPTER FORTY-NINE

THE WONDER OF WOMEN

———◆———

Journal Entry #383

WHEN YOU go to the movies in the summer, you can pretty much guarantee the movie options available to you—the action-adventure and the action-action-adventure. You go in, buy your tickets, and buckle up in the hopes that you will be entertained, thrilled and saved by the hero for the next two hours, making everything all right with the world again.

For the ride, you stop at the concession stand and purchase a giant drink you probably won't even be able to finish. Next, you get suckered into a super-sized popcorn that could feed a third-world country. And finally, a family-size bag of candy because now you are invested, and for the next two hours calories don't count.

You go in and find your seat. It is dark, but you still find the perfect spot and sit down. Never mind that when you get up to leave, you will have realized you actually sat in gum and melted chocolate. It's in a very unflattering spot and will be virtually impossible to rub out.

As you recline in your chair, ready for the show to start, someone sits next to you with a thirteen-month-old in her arms. On the other side, comes a woman with her six kids, who you know will be getting up fifteen times to go to the bathroom, trying her best to alleviate six little bladders for two hours without causing too much of a disturbance. The woman's purse hits you in the arm as she sits down. You know she has a convenience store-sized selection of goodies for her kids in there because she refuses to pay $10.00 for a bag of candy she can get for $1.99 at the store before she gets to the theater.

You, on the other hand, overwhelmed by the misfortune that you are sitting in the unluckiest seat in the theater, notice momentarily that the lights have gone down. The movie is starting, and you are taken back to that sweet escape you just paid a pretty penny for.

The movie doesn't disappoint. The opening scene starts with the hero leaping over a building, catching the bad guy, and teaching a relevant moral lesson to the kid who randomly witnessed it. All the while, waiting quietly on a street corner with his dog. The first two minutes foreshadow the rest of the movie in a predictable pattern of the hero always being at the right place at the right time—ultimately ending with good overcoming evil, and the hero fading into the sunset, humbly acting as if it was all simply done in a day's work. The credits begin to roll and you are startled back into reality. You leave the theater wondering why you can't have a life like that.

For a second, your mind lingers on that scene of those women with their kids. And you realize something, that maybe you hadn't given much thought to in the past—the wonder of women.

Women are used as God's champions and superheroes, too. They are breadwinners, child-bearers, problem-solvers, caregivers, innovators, ever-inquiring, the ultimate plate-juggler. The wonder of women is that most of them do all of these things with the constant concern to get it right. Sometimes too hard on themselves, and a lot of time, way too critical of their own work. They are the humble servants willing to be in the background. They aren't perfect. They've made countless mistakes. Frankly, they are somewhat of a mess. Oh, but what power they have been given.

You know how I know that? God said so. The Bible is filled with stories of powerful women, who, because of their belief in the Lord, and regardless of their ethnicity and past circumstances, were able to help save the future sons of Israel, testify to God's power, show unwavering faith, become disciples of the Word, and provide for Christ's ministry.

Women were the ones at Calvary when most of Christ's friends abandoned Him. Women became the first witnesses of His resurrection and brought back the most important message humanity has ever heard— that Jesus lives. The Lord knew what He had when He created woman. She was created in His image. She was the helper He always intended her to be. A woman after His own heart.

Thank you, God, for women. For allowing them to be a small part of Your story. Giving Jesus all the praise, glory and honor, first, women may boast in the Lord that with Him, it was simply all in a day's work.

Not bad. I think Lewis will like this one. Thinking more corporately, I began considering the church again. The Body of Christ as God's Bride, has been allowed to be a big part of His story, too. I just wished we would remember that.

CHAPTER FIFTY

WAITING IN THE WAIT

I HATE waiting rooms. The word *wait* simply means the anticipation of action. It would drive anyone crazy, but it always had me idling with the tension of an Indy racer at the starting line, with time riding my bumper.

Unfortunately, that became my sentence once a month, as I waited for my dreaded run in the infusion chair. Being roped into treatment for this neurological disorder, while I waited for it to slowly ravage my body, kept me in a perpetual state of unease.

On the other hand, at least in the waiting room, I was in good company. There were always people waiting with me in varying stages of this illness. We all had multiple sclerosis, many scars of our very own. Sitting in a sinking life-raft together was comforting, in a sick and twisted kind of way.

Contemplating the dead-end street my thoughts had turned down, a woman sat in the empty chair to my right. We made eye contact and smiled, knowing that even though we had never met, we shared something only the other could understand. We both said our token hellos and returned to the distractions we always brought to appointments like these. I had a book and she, her laptop. The woman was dressed in a suit, as this was probably just a pit stop in her very busy day.

I, however, was dressed in my fat pants, a sloppy, old-stained rock tee, and flip-flops. It was times like these I wished I had my job back. I couldn't help feeling insecure and inferior. I think that's why I initially struck up a conversation with the woman in the first place. She had to know; I did have a career, a profession, a position, and a purpose. *Boy, did I need therapy!*

We started talking about what we did for a living. I found out she was a sales rep for a pharmaceutical company and came in for her treatment in between business meetings. Then I proceeded to tell her I had been a nurse practitioner for several years and didn't know what was next. I told her I had been doing a lot of writing and read her one of my journal entries. She seemed to like it. "Why don't you become a doula?" She offered.

Why would she say that? We hadn't talked about me being a labor and delivery nurse at all. So, I asked her. "What makes you say that?"

"I honestly don't know. It just popped into my head."

"The reason I ask is that I was a labor and delivery nurse for fourteen years before I became a nurse practitioner. But you didn't know that."

The door to the infusion center opened, and they called my name before my new friend could elaborate. Saying "goodbye" I followed a tiny, pleasant-looking nurse into one of the infusion suites and sat down in the chair. The next several minutes danced by like a perfectly rehearsed Broadway number. This is how the steps went: weight, check, vital signs, check, questions about recent infections, check, blood draw check, and last but not least, the infusion. Check. Check.

Settling into a large, comfortable recliner I was relegated to for the next four hours, the nurse brought me a warm blanket and asked if I needed anything else. Simply shaking my head, I closed my eyes.

"Why do you think she told you that?" I knew that voice. Lewis.

"Who told me what, Lewis?" I knew what he was getting at. My intention, coyness. I know—a useless attempt to buy time for an answer I really didn't have.

"The woman in the waiting room. Why do you think she told you to be a doula?"

"I don't know, Lewis."

"Do you know what a doula is?"

"Yes, Lewis. A doula is a woman, typically without formal training, who is employed to guide and support a pregnant woman during her labor."

"Yes. But do you know where the word comes from?"

"No."

"The word *doula* comes from the Greek word *doulos*, meaning *bond-slave*. It refers to one person belonging to another with no ownership rights of their own. A *doulos*, especially with regard to the Bible, was any believer who willingly lives under the authority of Christ as a devoted follower.

"You needed confirmation. What better way to do it than by using a person you don't know, who knows little to nothing about you, as a messenger? A *doula* is bound to service those in labor to help them deliver. And they usually have no formal delivery training."

"Yes, Lewis. But you seem to forget. I do have formal delivery training."

"You have no formal spiritual delivery training, though. You did not go to seminary or spend countless years getting degrees in linguistics, theology, or religious studies. This is how God works. He uses the lowly and unknown to edify the learned.

"That one word the woman spoke over you in the waiting room was the perfect word, wasn't it? It fits perfectly with everything you have been told. It was a word divinely executed. Think about this for a minute. The woman made her appointment the same day as you, sat in the chair left empty next to yours, and then gave you a word that fits perfectly into the narrative of your story when there are so many words to choose from. This is the awe and wonder of God's majestic glory. And, even in the waiting room, He is speaking to you in a way only God can."

The alarm on the infusion pump signaled my time was up. Lewis was gone. The nurse came in, smiled, and told me I was done. She unbound my arm from the infusion tubing, and covered my infusion site with a flexible, colored bandage, and said I could go.

CHAPTER FIFTY-ONE

PARKING VALIDATION

—◆—

I PICKED up my things and made my way to the elevator. The woman I had been talking to earlier was no longer occupying the chair she had been sitting in. I couldn't help but think about what Lewis said as the elevator doors opened for me to step inside.

Rummaging through my purse for my parking stub with one hand while pushing the button for the first floor with the other was no small feat, but I managed. The elevator doors closed, and it began making a descent. Then the elevator opened on the first floor as I stood with my parking stub, method of payment, and car keys all in hand. Wanting nothing more than to get out of there, I rounded the corner to the lobby, only to find a huge line of people waiting to have their own parking validated. Was I ever going to catch a break?

I found my place at the end of the line, my hopes dashed that I would be out of there well before rush hour. The thought of an hour-long commute at a snail's pace flashed before my eyes, making my entire face sink. Looking to see what the hold-up was, I noticed a woman who was obviously not accustomed to the whole efficient parking validation method.

She was holding an umbrella that had formed a small puddle on the floor next to her. Great, that meant it was raining. Now I would be driving in rush hour slower than a snail's pace because the people where I lived didn't know how to drive in the rain.

My gaze shifted from the umbrella at the woman's side to a little girl staring intently back at me, on her other. Once our eyes met, she smiled and waved, totally oblivious to her mother's predicament. I smiled and waved back so she could apparently wave again. We played this little game for a couple of seconds before I broke eye contact to check my phone messages.

When I looked up again, the little girl was no longer standing with her mother. She was standing right next to me. She had to be maybe two or three years old. She grabbed my hand and brought me down to her eye level. It seemed she had something important to tell me.

"My brother is one-year-old, too." At least that's what I thought she said. She was speaking in broken Spanish, making it even harder for me to understand. So, I repeated, "Tu hermano es uno ano, tambien?"

A frown appeared across her little face as she shook her head. She repeated herself again. It sounded the same to me. I repeated what I heard again, making her apparent frustration even more evident by the deep indentation of skin on her tiny little forehead.

In that moment, her mother, who must have overcome her battle with the parking validation machine, came up behind her daughter. Nodding hello, she smiled politely, ready to get out of the lobby herself.

I told her that her daughter was trying to tell me something, but it was somehow getting lost in translation. The woman turned to her daughter and asked what she was trying to say to me. Her daughter repeated back to her what I thought I had already heard.

The little girl's mother replied with a funny look on her face, "She said, 'Mi hermano es uno angel, tambien.' I told her what you thought you heard, and she said, 'No.' She was telling you her brother is an angel too. He died last year. He was only a year old."

Telling the little girl and her mother how sorry I was to hear that she lost her brother, I offered her a hug. The woman took her daughter's hand, side-eyeing me with a goodbye, and headed for the lobby doors. The little girl turned to me and smiled once more before exiting the building.

I patiently waited my turn, and then my parking ticket was validated. I got to my car in the parking garage and jumped in. After adjusting the air conditioner vents and buckling my seat belt, I turned on the ignition and peered into my rearview mirror. I nearly jumped out of my skin because Lewis was there in the mirror. He smiled, got out of the car, opened the front passenger door, and slid in.

"Lewis, what did I tell you about this? Is there a reason you were sitting in my back seat?"

"Yes. I wanted you to see me in the rearview mirror's reflection."

"You're going to explain this to me, right?"

"Of course. I came to talk to you about mirrors. Hand mirrors."

CHAPTER FIFTY-TWO

HAND MIRRORS

"HAND MIRRORS?"

"Yes. Hand mirrors."

"You've got to give me more than that, Lewis."

"Well, let's start with what hand mirrors do."

"They reflect light." I snapped.

"Yes. But they also allow you to see your own reflection in them. And a mirror only becomes more effective the more polished it is."

"Lewis, are you saying I am a hand mirror now?"

"For this season, yes. You will reflect the light that comes from it and shed light on a mystery that has been hidden for two thousand years, so it can be made known to those who can't see it so clearly."

"Did you know during the times of the tabernacle and the temple, the bronze laver used for washing the hands of the priests in those days was made from the bronze mirrors of the women who served at the doorway of the tent of meeting? It was here where the priests could see a reflection of themselves and be cleansed."

"But, Lewis, wasn't it the water that enabled the priests to see, not the mirrors themselves?"

"It was both. The water was a reflection of the work of the Holy Spirit, given to us through the death and resurrection of Christ. And water is carried in a vessel. The laver was a vessel polished and rubbed smooth to shine so it could enhance the water within it and reflect the nature of what looked into it clean. We are vessels that need to be rubbed in order to shine, right?

"Hand mirrors, in antiquity, didn't get polished on their own. They were often carried with a pumice stone attached to them. The pumice stone was used to polish the bronze and make it shine. Isn't that what the Lord does in us and through us? The Lord allows the rubbing, so we can see for our eternal good.

"You are the hand mirror attached to the pumice stone to help people reflect on their relationship with the Lord, Jesus Christ. You are an instrument to help people acknowledge that the Holy Spirit is a real person dwelling in us, expecting to be heard.

"That is why the little girl gave you the message she did today. It was divinely spoken. You are an angel, a messenger appointed by God to deliver this word. What better way to confirm it than by giving it to you by a little child?"

"You are telling me this is another confirmation?"

"What? Do you need something else?"

"Yes, Lewis. I am starting to feel like an egomaniac. And this is a word I will continue to confirm, and rely on God for, because this must be His word and not mine. Where in this little scenario are the two stones we have been talking about this whole time?"

"They are there. Tomorrow, you will be going over to your mother-in-law's house. When you get there, go into the bathroom and look at the picture on the wall, and you will receive a word."

Making it home through the rain wasn't so bad. Lewis had vanished, once again, as quickly as he had appeared. I didn't get much sleep that night, wondering about my mother-in-law's bathroom. Wait, that sounded crazy. No, I wondered what I would find in my mother-in-law's bathroom. No. That didn't sound good, either. I resigned myself to stop thinking about it and finally drifted off to sleep.

The next morning, my husband and I loaded up the kids and headed to Beaumont for our weekly Saturdays with the grandparents. My father-in-law usually cooked ribs and we would end up playing dominoes all day long.

As soon as we got there, we unloaded the car, and I ran as fast as I could into the house to inspect the bathroom. I don't exactly know what I was expecting to find. Everything was in its place. The room was clean.

Nothing seemed new to me. Then I looked up at the wall and saw a picture I hadn't noticed before.

It was a picture I had taken in Israel. I had blown it up and had it framed for my mother-in-law. It was a picture of the Sea of Galilee as the sun shone its rays over the Golan Heights. I had gotten up early the morning the photo was taken and climbed out on the window ledge of my hotel room to capture the moment. It was beautiful.

At the bottom of the photograph, I added a scripture. It was from Matthew 5:16, stating, "Let your light shine."

Then the Holy Spirit spoke. "This picture of the Sea of Galilee looks much like what the bronze laver would have looked like, doesn't it? And even though your mother-in-law could have placed this picture anywhere in the house, she chose it for the bathroom—the *lavatory*. The place where someone is washed clean. Do you think this is a coincidence? Now, go and look up what the word for hand mirror is in Hebrew."

Leaving the bathroom, I grabbed my phone from my purse and typed the word hand mirror into the Hebrew lexicon app. As I typed the last letter and pushed the search button, I thought, *How can this be*?

There, in the results column, was one word, *gillayon*. It meant *tablets* or *hand mirrors*. It was derived from the word *galah,* meaning to *uncover* and *make clear*, *roll away* and *reveal*.

The Holy Spirit said, "That looks an awful lot like the name *Galilee,* which comes from the word *galal,* meaning to *roll away* or *to turn*. Here are the two stones.

"Could it be that the Word, the Ten Commandments, the perfect foreshadowing of Christ, are the perfect hand mirrors to reflect on our previous behavior and bring us to a state of repentance? Could the continual reflection and rubbing of God's Word make it smooth and clear in our hearts, ultimately making us a perfect reflection of His love and His Son in our outward behavior?"

CHAPTER FIFTY-THREE

TABGHA

———◆———

I AWOKE early the following day. I hadn't been sleeping well because of so many crazy dreams. Not terrific dreams, but dreams that were making me feel uneasy, all the same.

Last night, I had a dream I was an elevator operator. Standing quietly in the corner, I greeted people as they tried to enter. The only thing was that the elevator had no walls or buttons to operate it. It only had a door and a floor. And the only direction it went was down.

As the doors opened, I saw the look in the eyes of the people trying to get on. They were scared. They didn't want to get on, even though I urged them to come in. I kept repeating the same thing over and over again. "You have to go down to go up. This is the first step." The people refused. They just kept jumping off into the void, bypassing the elevator altogether. I woke up feeling so sad. What could the dream mean?

Contemplating that very question, I decided to go and make a pot of coffee. It was 3:00a.m. Who makes a pot of coffee at 3:00a.m.? *Me, that's who.* It was one of many habits I took from my labor and delivery days. I worked the night shift and had to have some way to make it through the night without falling asleep. I helped to deliver women while the rest of the world slept. I had to be on my game.

With the coffee pot finally in process, I opened the cabinet directly in front of me. I grabbed a random cup from the hundreds accumulated over the years. There were some given by grateful patients. Others had been hastily purchased at costly souvenir shops. And some, that frankly, had mysteriously found their way into my cabinet.

I poured myself a cup and walked into the living room. The lights were off. The silence in the house was almost deafening. I went to the end table at the corner of the couch and tugged on the lamp. As I adjusted my eyes to it, I recognized Lewis sitting quietly on my couch.

"Hello," he said. "I like your coffee cup," pointing to the one in my hand.

Pulling the cup up to take a better look at the one I had grabbed, I noticed it was the one I had picked up in Israel. Perhaps the randomness of my choice hadn't been so random after all. The cup had an image of the famous mosaic of two fishes and five loaves of bread found embedded in the pavement at the Church of the Multiplication, built near the edge of the Sea of Galilee.

"Do you remember where you got that?"

"Of course, Lewis. I got it at the gift shop near the Church of the Multiplication. It was where Jesus fed the multitude with what seemed like only a small portion."

"Yes. And it is also the place, recognized by the church, where Jesus confronted Peter and gave him instructions for shepherding His followers. Remember, He asked Peter three times if he loved Him after he had first denied Him three times. Both of those testing grounds were in sheepfolds—an open enclosure with four walls (the High Priest's house) and the open pasture on the side of a mountain where shepherds fed their flock (the place for the feeding of the five thousand).

"With every affirmation Peter professed, Jesus gave him instruction—to feed His lambs, take care of His sheep, and then finally, feed His sheep.

"This place, where Jesus gave these instructions, was given its name for a reason. He wanted Peter to reflect on the feeding of the five thousand. He wanted Peter to remember everything Jesus had taught him. To learn from His sufferings, His crucifixion, death, and resurrection. And share his own testimony about what Christ had done for him because that would help feed the crowd.

"Jesus wanted Peter to tell the people that He is the God of Second Chances. That He not only fulfilled the first Passover but the Second, as well. He came to save the tribes of Rachel and Leah, the strong and the weary, providing for and feeding them both.

"Peter had a testimony that could draw others to the Lord. He had a testimony that could encourage, feed, and preserve. A testimony of truth and light that could nourish."

"Lewis, sometimes that light and truth didn't look so pretty."

"That's right, and it wasn't meant to. People have forgotten that words of compassion, mercy, encouragement and love are meant to edify and build up. It is an edifying and building up that lead to truth. And edifying and building up never included trivializing and diminishing the unholiness of sin.

"Man's vision and understanding have always been so short-sighted. There are no excuses for sin. The way, the truth, and the life include recognizing the 'sin' in the sinner, humbling oneself by acknowledging the accountability of sin, and then turning from it. This is repentance.

"Sometimes, testimony isn't pretty. But what is beautiful and marvelous is the change occurring in a person who has received the gift of Jesus Christ in their lives. The beauty from the ashes is the testimony of it. That is what you are doing, testifying to everything you have seen and heard. You are still working the night shift, helping others be delivered, no longer as a labor and delivery nurse, but as a doula—a bond-servant to the Lord.

"That dream you had tonight was an important one. The elevator's descent represents men's need to sink down, be still, be steeped and immersed in humility and submission to the will of God, so they can overflow with the Holy Spirit.

"Unfortunately, so many people refuse to go there. They get on the elevator, but when they realize it is going down, they change their mind, acting like someone who forgot what floor they were going to. And once realizing it, take every measure necessary to find another elevator to jump onto. They would rather go their own way than God's.

"Now. I want you to look at your cup again. And instead of looking at the cup, look at its handle."

Taking the last sip of coffee at the bottom of the cup, I turned it around so I could see. Written in small lettering was the word *Tabgha*. I read it out loud. I repeated it, and then once more, letting the letters roll off my tongue for good measure. Lewis listened intently as the word enveloped the air in the space between us and said, "Do you know what *Tabgha* means?"

"No, Lewis."

"It means Seven Springs."

"Like springs of living water, Lewis?"

"Yes. And the number seven in Hebrew symbolizes completion and rest. It is like a chord of recognition connecting everything back to its origin. It's between the end of something and the beginning of something new, just like the seventh day of the week. It is a remembrance that everything that is or was always leads back to the Lord."

"Very interesting," I said, not knowing what else to say.

"There is also something hidden here for you."

"What's that, Lewis?"

"The name *Tabgha* sounds an awful lot like *Tabitha*, doesn't it? But that isn't all. The Hebrew word for cord, *tabothah*, also sounds a lot like it. A place named after a gathering cord of repentance, redemption, and the fulfillment of God's promise of mercy and second chances. You probably don't know this, but *Tabgha* wasn't mentioned in the Bible by name as the place for the Multiplication of fishes and loaves, nor Jesus' last physical encounter with Peter. Other men in history named it to be revealed to you. Another cord that is connecting you back to your God-given purpose."

Instead of getting up to leave, Lewis reached into his pocket.

CHAPTER FIFTY-FOUR

THE URIM AND THUMMIM

"I BROUGHT you something."

"You've brought me a lot, Lewis." That was an understatement.

"I know. We are almost at the end and at the start of a new beginning, so I brought you some more pictures to look at."

"More pictures!"

"Yep," he exclaimed as he pulled out another picture of two stones from his shirt pocket. One was black and rough, and the other white and smooth. The black stone had a rudimentary picture of a bull's head, and the white one, a mark like a giant "X" across its smooth surface.

"Do these stones represent Jesus, too?"

"Yes, they do. And like all the other stones in our conversations together, these stones are special. But something very different about these stones sets them apart from the others. They had unique names; one was called *Urim* and the other *Thummim*. Translated simply in Hebrew as *lights* and *perfections*.

"These stones were placed behind the breastplate of the Jewish High Priest of the Tabernacle and the Temple of the Lord. The stones were used to give guidance from God to the High Priest and the kings of Israel. Anytime there was a question about hidden truths in any given situation needing to be uncovered so that righteous judgment could be meted out, these two stones (or lots) were cast to reveal them.

"Interestingly, the word for *to cast* (as in stones) or to bring insight was the Hebrew word *yarah*—a word that looks remarkably like the word *yireh*, meaning *to see*. Remember, this is the same word used in the name for *Jehovah Yireh,* as in *God Will See to It*.

"The Israelites considered these stones God's divine provision because He saw to it that they were the vehicle of truth and righteous judgment.

"The special markings on these two stones were significant. They represented the first and last letters of the Hebrew alphabet—the *aleph* and the *tav*—implying that God's Word brought truth and righteous judgment.

"Not only that, but the markings crudely represented a sacrifice (the bull's head) on a cross (the X) because before the Hebrew alphabet was what it is today, letters were pictures of animals and objects. The letter *aleph* was the picture of a bull's head, and the *tav* was represented as a cross. A sacrifice on a cross? It sounds like Jesus, doesn't it?"

"Okay," I said. *And?*

"I can tell by the look on your face you are wondering what this has to do with you. Do not worry. I am about to tell you.

"In *Ezra-Nehemiah* in the Bible, a group of people could not authenticate their genealogy to be priests. They couldn't eat any sacred food nor perform any of their duties until a High Priest came ministering with the *Urim* and the *Thummim*. The priests couldn't be who they were supposed to be before God until then. Who do you suppose the High Priest is?"

"Jesus Christ, Lewis?"

"Yes. Jesus brought back the true holy priesthood. He was the only one who could bring perfect enlightenment, righteous judgment, and truth to God's Word—because He was God's Word.

"As Jesus made His triumphal return, He even proclaimed this. When the people were rejoicing and throwing their cloaks on the ground before His entrance to the city, the teachers of the law and religious leaders rebuked Jesus. They told Him to urge the crowd to stop echoing that he was the Messiah. Do you remember what Jesus said to those in authority?"

"Jesus said if the people stopped proclaiming it, then the stones would cry out," I replied.

"Exactly. Could He have meant *The Urim* and *The Thummim*? Another reflection of the Ten Commandments and God's perfect provision? He was the High Priest, bringing God's perfect Word—Himself."

"He was bringing an atonement, a reconciliation, and a relationship to the true understanding of love and righteous judgment that humanity could never provide for themselves. He was bringing a day of redemption and atonement for all nations. His *Yom Kippur.* Do you know what that means?"

"*Yom Kippur*? Isn't that the day the High Priest could go into the Holy of Holies and make atonement for the nation of Israel for their sins? It means *The Day of Atonement.*"

"Yes, but there is more to it than that. Written in Hebrew, it can literally be read as *A Day Like Purim.* And *Purim* celebrates a day of salvation in the history of the Jewish nation through the actions taken by one person who obeyed the Lord and walked in God's will, sacrificing themselves for the freedom of the collective whole.

"*Purim* means *lots* and refers to the stones cast to determine the day set for the annihilation of the Jews. That day was changed from a day of mourning to one of rejoicing, just like the day Jesus brought us through His own death and resurrection. He metaphorically took the *Urim* and *Thummim* (Himself) into the Holy of Holies. And even though they cast a light on our guilt, Jesus took it upon Himself, without regard to His own personal interests, to free us from the chains of sin.

"He turned *The Day of Atonement* into *A Day Like Purim* through circumstances that were divinely ordered by a loving and just God. Beauty for ashes, a wedding garment for graves' clothes. This was always how it was meant to play out."

I had never thought of it like that before.

"Okay. But again, Lewis, what does all of this have to do with me?"

"You are another one calling in the desert, proclaiming the High Priest's return with the true light and perfection of the Word so that the Jewish nation may see, turn, be healed, and take their rightful place in the holy priesthood. They have and will always be God's chosen people."

"Lewis, you are saying this word about the two stones will reveal the truth of Jesus Christ as the Messiah to the Jewish nation, and they will receive it?"

"Some will, yes. Did you know, in Jewish scholarship, a word from the *Tanakh* (The Hebrew Bible) is read every day, not just on the Sabbath? Some verses are read from the Torah, and others from the Psalms.

"On your birthday, May 30, 1975, here in the U.S., there were readings from *Numbers* and the *Psalms*. That day, Psalms 97-103 were read. Let's talk about a couple of them, starting in Psalm 97:1:

> *When the Lord will reveal His kingship, the earth will exult: the multitudes of the islands will rejoice.*

Psalm 98:2:
> *The Lord has made known His salvation; He has revealed His justice before the eyes of the nations.*

Psalm 99:1-3
> *When the Lord reveals His kingship; the nations will tremble, the earth will quake before Him; Who is enthroned upon the cherubim, before the Lord, who is in Zion, who is great and exalted above all the peoples. They will extol Your name, which is great, awesome and holy.*

Psalm 102:14-15
> *You will arise and have mercy on Zion, for it is a time to show her favor; the appointed time has come. For your servants cherish her stones, and love her dust.*

"There are many scriptures in between that are just as powerful. But these are the ones I wanted to show you. This is what was proclaimed on the day you were born. You think this journey started only a handful of years ago, but as you can see, the Lord isn't so short-sighted.

"Just like John, you are in the desert, directing those that can hear, where they can find something to drink that will always satisfy—the water of salvation only Jesus can provide. The perfection of Ten Words that brought enlightenment and became flesh so that humanity could be saved."

CHAPTER FIFTY-FIVE

SHILOH

———◆———

"THERE IS also another account in the New Testament that many people haven't seen a deeper meaning in. And it is another confirmation of this word for you."

"Where, Lewis?"

"In Matthew 22, right after the parable of the wedding banquet. In Matthew 22:15, the Pharisees went out to trap Jesus in His words. They sent their disciples to Him to ask if it was right to pay tribute to Caesar, hoping that Jesus would incriminate Himself by rebelling against Roman authority. But Jesus knew what they were up to and asked to see the coin of tribute. They offered Him a *denarius*.

"A *denarius* was a Roman measure of value, but the word actually translates to *consisting of ten*. Jesus looked at it and then asked those disciples whose face and inscription appeared on the coin's imprint. The guys said it was Caesar's. Jesus then replied in Matthew 22:21:

> *Therefore render to Caesar the things that are Caesar's, and to God the things that are God's. (ESV)*

"That seemed to stump the boys, and they left. Jesus was saying so much more here, though. The word used in Greek for *things* can be translated to *dabar,* the very same term used in Hebrew meaning *word*.

"Could Jesus have been saying to give back what currency mattered to the Romans—that denarius, back to Caesar? And give those things that resemble the currency of God—the Ten Words and actions of Christ back to the Lord? Remember, *denarius* meant the number ten.

"Jesus was sly in His response, not only in that respect. In those days, Caesar was considered the champion of the Roman republic. He deified himself, considering himself a god. Jesus very carefully insinuated that Caesar was no god at all by making the distinction between giving back to Caesar what he was owed and giving back to God what He was.

"Did you know that there is a Messianic name spoken of in scripture that speaks to this as well? You can find it in Genesis 49:10-11.

> *The scepter will not depart from Judah, nor the ruler's staff from between his feet,*
> *Until Shiloh comes, And to him shall be the obedience of the peoples. He ties his foal to the vine, And his donkey's colt to the choice vine; He washes his garments in wine, And his robes in the blood of grapes.*

"The name, *Shiloh,* in Hebrew means, *he whose it is* or *to him whom tribute belongs.* Could it be that Jesus was telling those disciples that He was *Shiloh*?

"The Hebrew word that makes up the name *Shiloh* is taken from the Hebrew word *shel,* meaning *whose, whom, who, which,* and *that.* It is the short form of another Hebrew word spelled exactly like *asher,* meaning *upright, straight,* and *level.* And it is this word that resembles another word in the Hebrew—the word *eser,* meaning *ten.* Because when two hands (with ten fingers) are filled, they are considered even, straight, and level—like two sides of a scale.

"And *eser* is the same word used for the word for *tithe* or *to give tribute.* This whole discourse revealed so much more than mankind thought—that Jesus is the perfect, physical embodiment of the Ten Commandments, the two stones, The Son of God with Us, The Tithe of Mankind, and is To Whom all Tribute Belongs.

"The disciples of the Pharisees didn't catch on to this little nugget and just went their way. Instead of Jesus getting trapped by their words, Jesus stumped them with His, showing everyone who the true Champion of the people was, and to whom all tribute was due. And it wasn't Caesar!"

CHAPTER FIFTY-SIX

THE CHAMPION

—◆—

MY MOUTH was dry. I needed a drink. Suddenly, I was so thirsty my tongue seemed velcroed to the roof of my mouth. I stepped into the kitchen, Lewis following not far behind. I offered him a drink, but he declined. The man was never thirsty. Glancing at the clock on the stove, I noticed the time. It was 5:00 p.m. which was quitting time, and my husband would be coming home from work soon. I poured myself a glass of water from the tap.

"We're not done for the day, Lewis?" The question was more of a statement than a search for an answer. The man wouldn't have followed me into the kitchen if we were done. If he had been, he would've just disappeared like he usually did.

"No, we are not. Before I go, I want to talk to you about one more thing." Taking his time to get started, he waited patiently for me to find a seat at one of the barstools and finish my drink.

"We have talked about so much, but I wonder if you remember what started our meetings together in the first place."

"Of course I do, Lewis. We started talking after I was delivered. As I recall, I was actually in a coma at the time. You came to me, and we started talking about the two stones and how they foreshadowed Jesus Christ in the Bible." Eyeing him, I gave his shoulder a nudge before saying, "Pretty good for a girl in a coma, huh?"

"Yes, it is. But do you remember what the first two stones were?"

"The word for a pottery wheel and birth stool. *Ha-a-be-nayim.* It means the two stones."

"That's right. And remember when I told you that God was working on you on that wheel? Well, the actual word used in the passage is the word *melakah*. It means a *piece of workmanship, deputyship,* or *ministry*. It is derived from the same root as the word *malak*, which means *ambassador, messenger,* or *angel*. He is working on His ambassadors.

"Every human being that has ever lived, He has had on that wheel. We are all messengers, conveyers of His will, whether we do so willingly or not. Imagine, if you can, every person that's ever been made or will be made has played a part or will have a part to play in His intricate design. This is His process. You have all been in His grip on that wheel, whether you knew it or not.

"The *pottery wheel* molds man into the life God created him to live for—standing firmly on the two stones, the *birth stool*, His perfect moral principles, to bear the load in every trial he goes through. This helps him endure it and brings him into a closer relationship with God."

"Wait a minute, Lewis. It sounds like you are saying we don't have a choice in what part we play."

"That's not what I'm saying at all. You have a choice. He shows the way to know Him, experience Him, dwell with Him, and submit to the grip He was always meant to have on our lives. He wants us to love that grip because we are His possession. He does not force anyone into a covenant-love relationship. You get the choice.

"You can choose His grip and walk in it, or you can choose to walk away from His hold on your life and take your lives into your own hands. But don't think for one minute, if you choose your own way, that He isn't still in control of the ultimate outcome and fulfillment of His will.

"God is the Potter, and the Deliverer, Jesus Christ, His Son, is His instrument in accomplishing the work of His hands. When Jesus became flesh, took our sin to Himself, died, and was resurrected from the dead, He made everyone an heir to God's throne if they repent and accept Him as Lord."

"You're saying all of mankind has a part to play in history, whether we know it or not?"

"Yes. You are all vessels and messengers. You just get to choose what type of vessel you want to be. Friend or enemy. God will use each vessel, in time, whether friend or foe, in the fulfillment of His will.

"Throughout the Bible, God used people all the time who had no relationship with Him to accomplish His will. They were just as much His vessels as the saints. They chose their own way. They may have walked in their own desire and power, but they always worked in God's design, even when they couldn't see it. From Adam to Caiphus, from Eve to Cyrus, God's will was always accomplished, even when it seemed as though evil was flourishing in the world. And our Champion, Jesus Christ, has been there for every part."

"Okay, Lewis. Then why are we revisiting the pottery wheel and the birth stool? There has to be a reason."

"It's because it looks very similar to another word. It is the word *hab-be-nayim*. It looks a lot like *ha-a-be-nayim*, the words meaning 'the two stones.' It appears in the story of David and Goliath, in the valley of Elah."

"What does it mean?"

"It is the word for a *champion*, but it literally means *the space between two armies*. In scripture, the word describes Goliath, not David. He was the Philistines' champion.

"Could it be that Goliath represented the Philistines' moral principles, religious and wisdom traditions—*their own two stones*? And God chose Goliath to reveal His own chosen instrument, *His two stones*—His Word, moral principles, and wisdom traditions through David, whose very name means love?

"David, then acting as Israel's champion, revealed not only the idolatry of the Philistines, but Israel's as well—in that, believing in a false faith, and not holding onto their very own was really one in the same. Remember, the Israelites felt like their God just wasn't big enough. That's how little David ended up on the battlefield in the first place.

"Jesus Christ, our Champion, is in that space between, the space where discernment and understanding help us choose to love, live, think and act the right way. He is there encouraging us to believe that His way, wisdom, and principles are strong enough to take on any giant.

"He stands in between two armies. He takes no sides. And that's right where He should be because Jesus never came to take sides but to take over. Remember when Joshua asked the Commander of the Lord's Army whose side He was on, Israel's or their adversaries? The Lord simply said, 'No.' God, Himself, confirms He is no respecter of persons, but delights in those who fear Him, and obey Him whomever they might be. To some, that comes easily; to some, a little harder; and to some, not at all.

"The Lord became flesh, in Jesus Christ, to show us these things and receive His free gift of salvation. He communed with the rebellious and the repentant, offering salvation to both, desiring that no one should perish. He is in the space between them, just as He appeared between them on the cross at Calvary.

"This is important for you to understand. You were not chosen to deliver this word because of anything you have done. You didn't deserve it or work for it. You are a sinner. You have been given grace, an unmerited favor, that has been offered to all people. You can choose to share this word or not. And if you don't, God will choose someone else who will. They won't have deserved it or worked for it, either."

"Lewis, so then why me, and why now?"

"Because God desires it so. If you want to know why now, I cannot say. But if you really want to know 'Why you?' I will tell you. Sit down."

CHAPTER FIFTY-SEVEN

A HEART OF FLESH

———◆———

SO I sat, not daring to take my eyes off him, waiting for some profound secret I'd been waiting for what seemed like a lifetime to hear. I was feeling nauseous, and my stomach—a hurricane of mixed emotions—was churning what little breakfast I had held down that morning. My skin was standing at full attention.

"Because you asked Him," Lewis finally declared. "You surrendered your heart to Him. You asked for His will to be done in your life. You stayed in an embracing pursuit of Him. Like Moses. Like Elijah. Like John. You asked Him to keep you in the center of His will. You asked for a deeper relationship with Him, didn't you?"

"Yes," I whispered.

"God put this word in your heart, through the Holy Spirit, to share with the world. He took your heart of stone and changed it to a heart of flesh. He made it soft and malleable so that through you, people might see—both Jew and Gentile. You asked for a double portion, didn't you?"

"Yes, Lewis."

"Well, He answered your prayers and then some. It's no coincidence this word has been about two stones. When you went to Israel and called out over the Galilee for Jesus to come to you, a man named Eli gave you two stones in your hand—a stone with a cross attached to it. Did you think that was a coincidence?" I just shook my head.

"And when you went to place your supplications at the Western Wall, what was your prayer?"

"Lewis, I prayed for the health of my family, and I prayed for the abomination of desolation to be struck down."

"At the time, what did you think this abomination of desolation was?"

"Well, honestly, at the time, I thought it was The Dome of the Rock."

"You must know that is not what God was talking about, per se."

"Well, I know there have been many abominations set up in the Temple throughout history; all put there to desecrate the God of Israel's altar and dwelling place. Baal idols. Asherah poles. A statue of Zeus. The exchange of the Jewish Temple sacrifice for pagan ones. They all found their way into the Temple. If it isn't the Dome of the Rock, Lewis, then what is it?"

"Embracing idolatry in any form and denying a meaningful relationship with the Trinity. It speaks to God's chosen people foremost. Jew and Gentile. God's creation has always chosen to hold on to what was tangible, to worship two stones instead of God, Himself.

"The tablets that carried the Word of God were more revered than the very wisdom they were supposed to impart. The *Urim* and *Thummim* were more revered than the righteous judgment and truth they provided. The Temple, more revered than the Lord who occupied it; the Brazen Serpent, more than its healing bite; Gideon's ephod, more than who truly brought the enemy's defeat; the ceremony and the sacrifice, more than the reason behind them.

"Mankind has never sought a meaningful relationship with God without some form of idolatry getting in the way. So, God gave them what their itching hands were asking for—their own king and separation between Him and them. He had them in His grip, and He let them go at their request, but He was still there, foreshadowing His presence and ultimate plan. Knowing all along, He would take their stony hearts and make them more malleable to His Word. He was going to make people cherish them in His time.

"God knew He would come in the flesh, to free His people, through Jesus Christ, His Son, and bring His Spirit to dwell in them. They would finally see that man-made objects, ceremonial exercises lacking true devotion, and earthly places where He no longer took up residence meant nothing to Him.

"It is a worshipping, repentant and obedient heart God desires. A true love for His Son's sacrifice He desires. It is a desperate pursuit of Him that He desires. God pursues you. Why wouldn't He want you to chase after Him? God has always sought the worship and covenant love that can only be accomplished by this type of relationship, and one that can only be embraced with a change of heart."

"Lewis, are you saying we are the abomination of desolation?"

"Yes."

"Then the Lord has never been talking about a certain object being the abomination, when He spoke through Daniel, and then again through John in Revelation?"

"Oh, no. He has also been talking about a certain object, just like those pagan tokens you mentioned earlier.

"You have to remember God's canvas is four-dimensional. He looks at things in ways we cannot. Biblical prophecy is usually fulfilled in cycles with a sort of preamble—a preliminary statement before the formal document manifests."

"Well then, what is the actual abomination of desolation, then, in my time?"

"You have seen it. You have touched it. You put your prayer request there."

Incredulously, I choked out, "You mean, The Wailing Wall?"

"Yes."

"You have to be joking, Lewis!"

"I am not joking at all. The Church and the Jewish people still have a wall up, don't they? How can they see *Moriah*, the place of provision, the place where God Saw to It, the place of His Love and the Great Exchange, with a huge wall blocking their view?"

"How can they see the son who was saved from the sacrifice, and God's own Son, given as a substitution, with their eyes still veiled? Many of them have come to worship that place, and the Temple Mount, the symbol of their struggle and their suffering, more than The One they built it for."

"Some people who profess Christ, and Jews alike, still don't see Jesus for who He is. That wall has become an idol, in some respect, just like so many other things that can occupy the place in our hearts where God should stand.

"So many people don't see Jesus as the fulfillment of scripture. They don't see Him as the perfect execution of God's love in the flesh and the consummation of their covenant through Abraham. But this word will help break down walls so people can see and hear in God's power and in His timing.

"God is fashioning a window to bring light into a very dark room, one that for so long had no doors and windows, to become a space with no walls. Make no mistake. Do not be confused. The Temple that will occupy the area on the Temple Mount is for *HaShem, Jehovah Jireh, El Shaddai.* You know this has been spoken about in scripture. Do you know where?"

"In the Bible, maybe?"

"Well, obviously. And I think it is appropriate you named this chapter what you did."

"What chapter are you talking about, Lewis?"

"The chapter in the book you are going to write."

"Well, are you going to help me out and tell me the name of this so-called book, or at the very least, what the chapter is going to be called?"

"No, but I can tell you that you get it from Ezekiel, chapter 11. And the very next chapter in that book foreshadows this time right now. Why don't you go and look it up for yourself?"

With that, he was gone.

It was way after five now, and my husband was coming home any minute. I ran to the Bible and began reading in Ezekiel. I got to Ezekiel 11:19 and started trembling.

> *I will give them an undivided heart and put a new spirit in them;*
> *I will remove from them their heart of stone and give them a heart*
> *of flesh.*

I started the chapter with Ezekiel being placed in front of the gate facing east and finished reading in chapter 12 as Ezekiel, during the day brought out the things he had packed for exile, and in the evening, dug through the wall as the Israelites watched, as a sign to them.

The Holy Spirit spoke to me and said, "Staci, if God's chosen people would prophetically be led away into captivity in this way, they would return in the same fashion, only to be held captive by the love of God and His Son, instead. So, start digging through the mortar, and let some light in. The way to the Temple Mount is not around the wall, but through it.

"If the *soreg* fell—the wall that separated the Gentiles from the Temple Mount—shouldn't the wall that separates the Jews from that very same spot fall as well? The Temple was meant for all nations. Not just Jew, not just Gentile."

CHAPTER FIFTY-EIGHT

THE HEAD-TURNER

"MAHER-SHALAL-Chash-Baz."

"What?"

"Maher-Shalal-Chash-Baz."

"Jason?"

Something had woken me up. Had my husband been talking in his sleep again? Turning over, I peered at the resting form lying beside me. I listened. Nothing. Jason was still chopping down a national forest in his sleep. No warbled utterances, just the occasional escaping gasp between thin, pursed lips. Repositioning myself in the bed, I closed my eyes again and tried to drift back to sleep.

"Get up, please. I need to talk to you."

Okay. I know that wasn't a dream. Shooting up in the bed, I sat for a moment, eyes still slammed shut, almost scared to see who was in my bedroom. Then I realized something. The voice was familiar. It could only be Lewis.

The clock on my nightstand screamed that it was 3:00 a.m. Turning to scan the bedroom, I noticed a man standing in the corner of the room.

"Lewis?"

"Yes, it's me. Can you get dressed and meet me outside?" Lewis said as he strode to the bedroom door.

"This can't wait for office hours, Lewis?" I griped.

"No. Meet me in the front yard in five minutes."

Grabbing some clothes still in a pile at the foot of my bed, I got dressed, hoping I had on something that matched as I walked outside.

Standing here, it was hard to believe somewhere else in the world people were already bustling around. Looking out at the lawn, Lewis was standing right in the middle of the grass, gazing up at the stars.

"This never gets old." He whispered, pointing up to the sky, "It's the picture of eternity."

"Yes. It is beautiful, Lewis. I guess that's why you wanted to talk to me now. If we waited until daylight, the stars wouldn't be visible."

"That's true."

"I am assuming you didn't come to talk to me about the constellations, did you, Lewis?"

"No. I came to talk to you about a name."

"Jesus?"

"No. It's the name, *Maher-Shalal-Chash-Baz.*"

"Who is that?"

"He was one of Isaiah's sons."

"What does that name mean, Lewis?"

"It literally means *Quick to the plunder, Swift to the spoil.*"

"Okay, so what is that supposed to mean?"

"This is difficult to understand because it has many different meanings all at once. There is one to be taken at face value, but there is an underlying subtext as well, just like every other name in the Bible. But for you, at this appointed time, it means *'Coming quickly' is a time for surrendering into captivity the wealth of the defeated. To make plain, a way, a hastening to make ripe the spoil, and a return to Him.*

"This is God with Us-*Immanuel.* Part of God's process is that He will allow a leading into captivity to bring about restoration, turning our heads back to what has true value, God Incarnate. It is in this name that ultimate victory is brought back to the house of David."

"Lewis, I thought the son's name was *Maher-Shalal-Chash-Baz.* You are saying his name was *Immanuel.*"

"Yes. It was spoken as a prophetic word in a time of distress for Israel. They were about to be led away as captives, but it wouldn't be the end of the story. Isaiah was proclaiming Israel's eventual restoration through the names of his sons. He was proclaiming a transformation of a nation who were led away, taken captive not only by Assyria but by the rampant idolatry that left a pervasive stain in the land and in the hearts of his countrymen.

"God allowed Isaiah to recognize that Israel would be lost and scattered to the wind because of their own rejection of the Lord. But Isaiah also saw a much bigger picture through God's eyes.

"Isaiah saw that even through men's corruption and rejection of God, He would still transform it into glory, purification, and fruitfulness. Israel would become the spoil, but in the end, they would be taking the plunder, and broadening their tent, on the way out.

"Don't we find this in the life, death and resurrection of Jesus Christ, God's Son? Jesus was dispossessed by the Jewish people, so He could bring a double portion, an abundant harvest, and hope enough for the whole world.

"This is why Jesus so perfectly pointed out salvation came from the Jews. It was true just as much in the Old Testament as it is in the New. This is how Isaiah's progeny became a sign to Israel. These names pointed to Christ, God with Us. He would be *Maher-Shalal-Chash-Baz*, as the spoil. But in the end, Israel would see Him for who He truly is, and receive Him back from the Gentiles, *Immanuel*, bringing a plunder, and holy remnant much bigger than they could have ever imagined. And incidentally, the meaning of Isaiah's other son's name—*Shear Jashub*—means *A Remnant Shall Return.*

"Another interpretation of this name, *Maher-Shalal-Chash-Baz*, is *Esteeming lightly God's order, One He so generously brings to instruct and teach us, hastens the rub, the rebuke, the revelation, and the return.*"

"People fail to realize that everything in God's divine order benefits us. Humanity's need for instant gratification has never been able to comprehend that. It is only as we let go that we realize the only value in a set of circumstances can only be truly measured by an unchanging and just God. And that's the way we should want it, right? The whole universe being ordered, arranged, and known by the author who sits above it?"

Lewis pointed to the stars and said, "Can you try to connect the dots in the sky, starting from the first star to ever bring light until now?"

"Lewis, that's impossible."

"No, it's not. Not for God. Did you know one little line from one dot to the next in the vastness of space is the story of your life and His order for it if you choose to walk in it? Your life can be one little line that helps to connect the dots. It doesn't seem so big compared to the whole of the universe, but to God, it holds immense value, one you could never fully comprehend. This is His love carefully concealed, that when exposed, reveals His presence and glorifies the only one it should: Him.

"It is a love that clearly can be seen by those who seek Him, through Jesus Christ, The Messiah, The Word, and the only way to the Father. He acts as the Head-Turner, through us; through our lives, through our brokenness, our restoration, and our witness to His love for us. He is constantly with us, even when we go into captivity. And He will always be there to loosen the chains that bind us there and lead us out if we let Him."

I looked up at the stars again, seeing eternity for the first time in my life.

CHAPTER FIFTY-NINE

TRUE TREASURE

—◆—

Journal Entry #400

THERE IS nothing more frustrating than looking for something and not being able to find it. It could be your car keys, your phone, or the partner to the sock you've already committed to wearing. It brings a most exasperating feeling when you find what you have been searching for the last hour, right in front of your face; hiding in plain sight, eyes quickly unveiled to the misplaced token. A small treasure found, feeling like you've just hit the lottery.

In a very busy life, things often go missing: love, fellowship, time, those things that truly enrich our lives with meaning and purpose. Now purpose—that's a powerful word. It builds. It sustains. It endures. Its design is the process of a just, unchanging, and merciful God. Often ignored is God's plan for our lives, our egos choosing instead to live from a treasury filled to overflowing with our own interests.

This is a storehouse that will never be filled, never quite sustain, and more often than not, leave the owner wanting—well, just more. Only a proud heart could contrive to ever believe the desires and longings of a mere mortal could ever be the better alternative. The love, however, given by our Heavenly Father, gives us the choice of one. You see, He wants a love freely offered, rather than one begrudgingly given.

The true treasure we can take from this life can be found if we remember God has impeccable timing and His ways are so much higher than ours. He wants us to come to that conclusion, at least. Always giving us the free will to do so. He wants us to see His joy as our joy. His delight is our delight. To know that His plans were always meant to prosper us, no matter what the devil has in mind.

In a fallen world where the devil is the morning star, the selfish desires of this life can shine so much brighter than living a life of love, contrition, humility, and service. How can the purposes of God compete with the dazzling, blinding lights of the enemy?

The answer is—God doesn't compete. He is God. The devil has already lost; he just doesn't know it yet. Think of God as the universe's best chess player. His moves are carefully laid out before the beginning of time. For every one of the devil's moves, God has a perfectly calculated countermove. Every opportunity the accuser takes to destroy, God uses to lift up if we walk by faith. The devil only sees the destruction of the sinner, but God sees the possibility in the worst of sinners. This is His love for us.

Those seasons of adversity that put chips in our vessels, here on earth, where the adversary has a momentary monopoly; God uses for change, growth, and a time for drawing nearer to His children, which in turn, creates a longing for intimacy. You see, relationships are always deepened and strengthened when sought. People have somehow forgotten that.

God loves us so much that He allows a binding, rubbing, pressing, stretching, and loosening; a letting us go so that we seek Him, long for Him, chase Him, search for a treasure that ultimately brings glory to His name, so that when found in Christ, lasts an eternity.

CHAPTER SIXTY

THE FIRST OF TEVET

I WAS starting to think I had missed the mark in some way. Had I turned to the right or to the left? I thought I had my eyes firmly set in the middle of the path, but I hadn't seen Lewis in a while. Spending hours in the Word and in prayer, I felt closed off from my family. They had become irritated that I was so devoted to God.

"You are spending too much time on this," my family constantly told me. All I could think about was what Lewis said. I needed to finish this, whatever this was. I didn't want to talk about anything else but Jesus. He consumed my thoughts, my sleep, and my wakefulness.

Sure, I did things that were expected of me. I picked the kids up from school, helped them with their homework, and spent time with my husband, but in the back of my mind, Jesus had usurped the space once occupied by frivolous things.

I had fallen in love with Him. He had painstakingly rubbed His mark clear across my soul. There wasn't a space left that hadn't been touched by Him. I started seeing Him everywhere, touching every part of my life, filling all those chinks in my armor with the precious metal of His love. He was my addiction, a high I couldn't shake; a feeling, quite frankly, I never wanted to end.

I was still reading the Word and spending time in worship and prayer. So where, in crying out loud, was Lewis?

One night after church, I went home, crawled into my bed, and actually prayed to see him again. I missed the guy. I opened my Bible and started to read from Esther, feeling like I related to her in some way. Lewis had spent years drilling into my heart and head that I was chosen for this appointed season, just like Esther had been so long ago.

A knock at the door jarred me back to the present. Opening it, I found Lewis standing there. "You missed me?"

"Yes, I did, Lewis." Then, smiling, I moved out of the way so he could come in.

Eyeing the Bible lying open to Esther on the bed, he said, "You know this is the only book in the Bible that never mentions God's name. He is there between every line, though. It is a book about doing what's right in God's will and timing. And poetically reveals there truly is a season for every person's purpose under heaven. Every manifested circumstance has one hidden underneath. Every moment has borders that connect it to another one, and on and on. It's really quite beautiful if you think about it.

"Esther was at the right place, at the right time, doing the right thing. Every exquisite moment marked by God, on an elevated track, fixed, with a specific destination in mind.

"All of mankind are types of Esther, Staci. Or at least, they can be. Each person has a purpose and time under heaven waiting to be illuminated to expose Jesus Christ in them and in the world around them.

"You have honestly still been questioning this?" he asked, raising a brow.

"Well, yes, Lewis. I thought maybe I missed it. Maybe I hadn't hit the target. I haven't seen you in such a long time."

"I have been here. And I have come to tell you something. You are on the right track to fulfilling your destiny. The Lord heard your call and wanted you to know that today is a very special day. God is calling you into His presence. It is the first of Tevet."

Pointing to the book I was reading, Lewis continued, "In the book of Esther, it was the day Esther was called to the palace. She spent one year getting ready to see him. She spent twelve months being beautified before she could. This is what this time has been for you.

"You have been undergoing your beautification to become a beautifier of His Word. You have spent every moment up until now being rubbed with oil, salt, light, affliction, sorrow, repentance, joy and grace to prepare you for who God has destined you to be. He has been next to you through it all.

"God has been transforming the description of your personal qualities to be so closely associated with His that the mere mention of your name calls Jesus to mind. Isn't this who God calls us all to be? This was Esther. Her name means *star*. She was the reflection of Christ, shining a light in a dark place. And today is the day!"

"The day for what, Lewis?"

"The day He has called you up."

"But what does that have to do with today?"

"What is the date today?"

"Um. I really don't know. Let me look." Running to get my phone, I looked at the date. It was December 9, 2018. Going back to the bedroom, I told Lewis as much, not recognizing the date as one of any significance.

Lewis looked straight at me and said, "Yes, today is December 9th, 2018, but it is also a special day for the Jewish people. It is literally the first of Tevet."

No way. I sat there in wonder for a long time and couldn't speak. I couldn't do anything but sit down on the bed and cry.

CHAPTER SIXTY-ONE

THE WHETSTONE

"WHY ARE you crying?" Lewis whispered.

"You have said I have this big calling. It is hard for me to wrap my head around. My tears are filled with reverence, and frankly, a little fear. I don't want to mess up."

"The wonderful majesty of Almighty God should provoke those feelings in every single one of His people. He has given you the heavy weight of His glory so others can see what His power can bring through mortal man. He doesn't want you to mess up, either," Lewis encouraged.

"But if you do, it's not like failing a test. He'll keep bringing it to you until you pass. He always allows a do-over. Remember, He is the God of Second Chances. God is and has always been in your corner. And He had already marked you for salvation when you gave your heart to Him. There is no going back from that, but there are still growing pains to encounter, convictions to experience, confessions to give, and grateful hearts to be offered.

"The tears are evidence of God engraving Himself on your heart because that's just what He does. He cuts to the heart of those who love Him to leave an extension of Himself. It's an impression that won't fade or be worn away with time but will be made more apparent every day in your walk with Him.

"You know, there is another stone I want to talk to you about today that kind of deals with this very topic. It is called a whetstone."

"A whetstone?"

"Yes. You would think by its name this stone would be full of moisture, but this *whet* means to sharpen or make keen."

"So, Jesus is the whetstone?" I asked.

"No, not exactly."

"Then who is, Lewis?"

"Everyone who belongs to Him. Elijah was a whetstone in the Old Testament, just as John the Baptist was one in the New Testament. They both called people to repentance. And that is what you are all called to do. You are a whetstone encouraging others to accept Jesus as their Savior and their Lord.

"Everyone has a part to play, their own grateful tears to cry, their own hearts to give, their own testimonies to declare, and their own God-willed purposes to fulfill. Your purpose has been wrapped up in this book and what will come from it. They are the perfect marks in life, moments captured with utter precision to reveal God and His love.

"This book is a watercolor of His glory in your life. It will be written to encourage others to find their way back to the Bible, prayer, and a relationship with Jesus Christ and the Holy Spirit.

"God wants people to stop hiding behind walls that separate them from His love. From the beginning, mankind has always wanted God at arm's length, elevated and hidden from them, but this is never what God wanted. He wanted to walk in the garden with them, in the cool of the day.

"God wants man to accept His authority and let go of their own. He wants man to willingly obey Him and worship Him openly. But that's not what man wanted, so He became a love carefully concealed to bring revelation. Every memorial stone in every field, in every home, in every mill, in every press, in every fortified tower, in every wall, in the Temple, in the Ark, and on the altar, He walked with them, however obscured. But God changed all that when He brought Himself down in the flesh, through Christ, to find a way into their hearts, to be concealed there, instead."

CHAPTER SIXTY-TWO

THE TOUCHSTONE

"DO YOU remember the five-minute sermon you gave on the Sea of Galilee?"

"How could I forget, Lewis? It was probably one of the best moments of my life."

"Did you prepare for it?"

"You know I didn't."

"Out of all the amazing testimonies and miracles surrounding that area, why do you think you picked the account that you did?"

"The Holy Spirit?"

"Yes, and it was a powerful five-minute sermon about two men in chains from *Gadarenes*, both living in the tombs, possessed by demons, and begging the Lord not to torture them. They demanded to be cast into a herd of pigs instead of remaining in the sheepfold. That's what *Gadarenes* means—*sheepfold*.

"The word used in this scripture, in the Greek, for torture is the word *bastanizo*. It comes from the word *basanos,* which means *touchstone.* Do you know what a touchstone is?"

"No, Lewis, but I have a feeling you are about to tell me."

"That's right, I am. A touchstone is a black silicon-based stone used to test the purity of precious metals like gold. For all intents and purposes, it was considered a testing stone because rubbing pure gold against its surface left a singular mark, proving its worth.

"Those spirits were clinging so tightly to those men it made them wholly unrecognizable, and they didn't want Jesus to rub them. It was because they knew they weren't walking in right standing with God. They were living in the flesh, and there was nothing precious about them.

"Those spirits knew they were fool's gold. And they wanted to continue doing what they wanted—filling themselves up and feeding their own appetites with depraved inclinations, marking themselves with the impurity only sin can leave, instead of being filled with the presence of God and the freedom and peace only His love can bring. They were more concerned with holding onto those things that could only satisfy for a moment.

"They knew Jesus was a game changer, a tester of their metal, and the gold standard. They only saw it as torture because they didn't want the change. They liked walking in their own will. Being foolish felt good. Who wanted to be considered precious? Certainly not them.

"Those spirits couldn't even accept Jesus' gentle approach. Did that which Jesus brought to them involve self-examination? Yes. But in the end, what was rubbed away would make those men, whole in their right minds, dressed in self-control, compassion, mercy and love.

"Don't you see? God allows the rub, desiring in us, to be proven pure when presented with the selfish desires and painful circumstances sure to come in the many seasons of this life. We have all kinds of days, and Jesus just wants to be Lord of all of them. It is the only way home.

"It should be apparent to you, by now, that God allows division, folding and separation in His ultimate plan for increase. This is seen throughout nature, is it not? This is the Lord's covenant love. It is not like the way we love. God's love has always involved compassion, grace, rebuke, chastisement, and discipline.

"And it is with a firm but gentle hand that he gives this love—never for His own benefit, but yours, as unpleasurable as it might feel sometimes. He loves without prejudice. God's justice is pure. He is the truest of all dividing lines. The Lord expects us to love others like this. He expects us to love without limits and without cutting or stabbing others with our words or deeds. But we are called to test their metal, too, just as we are called to learn to recognize the agony and pain in others, so we can rub them with the appropriate measure of firmness.

"We are to love people blindly, but not to lead them blindly. We are not to encourage them blindly, nor instruct them blindly. We are called to speak the truth covered in wisdom, instead of placing a weighted vest of cruelty on an already drowning man. We are here to rub each other in due measure to reveal God's love because restraining that touch to hide the light of the truth isn't love, either.

"There are so many people who misunderstand this part of it. They lead by cutting others down and call it righteous rebuke. Now, don't get me wrong, there are seasons when our rubbing will seem rougher than others. It will offend some, and the only way to discern those times is to check your heart, asking God for guidance as you are doing it, and examining the motivation behind it."

Lewis stopped talking. Did he expect me to add something here? I had nothing.

Then something sparked in me. "I just had a thought, Lewis."

"And that is?"

"You once said God's purpose for me started in a delivery room. I think I know what you mean by that, now.

"In labor and delivery, there are several instances where rubbing is involved, the kind of rubbing I think that you're talking about; the kind God expects to see in us.

"There are actually two deliveries in every labor process—the delivery of the baby, and the delivery of the placenta.

"In the past, after a woman delivered, I would take the baby from the doctor and place him on the mother's abdomen. The cord would then be cut and the baby would be handed to a nursery nurse.

"Most of the time, I would stay with the mother until the placenta was delivered because its own delivery can be a tricky thing. It must come out, and occasionally, it can become quite dangerous.

"As a baby's only lifeline in-utero, the placenta embeds into the uterine wall to provide the much-needed nutrients and oxygen the baby needs via the mother. When the placenta is delivered, it's like pulling a plug out of a well-crafted dam. All of these free-flowing blood vessels are left exposed and open, ready and willing to help a mother bleed out.

"Most of the time, the uterus contracts down around those vessels and keeps the mother from bleeding to death. However, sometimes the uterus doesn't respond as it should, and the nurse is called to roughly massage it to urge it to clamp down.

"This is never a process the mother enjoys because it's painful. In my experience, this always ended with her grabbing my wrists and begging me to stop, never understanding that she could die if I did. Only after I shared this information with her, would she bear the pain because she knew where my heart was coming from. The rub was never meant to torture her, but to save her life.

"If the mother was stable, and the placenta delivered without incident, I always turned my attention to help with the care of the baby. It usually didn't take long. It always started with rubbing the baby with a towel, vigorously drying him off, encouraging him to clear his throat, and take his first breath. Without the rub, the baby lacked initiative.

"Once the baby was stable, dried, and swaddled in baby blankets, he was handed back to the mother to initiate breastfeeding.

"Now, babies usually have a natural instinct to feed, but sometimes they need a little help. During those times, I put my gloved index finger in the baby's mouth and rubbed the roof of it to stimulate the suck reflex, encouraging the baby to take a drink. I don't know; when you said all that, it reminded me of the type of rubbing God prefers."

Lewis confirmed my thoughts. "I think that is precisely the rubbing God calls for. The Holy Spirit has spoken to you. Did you know the word for finger in Hebrew is *etsba,* and an anagram for the word *tseba,* meaning to *wet, dip, dye,* or *mark*? Maybe, to point out, perhaps? That's what fingers do. And this word looks a lot like the word *tsebi,* doesn't it?"

"That word looks familiar, Lewis."

"It should," he continued, "because it is the word for *gazelle.* It also means *to be beautiful* and *to shine.* To the Hebrews, pointing out something, thus making it clear, made the agents that brought such illumination and insight, beautiful and bright. Could it be that God has made you a beautifier of His Word, to point it out and rub others with the testimony He has given you?"

"I just thought of something else, Lewis. The baby, before he was handed over to the mother, was always swaddled. He was wrapped so tightly in blankets that it restricted his movements. You would think it made the baby irritable, but it soothed him."

I continued, "Scientists believe it's because being tightly bound reminds the baby of the intrauterine environment, another swaddling, of sorts. The uterus was a type of network of cords that bound the baby and protected him in love."

"It's very interesting that you say that because one of the Hebrew words for love and uterus is the same in the Hebrew language. The uterus is a type of cord of love in restraint. And isn't that what the Ten Commandments are? Cords of Love in Restraint? And Jesus, a Bond of Love in Restraint? So we were always meant to resemble Him, being cords of love in restraint ourselves.

"Your call has always been to point people towards Jesus and remind them God has always governed in the affairs of man, whether visible or unseen, even before the womb, and that He has always done that in love through His Son. People must see this love and realize it has two sides; the rub and the return. It is this duality that leads to reaction and revival. The time is now to remember that because there isn't much time left."

"That makes sense, Lewis."

"And now, I can reveal something else to you—the reason why you were given the scripture you woke up to so many years ago about preparing for the First and Second Passover.

"We know that God is the God of Second Chances, but time is running out. Jesus passed over once, and He is about to do it again soon. There won't be any second chances after that. This world has become an urn of desolation, filled with the dust and dregs of men's hearts. And it is about to be poured out. Something big is coming, and mankind needs to be ready for what follows.

"If you are willing to receive it, God has foreshadowed this very moment over thousands of years and how you were always meant to be a part of it."

"Okay, Lewis," I said with a sigh, not thinking my heart would be able to take any more of Lewis' surprises.

"There was a man who went to Israel a very long time ago. On the last Sabbath day that he was in Jerusalem, something was read. As you know, on the Sabbath, a part of the Torah is read. On that particular day, Deuteronomy 29:22-23 was read.

> ... *A stranger would come from a distant land, when they see the plagues of the land and the diseases, with which the Lord has afflicted it, will say, 'All its land is brimstone and salt, a burning waste, unsown and unproductive and no grass grows in it...'*

"This man went home and wrote a book that would be read all over the world speaking this truth. He wrote about Israel's desolation. And you will do the same—only you will speak to the desolation, wastes, plagues, and diseases that have afflicted the world and the church, making them both barren and unproductive.

"You see, you were at the Wailing Wall in Jerusalem on the last Sabbath day of your trip. It was September 16, 2017. You put your prayer in that wall, calling for the idolatry and desolation, with all its manifestations in the world, to fall so man could reflect God's abundance again without fully understanding the gravity of it.

"The day you were there, a reading from the Torah was also spoken. It was from Deuteronomy 29:22-23. Those were the exact words spoken one hundred and fifty years prior when it was spoken before another man appointed to tell his own story about the desolation he saw. And the man who wrote the book that would be read worldwide long before you were born—Mark Twain.

"He set sail on his journey June 8th, 1867, with no natural inclination that he was fulfilling Bible prophecy. He hadn't known at the time that he was part of something hidden and so much bigger than himself, and neither did you. This is true of everyone's story.

"Your story points out the desolation, but it also points to the hope and revival that can spring from it through Christ. Your story points to the fact that God knows every moment beforehand and that His timing is perfect in every instance to bring about something so much bigger, something so much more than anything we could ever desire—His Manifest Presence."

CHAPTER SIXTY-THREE

LOVE SO CAREFULLY REVEALED

"TABITHA, ARE you awake?"

I was staring at Tabitha again. Back in her cramped little office, I found myself waiting for something. Maybe I was waiting for her to fall out of her chair. Who knows? The tension in the room had her body pressed into the cluttered desk in front of her. Her eyes were closed, not daring to move a muscle since I asked her that question.

Honestly, I didn't think she knew what to say at this point. And I still had two more pictures to show her. I pulled out the first one and laid it gently on her desk as she opened her eyes.

"What's this?" She said as she leaned over the desk to get a better look. It was a list of Jewish holy days from this year.

"It is my confirmation that everything I've told you is the truth. This generation will not believe without signs and wonders. And they need to believe because we must prepare for something that is coming."

After glancing over the dates, she slid back in her chair, completely unimpressed. I think she was expecting me to call fire down from heaven or make it rain in her office. "These dates mean nothing to me," she boasted.

"I know, but they mean everything to me. You see, one day in June of this year, I was feeling really discouraged about the so-called book I was supposed to write.

"I was second-guessing everything God told me about it. I had written it, but I still found myself sitting in the shower, crying out to the Holy Spirit to show me that I wasn't crazy. He came into that place with me and said,

'There is no coincidence that you have been given this word at this time and in this season. Today is June 9ᵗʰ, 2019. And today is Shavuot (Pentecost), commemorating the deliverance of the two stones, the Ten Words—The Ten Commandments, from God to Moses on Mt. Sinai. This same season corresponds to the receiving of the Holy Spirit to the first Christians in Jerusalem.

"'When you get out of the shower, I want you to go and look up what day Shavuot fell on the year you were married.'"

Tabitha looked at me, wondering where in the world I was going with this.

"I finished my shower, got dressed, and went and laid down on my bed because the heat from the shower always exacerbated the arm and leg weakness I suffered from. I grabbed my cellphone and typed the words *Jewish Holy Days in the year 2008* into the internet search engine and waited. A list of sites emerged. I picked the first one on the list and clicked it open. My heart started to pound, and the hair on my arms proverbially rose." The list read:

> March 23: *Shushan Purim*
> May 19: *Sheni Pesach*
> May 23: *Lag be Omer*
> June 9-10: *Shavuot*
> October 9: *Yom Kippur*

Tabitha read them aloud and then looked up at me, completely unfazed.

"My heart pounded and the hair on my arms suddenly stood at attention. Not only because Shavuot fell on the same day of the year as this one, but because all of these other dates meant something to me specifically. Not that I knew it back in 2008 because some of them hadn't happened yet.

"March 23 is my daughter, Zoe's birthday, but she wasn't born until 2009. May 19 is the day my firstborn son made a public declaration of his faith, at the age of 18, with water baptism. May 23 is my husband Jason's birthday, and October 9ᵗʰ is my wedding anniversary. These days were appointed before I had a true relationship with the Lord, before my daughter was born, and before my firstborn expressed a token of his faith. And they all matched the dates of the Jewish holy days."

Tabitha looked at the dates and then, sounding unsure of the situation, said, "Okay. I must admit that *is* pretty interesting. Frankly, it is freaking me out a little. What do these dates have to do with this book?"

"Well, to start, every one of these holidays has something to do with two stones. March 23 was *Shushan Purim* and was the day Jerusalem celebrated *Purim*. *Purim* means 'lots' in Hebrew. They were two stones of decision and were considered, by the Jews, to be a mark of God's divine judgment. *Purim* celebrates the date of the casting of lots for the destruction of the Jews in Persia but used by God as a day of destruction for Israel's enemies instead. The two stones were the lots cast to pick the day. It was chosen as a day of destruction according to man but turned into a day of salvation by God.

"My daughter, Zoe's name means *God-driven life*. When we went to deliver her, we hadn't picked her name yet. While pacing in the waiting room, my mother-in-law found a book among the secular reading material. The book had a peculiar title: *Zoe: The God-Kind of Life* by Kenneth Hagin. She liked the name and gave it as a suggestion. I wasn't walking in step with the Lord at the time. I wasn't even going to church, but that name and day found its way into my story. So, on *Shushan Purim*, God brought to birth in me a God-driven life, whether I knew it or not."

I looked up to make sure Tabitha was still keeping up. I thought maybe she had dozed off, but to my surprise, she was hanging on to every word.

So I continued. "May 19, 2019, *Sheni Pesach*, was Second Passover. Remember the scripture about preparing for the First and Second Passover the Holy Spirit told me to read in a dream? That was long before the first fruit of my womb would be baptized as a token of his faith in Christ or before I started walking in step with the Lord myself. The Passover lamb was chosen by the casting of lots—two stones.

"In the Old Testament, Second Passover was the day Moses granted those traveling on a long journey, or in contact with a dead body to celebrate the Passover if they couldn't participate in the first one. It was a holiday of second chances. I think if I could sum up God's nature in just two words, it would be these—second chances. I think they define one of God's most basic character traits.

"The dream was telling me to prepare people for the God of Second Chances. His covenant cut and sealed with Jesus' blood, was First Passover and the Rehearsal Dinner. And the Second Passover to come, represents His Wedding Reception. The dream was telling me to declare that He came once in blood to redeem, and He is coming once more to reign, and it is soon approaching. A time was also coming when His nation of first fruit would recognize Jesus for who He is—the Messiah.

"May 23, *Lag be Omer*, is the commemoration of the 33rd day between Passover and Shavuot. It represents a time of eager anticipation between the redeeming work of Jesus at Calvary and the outpouring of the Holy Spirit at Shavuot. It fell on my husband's birthday.

"My husband's name is Jason. *Jason* is a Hellenized version of the name *Joshua or Yeshua—Jesus. Lag B' Omer* is the counting of the days from Passover to Shavuot. And the ultimate realization of Jesus' true value— His words and His promises in our lives, just like the weighing of two stones on a pair of scales. It is the only day during this time, in the practicing Jewish community, when there is dancing and joy. And the only day when weddings are encouraged to take place.

"June 9 was *Shavuot*, commemorating God bringing the two stone tablets to Sinai and the coming of the Holy Spirit at Pentecost. This day is special to me for a couple of reasons. It was my first day of work as a nurse practitioner, and it was also the day I started having symptoms of my MS. The day my birth pangs began, so to speak. June 9th marks the beginning of this voyage for me in returning to the Lord and bringing this message. It marks the day of *my* deliverance.

"October 9, *Yom Kippur*, was The Day of Atonement. It's considered, by the Jews, to be the day they are reconciled to God. This is my wedding anniversary. I got married on *Yom Kippur* in 2008. It was the day I married Jason. *Jesus.* And *Yom Kippur* commemorates the return of Moses with the second set of unbroken Ten Commandment tablets to the nation of Israel.

"I can tell you I didn't get married that day because it was the highest Jewish holy day of the year. You can ask any of my friends at the time; I was beyond prodigal. These dates can't be changed. It goes back thousands of years, but they are perfectly woven into this word and the story of my life. That is the power of God and how He works.

"And there is something else. Something even more powerful than this. Another confirmation of this word."

I looked at the dates once more. "These dates should mean something to you, too."

"Why would they mean something to me?" Tabitha asked, completely puzzled.

"These exact dates fall on the same Jewish holidays in another year that might be of interest to you. They appear again in the Gregorian year 2239 but in the Hebrew year 5999. The Jewish New Year starts on *Rosh Hashanah*, which falls in the Jewish month of *Tishri*. *Tishri* usually occurs during September and October on the Gregorian calendar.

"So, *Rosh Hashanah* or *Yom Teruah* (Feast of Trumpets) in September of the Gregorian year 2239, changes to the Jewish year 6000, making *Yom Kippur, The Day of Atonement*, in the Jewish year 6000, October 9. Remember, this is the day that commemorates the reconciliation between God and the Jewish nation."

Tabitha responded, "Didn't we already talk about this? How does it have anything to do with me?"

"According to Jewish tradition, the end of the age occurs in their 6000th year, ushering in the Messianic Era."

"Are you talking about the end of the world?"

"Well, more specifically, the end of this dispensation. And if you can receive it, this word doesn't reveal the day of the end of it. The date is just a confirmation that this word is supposed to help people prepare for their wedding day. It is a countdown. My actual wedding anniversary is 10-9-8. It would seem God isn't without a sense of humor and is meticulous to the last detail.

"This word is a confirmation, that through the guidance of the Holy Spirit, people *should live with joy, a God-driven life, immersed, baptized, and delivered in God's love, getting ready in eager anticipation for the return of His Son, Jesus, and their wedding reception.*"

Tabitha stood from where she was sitting and said, "I need to take a breather. I am going to stretch my legs for a second," and then left the room like her pants were on fire. I don't know where she went, but it couldn't have been far because she quickly returned and sat back down behind her desk. "You said you had another picture to show me?"

"Yes." I pulled out the last photo in my story. Composing myself, trying desperately to restrain the tears itching to break free. "I only saw Lewis one more time after this," I offered, as I handed her the picture. "It was the day he gave me this." She took it, stared at it for a moment, and then asked point blank, "What did Lewis say about it?"

"Lewis explained that this picture embodies God's love and how His love is exposed. He started by giving me a history lesson on how cameras capture multiple exposure frames and the inner workings of fiber optics. Let me tell you, I was not the least bit interested at the time.

"In a nutshell, he explained that cameras can be programmed to take multiple pictures over short, mathematically calculated bursts to enhance the photograph being taken so the true essence of the photograph can be captured. Then those frames can be folded back on themselves to reveal a story the photographer wanted to be expressed. The picture might not be clear or whole at first. But each splintered memory becomes a broken sherd carefully pieced back together, not only revealing something so much bigger, but the genius of the artist as well."

I pointed to the picture Tabitha was holding. "Lewis told me this is how that picture was taken. Dates were set for the exact moment in space and time to achieve this breathtaking work. Multiple exposures calculated and appointed and folded back together to reveal it. And it did, didn't it?" Tabitha, not wanting to look up from the photo, simply nodded her head.

"And the kicker is, the light you see in the photograph, scientists say, is an optical reflection of the lens from the light of the sun streaming off it. Strange, isn't it, that one of those rays of sunlight, reflected perfectly on the lens to reveal the Earth in the vastness of space? A tiny point that looked like a speck of dust to the observer reviewing the pictures."

"This picture is famous, isn't it? It has a name too, right?" Tabitha asked.

"Yes. This specific picture is called *The Pale Blue Dot*. The picture was captured while NASA was trying to take a picture of our solar system as Voyager 1 was leaving it, taking its own long journey. The picture had no scientific value, but was taken regardless, and bestowed God-given value.

"Lewis said our lives are a lot like this. Multiple moments captured over space and time to reveal something in us—a speck of *dust,* willing to walk in the light, sprinkling mankind with the testimony of God's divine majesty in our lives through Jesus Christ. Or revealing instead—a speck of *dust*, moments from being swept away into the vastness of an empty vessel.

"When I look at this picture, I think of myself as that little dot. I see every circumstance in my life that created and fed the darkness around it. But then I see the light shining around that little dot. I see every circumstance the enemy attempted to push me into the void, turned into thousands of tiny strings of light—divine appointments, bound together in Christ, leading me back to the Father, and filling me with His love. That is mercy. That is compassion. That is grace. I didn't deserve any of it."

"I don't think I will ever be able to look at this picture the same now," Tabitha said.

"I know I can't. Lewis told me one other thing you might find interesting about the picture."

"What's that?"

"The date chosen to capture this image was February 14th, Valentine's Day. A day humanity celebrates love, and named after a saint, who was martyred, and reportedly used by the Lord to help a blind man see."

I know Tabitha wanted to ask me a question. I could see the battle she was waging with herself to get it out. "Can I ask you something?"

"Of course," I said, moving to a standing position to put my coat back on, knowing it was time to go. I made my way through her door to the lobby, hoping she would catch up and ask me her question. I turned back, reached the reception desk, and nudged the conversation forward. "What's on your mind?"

"I feel like I am missing something. You said in the story how Mark Twain's own experience foreshadowed this moment and this book. How do you know for sure? There must have been thousands of people over the years that have gone to the Wailing Wall on the day that scripture is read. And how do you know, without a doubt, that Jesus is coming soon, and that you were one of many sent to help open people's eyes to the fact?"

Tabitha was handling this with a stream of relative calm. But I had a feeling I was about to test those waters. "You know those dates I shared with you that are so important to me? Those Jewish holy days that seem so woven into my life? They correspond to the same Jewish holy days in the year 1867—the year Twain journeyed to the Holy Land and brought back his own story to tell. And his journey started on the same day mine did—the evening of June 8th, 1867. It was the start of Pentecost or Shavuot.

"And regarding your second question, two readings are offered in the synagogue on the Sabbath. And two were delivered the day I was at the Wailing Wall. The one I shared with you from Deuteronomy. And a second reading from Isaiah. First, 61:10-11:

> *I delight greatly in the Lord; my soul rejoices in my God. For he has clothed me with the garments of salvation and arrayed me in a robe of his righteousness, as a bridegroom adorns his head like a priest, and as a bride adorns herself with her jewels. For as the soil makes the sprout come up, and a garden causes seeds to grow, so the Sovereign Lord will make righteousness and praise spring up before all nations.*

"And Isaiah 62:1-5:
> *For Zion's sake I will not keep silent, for Jerusalem's sake I will not remain quiet, till her vindication shines out like the dawn, her salvation like a blazing torch. The nations will see your vindication, and all kings your glory; you will be called by a new name that the mouth of the Lord will bestow. You will be a crown of splendor in the Lord's hand, a royal diadem in the hand of your God. No longer will they call you Deserted, or name your land Desolate. But you will be called Hephzibah, and your land Beulah; for the Lord will take delight in you, and your land will be married. As a young man marries a young woman, so will your Builder marry you; as the bridegroom rejoices over his bride, so will your God rejoice over you.*

"And Isaiah 62:10-12.

Pass through, pass through the gates! Prepare the way for the people. Build up, build up the highway! Remove the stones. Raise a banner for the nations. The Lord has made proclamation to the ends of the earth: 'Say to Daughter Zion, See, your Savior comes! See, his reward is with him, and his recompense accompanies him.' They will be called the Holy People, the Redeemed of the Lord; and you will be called Sought After, the city No longer Deserted.

"And Isaiah 63:1.

Who is this coming from Edom, from Bozrah, with his garments stained in crimson? Who is this, robed in splendor, striding forward in the greatness of his strength? "It is I, proclaiming victory, mighty to save."

"Do you remember when I told you that my mother-in-law and I blew the shophar in Petra for the Jewish New Year in 2017?"

Tabitha silently nodded, urging me to go on.

"The blowing of the shophar wasn't only a proclamation to rally an assembly together, or a call for alarm, introspection, remembrance, and celebration. Most importantly, the person blowing the shophar proclaimed the coming of the dawn. It announced the Return of the King, and the coming of Messiah.

"According to many Jewish and Christian commentaries, Messiah will come first from Bozrah, in the land of Edom, on the day of the Lord, which is in present-day Jordan. Isaiah tells us there will be people to prepare the way for others and build up a highway proclaiming that the Savior has come.

"It would make perfect sense, then, for my mother-in-law and I to blow that shophar where we did, to announce the imminent Return of the King, the Return of Messiah, because the place where we blew that shophar was in a hotel located in Petra, right along the *literal* King's Highway. And Petra is the Greek translation for the Hebrew word *batsur* meaning rock. Looks a lot like Bozrah, taken from the word *batsar*, doesn't it?

"And here's a bonus. The word for messenger or envoy in the Hebrew has a cognate association to these words. It is the word *tsir*.

"In antiquity and throughout Hebrew scripture, the midwife was always the official witness of a son's birth, lineage, or pedigree. So, it stands to reason that a midwife, among others, would declare that the Son of God was soon in coming.

"In Genesis, there is a scripture that speaks of this very moment."

"Where?" Tabitha questioned impatiently.

"In Genesis 38:28-30, with the birth of Perez and Zerah. It was a midwife who assisted in their births. Zerah's hand came out first and was marked by the midwife as the firstborn with a scarlet thread. It was she who marked his arm. His hand then returned to the womb and Perez broke through. And then Zerah came again. Doesn't this sound like the First and Second Coming of Christ?

"Zerah's name means *the rising of the sun or the coming of the dawn*. Isaiah clearly speaks of the Messiah coming from Bozrah. And even though these names aren't spelled the same, they were meant to kindle an audible relationship.

"The name *Bozrah* then becomes to a Semitic ear *Here Comes the Dawn*—the most important reason someone would blow a shophar to begin with. It's the coming of the dawn, the King, the Messiah—the Coming of Zerah, the Righteous, Redeeming Arm of the Lord, who was and is to come.

"The name *Bozrah* actually means *sheepfold*, but sounds remarkably like the word *besarah*, which means *to bring tidings of good news*—that being, the coming of a son, in the flesh. Who better to declare that than a midwife? And remember those two midwives' names back in Egypt sounded like 'Blow (Puah) the Shophar (Shiphrah).'

"Lewis told me all of this, but I still wasn't completely convinced. That's when he reminded me of the Law of Double Reference."

"I don't understand," Tabitha said.

"Well, Lewis reminded me of the sermon I gave on the Sea of Galilee about a town called *Gadarenes* and two guys who didn't want to be proven fool's gold. *Gadarenes* means *sheepfold*—just like *Bozrah. Bozrah* takes its name from *batsar*, meaning *fortress*, but is spelled the same as *betser*, meaning *gold*.

"He told me there was no coincidence that I preached about Jesus in *Gadarenes*, just as it was no coincidence that my mother-in-law and I blew the shophar in *Bozrah*. If I proclaimed that Jesus was the Messiah and the Gold Standard upon whom men's metal should be tested west of the Jordan, then it would have to happen east of the Jordan as well.

"And then Lewis said this proves that Jesus and this account I have been commanded to bring are the real thing.

"My mother-in-law and I didn't know any of this at the time. I didn't plan to be at the Wailing Wall the same day Mark Twain was when that scripture was read. Those dates that match all the days in my life to the year he took that trip weren't contrived by me.

"And I didn't know I would even be asked to speak on the Sea of Galilee, much less what testimony about Christ I would bring.

"My mother-in-law and I didn't know we would be blowing the shophar on the King's Highway or in a place (*Petra*) that would cross-translate as Bozrah. We were just a couple of ladies wanting to glorify God and spread the good news of His Son.

"We didn't know the second reading the day we were at the Wailing Wall was the Bozrah prophecy, but God did.

"I am here to tell you there isn't much time left. He passed over once, and He will pass over once more. And we must be ready."

Tabitha appeared at a loss for words, but she seemed to choke out, "Please tell me your name. Your real name."

A phone rang in the lobby, thundering through the halls like a voice crying out for a response. The receptionist answered, listened to the caller on the other end, and replied, "One moment. Please hold for Tabitha."

I turned to her and said, "I already did." I looked at the phone being extended and added, "You better get that. You have someone who is holding."

Tabitha reached for the phone, a little puzzled by my last comment. I just smiled a little to myself, making my way to the elevator, feeling for the first time in my life that I was right on time.

THE ELEVATOR door opened, and I entered, relieved I had finally done it—kept my word to God. The book was in somebody else's hands now, and I was off the hook. The doors closed as my own chest expanded, finally able to take a deep breath.

The elevator descended a couple of floors, and slowly opened again to take on more passengers, but only one man got on. It was the old man with his little compass. His appointment must have run over, too.

"Hello," I said, half-excited to see a familiar face after finishing this journey, which started so many years ago for me.

"Hello, there. Did everything go the way you wanted it to?" He probed as he peered at the lit-up buttons on the elevator's display panel. Following His gaze, I noticed the numbers eleven, nine, and one were still lit up. *Great.*

"I suppose so. God said He would take care of it if I just did what He told me to."

"Well, then, I am glad for you. But I have a feeling you are not done quite yet," the old man mused. His hand rubbed his compass in the same worn-out place I had noticed earlier.

"Oh, yeah? What makes you so sure?" I said, lifting my brows.

"Did you ever notice that most of the scriptures in your book had the numbers nine and eleven in them, in one form or another? Those numbers have been coming up quite a bit for you, haven't they?" He said as he pointed out the numbers lit up on the elevator floor panel. "You had to be in Israel on September 11th. And the numbers keep popping up every time you look at a watch, a license plate, or a cash register receipt."

"Who are you?" I said, half-wanting to crawl into my coat and wait for the elevator to reach the lobby.

"I think you know who I Am? Haven't you ever wondered why those numbers kept coming up?"

Not waiting for me to say anything, He continued, "Did you know the number nine in Hebrew is the word *tesha* or *tav-shin-ayin*? And the number for eleven comes from the original word *ashath* or *ayin-shin-tav*. They are mirror images of each other. The word *tesha* is derived from the word *shaah,* meaning *to turn your eyes.* And the word *ashath* not only renders the number eleven, but means *to shine or to be bright.*

"These two words together infer a sense of turning away from sin and being made whole because brightness, in Jewish thought, is a reflection of overflow and abundance. This makes perfect sense because nine implies lack or just coming up short, and eleven is more than ten fingers can hold. Wasn't this John's message before Jesus came the first time? A call to repentance—to turn your eyes away from sin and be brought to wholeness and abundance."

"I've never put that together." I had done countless word studies in Hebrew and knew the Hebrews loved wordplay. I couldn't believe this one had escaped my notice.

"You weren't meant to put it together until now. Things come together in this way for a reason. Don't beat yourself up too much about it."

"I guess I'll try not to," I smirked.

"Before we get to the bottom floor, I wanted to ask you if you've ever heard of something called a 'palindrome?'"

"I think so. Isn't it a phrase or word reflecting itself, both forward and backward, meaning the same thing no matter how you read it?"

"That is exactly what it is. A reflection of the past and the future at the same time. It is a foreshadowing of its very own, encapsulated in a row of conjoined characters that can be seen by some but hidden to many."

"Why are you telling me this?"

"Because your journey isn't over. We have another trip to take. I thought I would give you a head's up. And I also thought you might need this," He said as He tossed me the compass He was stroking in His right hand.

Catching the compass and placing it in my pocket, the doors opened as He stepped out. "Are you coming or not? You know you're not supposed to stop moving, right?"

"I am coming. Where are we going, anyway? Do I need a passport, visa, and a change of clothes?" I was having a hard time keeping up. The old guy definitely had a spring in His step, but I shouldn't have been surprised.

"No. You won't need any of those things. We will be back before you know it. Remember, 2 Peter 3:8 says:

> With the Lord, a day is like a thousand years, and a thousand years are like a day.

"We will be traveling the way I like to travel. *Through* time—not subject to it!"

The Two Mites *(Referenced in Chapter 36)*

A "mite" was the smallest of the bronze coins in Jewish currency.

The Hand-Mill *(Referenced in Chapter 11)*

This object was used for grinding grain with a stone, ground against another stone that was turned.

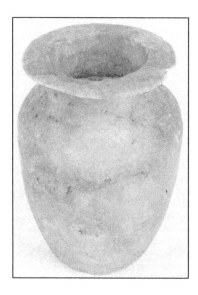

The Alabaster Jar *(Referenced in Chapter 38)*

The woman came to Jesus with an alabaster jar of expensive perfume, which she poured on His head. It is a symbol of strength, beauty, and purity.

The Birth Brick *(Referenced in Chapter 6)*

These bricks or stones were used to support and raise the mother while she crouched during childbirth.

The Roman Mile *(Referenced in Chapter 34)*

This was a small stone pillar that designated the starting point
for measurements of distance.

The Pottery Wheel *(Referenced in Chapter 34)*

This disc-shaped stone represented the hands of God. The prophet Jeremiah
compared God to a potter and us to the clay in his hands.

The Roman Denarius *(Referenced in Chapter 57)*

The denarius was the standard Roman silver coin, minted around 211 B.C.

The Olive Press *(Referenced in Chapter 12)*

In biblical times, the olive press was positioned near orchards and was used to extract
the oil in a three-step process.

The Ten Commandments *(Referenced in Chapter 8)*

According to the Hebrew Bible, the Tablets of the Law or Ten Commandments were inscribed when Moses ascended Mount Sinai, as written in the Book of Exodus.

The Tannur *(Referenced in Chapter 16)*

People baked unleavened bread in this mud oven, referenced numerous times in the Hebrew Bible.

The Lodestone *(Referenced in Chapter 13)*

This naturally magnetized stone is made from the mineral magnetite. In early navigation, pieces of this were suspended so they could turn, providing the first magnetic compasses.

The Sheepfold and Sheepfold Gate *(Referenced in Chapter 17)*

The Sheepfold was a strong fence or enclosure, typically made of layered stones and used to protect the sheep gathered within.

The Capstone *(Referenced in Chapter 33)*

In ancient architecture, the capstone is the final stone placed on top of a wall to hold the wall together. It is also a metaphor for Jesus' prominence as the head of the church.

The Touchstone *(Referenced in Chapter 64)*

This was a tablet of dark, finely grained jasper used to determine the quality of soft metals. The Lord, himself, was a touchstone by which men of His day were tried.

The Hand Mirror *(Referenced in Chapter 53)*

This object had a circular shape with a metal handle that often resembled the form of a female figure. The face of the mirror was left unadorned.

Jacob's Well *(Referenced in Chapter 35)*

This well was constructed deep into the bedrock of Samaria and has been associated with Jewish tradition for over 2000 years. It was a place where a sinner could come and encounter Jesus as their Savior.

The Anvil & The Hammer *(Referenced in Chapter 15)*

This was a weapon of warfare to keep enemies at bay.

The Whetstone *(Referenced in Chapter 63)*

This stone had a dense, quartz-like binding used to sharpen blades.

The Distaff & The Spindle *(Referenced in Chapter 14)*

The Distaff was a device that held a bundle of natural fiber. The fiber was then drawn off the distaff and spun into thread. The Spindle was the rod used for spinning the fibers and then winding them.

The Mortar & The Pestle *(Referenced in Chapter 39)*

This was a set of two simple tools that crushed or ground ingredients into a fine powder used in cooking. The Mortar was the bowl that held the ingredients, and the Pestle was the blunt club used to grind them.

The Wailing Wall *(Referenced in Chapter 57)*

This sacred Jewish site is believed to be the last remaining wall of the second temple of Jerusalem (the temple itself was later destroyed by the Romans).

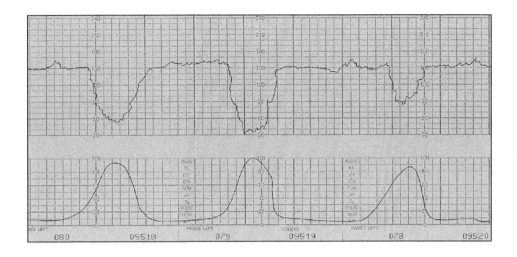

An Example of a Contraction Pattern & Fetal Heart Rate
(Referenced in Chapters 3 & 17)

The Pale Blue Dot *(Referenced in Chapter 63)*
This is an iconic photograph of the Earth taken aboard the
NASA Voyager 1 spacecraft.

BIBLIOGRAPHY

Bentorah, C. (2016). *Cure: Rapha: Hebrew word study: Revealing the heart of God.* (pp.110-113). New Kingston, PA: Whitaker House.

Fleming, J. (1983). The undiscovered gate beneath Jerusalem's golden gate. Biblical Archaeology Review, 9 (1) 24-37.

"God's Timepiece: Understanding the Times." (2021, May 3). In *One for Israel.* https://www.oneforisrael.org

Green, J.P. (1986). The interlinear Bible: *Hebrew-Greek-English: with Strong's concordance numbers above each word.* Peabody, Mass: Hendrickson Publishers, 1986.

Merriam-Webster's Collegiate Dictionary (11th ed.). (2005). Springfield, MA: Merriam-Webster.

NIV study Bible. (1995). Barker, K.L. (Ed.). 10th anniversary ed. Grand Rapids, MI: Zondervan.

Steel, F.A. (1918). *The story of the three bears: From English fairy tales* (pp. 17-22). London, England: Macmillan and Co., Limited.

Strong, J. (2010). The new Strong's expanded exhaustive concordance of the Bible (Red letter ed.). Thomas Nelson.

The English Standard Version Bible: Containing the Old and New Testaments with Apocrypha. (2009). Oxford University Press.

ABOUT THE AUTHOR

A DIAGNOSIS of multiple sclerosis derailed the life Staci Biscamp had made for herself, where she had spent most of her adult years as a labor and delivery nurse—helping to save and bring new life into the world while systematically destroying her very own. But in one night, all of Staci's scars (*that's what multiple sclerosis means*) thrust her train onto a very different track. Destined to collide head-on with the Almighty, it ultimately culminated in this genuine account of one woman's realization that she was never enough without Jesus. And that with Him, she was always meant to write *A Love So Carefully Concealed* to reveal to others the undeniable reality of God's providence in their lives. And that they all have a purpose and a story to tell, just like this one.

It seemed God didn't much care if the letters behind Staci's name had anything to do with literature or identified her as a master in storytelling or theology. He didn't want or need a Nobel laureate's words reflecting His glory. He wanted Staci's. And He wants yours.

Retired as a nurse practitioner, Staci now volunteers in women's ministry, performing ultrasounds to make visibly tangible the heartbeats

318 · STACI BISCAMP

of the "least of the least of these" to mothers who are contemplating abortion. And she hopes, with the power of the Holy Spirit, to do the same with this book—to make visibly tangible the hearts of those who are the weakest so that they can be strengthened in God's love and by His Hand.

Staci is a native Texan and a married mother of four. She loves Jesus, full stop. But it doesn't keep her from asking and hoping for beef ribs, buttermilk pie and Dominoes *(the game, not the pizza!)* in Heaven.

Made in the USA
Coppell, TX
12 May 2025

49258912R00175